THIS AIN'T
the
RITZ

NEIL D. MARTIN

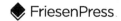 FriesenPress

Suite 300 - 990 Fort St
Victoria, BC, Canada, V8V 3K2
www.friesenpress.com

Copyright © 2015 by Neil D. Martin
First Edition — 2015

front and back cover photo courtesy of neonguy.ca

These stories are works of fiction. All incidents and dialogue, and
all characters with the exception of those who appear with their
permission are products of the author's imagination and are not
to be construed as real. Where real life figures appear, the situations, incidents and dialogue concerning these persons are entirely
fictional and are not intended to depict actual events or to change
the entirely fictional nature of the work. In all other respects, any
resemblance to persons living or dead is entirely coincidental.

ISBN
978-1-4602-7831-4 (Paperback)
978-1-4602-7832-1 (eBook)

1. Fiction

Distributed to the trade by The Ingram Book Company

ACKNOWLEDGEMENTS

It has taken me 'way too long to put this collection of stories together and it would have taken a good deal longer without the generous help of a few special people.

I know I'm going to forget someone but I can't forget to thank Doug Jamha for his time and his kind advice.

Thanks to Myrna Kostash, who generously took the time to read some of my pages and pointed out that what I was writing was fiction. Thanks, also, for using the word "gripping" to describe my prose. You have no idea what that meant to me at the time.

Thanks to Gary Pon, Percy Marshall, Doug Jamha and Bob Zawalski for living through those days with me and helping me to remember them.

Many thanks to the good folks at Friesen Press who waited patiently as I dithered and dawdled and fussed with my manuscript when I could have just sent the thing in and gotten the help I needed.

Lastly, thanks to all the many fans and friends of Captain Nobody who have offered their encouragement and recollections to me as I put this book together. If there's no audience, there ain't no show.

TABLE OF CONTENTS

FOREWORD

These stories are dedicated to the members of Captain Nobody and the Forgotten Joyband. You know who you are.

The writing of these stories was made less difficult by the remarkable resemblance some of them bear to things that really happened to us in the course of those years, playing in that other band of the same name. It was, however, never my intention to set down a factual chronicle of those experiences.

If, while reading these stories, you find yourself thinking-"Wait! It didn't *really* happen that way..." or something like that, bear in mind that these are works of Fiction.

Trying to decide how to approach this book, I decided that, in the spirit of the way Captain Nobody played the music of that time, what I really wanted to accomplish here was to convey something of the *feel* of the time we spent together. I didn't want to, as somebody said, "Let the truth stand in the way of a good story."

And what good stories there are. Even given the distance that time loans the telling, the heart of these tales lies in the living of the lives they are based on. It was a special time in my life, as I know it was in all of our lives. I never once found another place where I felt as good creatively.

As I mined my memories and yours for the jewels to set in print before they become lost forever, I became more and more aware of the wealth we share in these tales of the times we knew.

It was such a perfect time to do the things we did. We were all so suited to our roles and the caste of characters who were our friends and lovers and our audiences provide a perfect backdrop to the funny, outrageous, heartwarmingly weird and ridiculous things we did.

We rode the crest of the big wave of our times and in doing so helped each other to fulfill our potential as musicians and as people. This is not the common experience. Such a wealth of splendid memories we share that telling them makes those who weren't there burn with envy and disbelief. But we remember. Forgotten Joyband, indeed.

Lucky, lucky men to have shared such a treasure of experiences together. Lucky still, to be able to revisit them in memory and share the joy of that.

Neil D. Martin, July 21 2015

THIS AIN'T THE RITZ

Coming into town, it's not looking good. The buildings are a uniform grey, the last flecks of paint long gone, leaving the exposed wood to weather. Sidewalks crumble, past repair, in front of storefronts that have been closed so long the sun has burned the words off the signs in the windows.

The few vehicles on the street are all pickup trucks, old and new, each one with a gun rack in the window behind the seats. Every one of them has at least one rifle in it.

The hotel is where we knew it would be; on the corner of the main street, the only three-story building on the block. We turn into the alley that runs past the building to the parking lot, looking for the back door that might lead into the tavern. It's there, under the old wooden fire escape.

A big blue dumpster is parked in front of the door, throwing the doorway into shadow. I can just make out a figure there, leaning against the wall by the door. As we pull up, the glow of a cigarette illuminates a face looking back with open disinterest.

Doug rolls down the window.

"Hello."

"Hello, yourself."

"Is this the Dallas?"

The guy takes a last drag and flicks the butt at the dumpster. Sparks blossom briefly as he peels himself off the wall. Turning to the door, he spits towards the truck out of the side of his mouth.

"Well, it ain't the Ritz."

"Great, thanks. This is it, guys."

As the door opens, a blade of yellow light cuts across the darkness of the parking lot. Sounds of awakening come from the back seat of the van. Blankets are tossed aside, bleary eyes blinking in the harsh light.

We'd left the last gig at three thirty in the morning after breaking down the stage and packing all the gear into the back of the truck. We've been on the road ever since.

"Where the fuck are we?"

"We're here, man."

"Where the fuck is here?"

"We're at the gig, man. Get your shit. I'm going to go find the manager, get some rooms happening. Half hour to freshen up and then back here to load in and set up."

"What about breakfast?"

"Breakfast? It's seven o'clock in the evening, man. The restaurant's probably closed."

"Shit, man, I'm hungry."

"We'll see what we can dig up later. Everybody; get your personal stuff and meet in front of the stage. I'll get room keys."

Groaning and yawning, the group manages to get themselves and their gear out of the truck and into the tavern. The familiar pong of an old bar assaults our nostrils as the inadequate lighting begins to reveal the character of the place.

The carpet is so worn it's practically non-existent in spots. All the little round tables are naked. A pile of dirty red towel-tops sit on a chair in the corner, waiting for a long needed trip to the laundry. The chairs, turned upside down on the round tables for the cleaning staff, show extensive need of repair. Attempting to pull one down for a seat, Percy accidentally rips off a leg.

"Jesus Christ, man."

"Go ahead-wreck the place."

"Too late, man. It's already a wreck."

"Hey, guys; check out this stage."

"What the hell?"

"No, no-this has got to be a joke, man."

"It's a joke, alright."

The item in question is a corner of the room that's been filled with stools; twenty or thirty of them, all identical steel-framed stools with wooden tops, packed in side-by-side, covering an area about ten by ten feet. Four sheets of plywood have been placed on top of the stools to form what could euphemistically be called a stage.

"They can't be serious. It's not even nailed together!"

"No way am I putting my stuff up on *that.*"

"Agreed, man. There's no way this rig is going to support the weight of our amps and us, anyways. And then there's the drums."

"Fuckin' A, there's the drums; with me sitting on them, man. How do we know these stools don't start shifting around under there when things start rockin' and rollin'?"

"Not to mention the keyboards."

"Forget it man. How much are we getting for this gig? I say we blow this dump off and go home."

"Yeah, man-if this is the best we can do for a stage...we probably won't ever get paid anyhow."

"I agree. Let's just get back in the truck and keep on drivin'. We'd be home by midnight."

This train of thought is interrupted by Doug, returning from the front of the hotel with a handful of room keys.

"We would, if we had enough gas to get there, which we don't. Nor any funds with which to buy some. The last two gigs paid by cheque, guys. We are ten business days away from seein' any dough and we are *broke*, boys and girls. The only way we are going to eat tonight is if I can wangle an advance from the owner here."

"What?"

"Oh, man; this sucks."

"You gotta be kiddin', man."

"That's where we're at, guys. We got no choice, here. We gotta do the week."

"All right, but shit, man; what about this fuckin' stage? You don't really expect us to try and get everything on this thing, and try to play on this?"

"Yeah, come on. I mean, we gotta draw the line somewhere."

"No, I get it about the stage, guys. Lets just leave the stuff in the truck for now, lock up and get upstairs, clean up a bit and meet down here in half an hour, all right? Maybe we can think of something by then."

We collect our suitcases and packs and trudge wearily up rickety stairs to the second floor. There are no windows in the halls. Naked light bulbs hang from frayed cords too far apart to light our progress. I find my room and try the key. After a little convincing, it opens the door.

The room is typical of what I've come to expect in these small town hotels we've been playing in but somehow it's just a little bit more depressing than most. The spongy floor is covered with ancient carpet, threadbare and stained. The furniture is spare and Spartan, the mirror on the bureau cracked, the mattress swaybacked and smelly. There might be wallpaper but it's hard to say for sure, the walls are so grey and washed out. The curtains on the single filthy window hang like ancient campaign flags in some forgotten tomb, the fabric left untended so long that it's begun to unravel under it's own weight.

The door has been trimmed along the bottom to keep it from binding on the heaving floorboards. There's a space of two or three inches between it and the floor, a guarantee of no privacy from, or for, the people in the hall. The door to the bathroom is similarly customized, with the added feature that it doesn't close properly and swings open when left to it's own device. There is a big stainless steel bottle opener screwed onto the side of the vanity, the only thing in the room that might be called an amenity.

It's not like there's one single item I could point to and say *that's* the reason this room seems somehow drearier than all the rest. There's nothing here that I haven't found in all the other places we've been. Maybe it's just the fact that this one has *all* the possible shortcomings that makes it feel more decrepit. Or is it something else?

I sit down hard on the edge of the bed. A wave of fatigue washes over me. I look disinterestedly out the window at the dreary sight of the main street, so like all the other main streets of all the other small towns I've seen in the past four years. How many, now? Two hundred? Three? Maybe three hundred, I decide, counting repeat engagements. Surely, not four.

"Please tell me I haven't done this four hundred times."

Sighing heavily, I force myself up and into the tiny bathroom, where I wash my face. I look about for a towel. Standing there, dripping wet, I see none in the room. Trying not to drip on my shirt, I step out to check if there's a towel rack on the outside of the bathroom door. No luck.

"Fuck."

Can it possibly be too much to ask, to have a towel in the bathroom? I'd been planning on a shower after I help carry all the stuff in from the truck and set up my drums. Freshen up before a light dinner and hopefully shake off this fug. At least I hope that's what it is; fatigue and not something else, something more that has been dragging me down the last few days.

Longer than that, really, if I'm honest with myself. Months now, I've been feeling...out of sync with the whole thing. The road, the gigs, the travel, even the guys; it's all just no fun anymore.

Worse than no fun. And not just dead boring. Face it; it sucks. I need a break.

But how to do that, when I never get anything ahead? The weeks we get off between gigs are spent rehearsing, trying to update the song list so we aren't playing the same show in the same places.

The band dared not turn down a gig when one was offered, for fear of alienating an agent and losing their spot on the pecking order. Now that the Liquor Control Board had OK'd dancing in taverns, forcing bar owners to choose between giving up more tables for the dance floor or giving up bands altogether, there were only so many rooms that still hired a rock band.

Mostly it was the ones that couldn't lure people in any other way; the places where the security was a little lax, where they didn't check I.D.' s as much as they might. The kind of places where the fights didn't get broken up, just moved outside to the parking lot. Places like this.

I heave another sigh and sit back down on the bed. Feeling a weariness that goes deeper than being worn out, I let myself fall back on the bed, cooties be damned.

So, what was the answer? I didn't know. The guys didn't, either. We spent endless hours talking about it and never arrived at a plan to somehow pull out of this vicious circle.

The equation was a simple one. If a band was good enough to find work on the road, they could expect to be on the road most of the time. There was little co-ordination between the hotel owners and the booking agents, who were constantly competing with each other. The upshot for the bands was that the gigs could be arranged on schedules that made no sense whatsoever. They might be playing somewhere hundreds of miles north of the city and receive a call from the agent that they would need to be somewhere in the extreme south for the following Monday. It meant packing up gear after the Saturdays' performance and driving twelve or thirteen hours to have time to set up and hopefully get a little rest before the next show. It was exhausting. Sometimes it was more than exhausting. Sometimes it got down right dangerous. And the driving wasn't the worst part.

It was the endless hours of nothing to do, sitting around in hotel rooms with the weather too cold to go out, the TV non-functional and no one in the place to carry on an intelligent conversation with. It wore a person down.

Band members became their own mutual support group in an ongoing battle to retain some semblance of sanity, in the face of boredom off the scale.

The only way out of the vicious cycle of the road was to get in with the in-town circuit. That meant waiting until one of the established in-town acts had to cancel a gig at the last moment when your band was in town and available to fill in.

An agent that controlled the booking in one or more of the downtown venues would not risk putting an unknown band into one of his rooms, so if you wanted to get a shot, it meant first talking someone from one of the top agencies into coming to a gig to check the band out. If he liked what he heard, you might get a spot on the list. If you got a shot, you had to play the gig of your life and hope it wouldn't be marred by equipment failure or anything else.

The band had gotten gigs in town. We'd filled in for one of the established groups in two different in-town bars in the last six months and had done well both times but still the downtown gigs didn't come. We had to believe that we were on the brink, that it was going to happen for us soon but it was cold comfort, facing another week in a shithole like this.

Facing yet another week of it, I don't have the strength to go on. I find that I can't even martial the energy to get back up off the bed. I lie there, staring at the peeling paint on the ceiling and thinking, over and over-how did I get here?

A sound out on the street finally brings me to my feet. Through the grit on the window, I can make out a couple of people getting into a truck on the street. The one man is fiftyish and fat, carrying a case of beer, which he places on the seat before pulling himself up behind the wheel. The other man, younger by a decade and dressed in hunters' camouflage, pauses to take a leak in the gutter before getting in the passenger side.

One thing that I can't complain about is the music. There was no arguing with the fact that something had resulted from all the constant gigging and the relentless rehearsal between gigs; we'd gotten good.

The songs are well chosen and the arrangements are clean. Everybody knows their parts and the song order is well thought out, to give the show a conscious flow from start to finish. We're comfortable and relaxed on stage and able to get a good rapport going with the crowd.

We know we're good enough to be playing the in-town rooms, so why are we still stuck playing in these funky backwater towns? It is a rhetorical question, by now.

I turn to the door, wiping my hands on my shirt. I meet Percy in the hall and we walk together to the stairs.

"What a fucking dump, eh?" said Percy.

"Like the guy said; it ain't the Ritz."

"He got that right."

"You got any towels in your room?"

"Why, don't you?"

"Nope. Not one."

"I think there's a couple. You're welcome to one. You don't think you could just ask?"

"I don't know, man. After all, like the guy said..." as we round the corner to the tavern entrance, Percy joins in on the chorus, "THIS AIN'T THE RITZ!"

Back in the tavern, we come upon a scene of some industry. The plywood has been taken down off the "stage" and the stools are being stacked at the back of the space.

"C'mon, guys, lend a hand," Doug calls.

"What, so we're just going to play on the floor?"

"It's the best we can do. At least it'll be safer."

"Safer for who?" I grumble. Even behind the drum kit, I've always felt exposed playing on the floor. It removes more than a physical barrier between the band and the audience. Playing with no stage makes the band seem more approachable, not only to the nice folk who just wanted to relay a request or just to chat, but to the drunken fools and the assholes, too.

There is no telling what the next guy or gal who approaches the stage in a tavern might have on his or her mind. I've seen lots of women try to kiss one of the guitar players while he was singing.

The men generally wanted to sing, having found courage in the bottom of their tenth or twelfth beer. Occasionally, they wanted to play guitar, but not as often as they wanted to play drums.

Guys often wanted to play the drums; there was and is a generally held belief that anyone can play the drums, akin to the conviction a lot of people have that, given the time, they could just up and write a novel.

Luckily, the logistics of maneuvering oneself behind the drum kit on a crowded stage was too much for the average drunk and they usually gave up before any real harm was done. Usually.

And then, there were the ones that had a beef with one of the band members, stemming from some imagined slight or just the way his girlfriend was looking at the member in question.

There is a psychological advantage to being up, even just a few inches, on a stage. Without it, things could get nasty a whole lot faster. Now, facing the prospect of playing in a familiar-looking establishment without the benefit of a stage to separate us from the crowd, I was apprehensive.

Working together, we stacked all the stools and moved them out of the way, so we could put the plywood back down on the floor. Then we began the practiced tasks of setting up the equipment.

We'd set up our gear hundreds of times in various conditions, so it wasn't often we ran into a stage that we couldn't cope with. Some taverns had nice, big stages with ample room for all the gear and performing space left over but this was rare.

Most places, the stage was an after thought-an area that once housed the shuffleboard table or a couple of pinball machines, barely large enough for four players to stand in front of the drums. I'd learned to make the footprint of my drum kit smaller by choking the cymbal stands' legs together, which saved room but reduced their stability.

It was a practice I abandoned after one fateful evening when I hit my ultra-thin crash cymbal and knocked it over. The knife-edged disc fell straight and true, digging itself a half inch into the side of Gary's prized Flying V guitar. The look on his face as he perceived the damage was all I needed to insist on room enough to set my stands out at their full width from then on.

At times, there just wasn't room on the riser for anything but the drums, and the lads ended up standing on the dance floor. On those occasions, we'd learned to set the speakers out on the floor as well, so that they defined an area that the dancers respected, mostly. And then, there were times when there was no stage at all.

"At least the plywood makes the impression of a stage," said Doug hopefully.

"3/4 of an inch doesn't make that much of an impression after midnight," Percy mused.

"You know this from personal experience?" asked Doug.

"Just from watching you, man."

Percy and Doug always roomed together and were forever chiding each other about the imaginary sex that supposedly took place in their room.

"Size isn't everything."

"That's right, man; it ain't the flick of the prick that does the trick..."

"It's the throb of the knob that does the job."

Gary interrupted.

"So, what's going to happen is, these drunks are going to come traipsing towards the front of the non-stage area and trip on the edge of the ply. They'll be going down for a face plant on top of all your pedals and shit, so be ready to catch 'em, alright?"

"Fuck; now we gotta play lifeguard for a bunch of drunks?"

"Comes with the territory, boys. Get over it."

"The manager told me that he owns the café on the corner, too. He phoned them and arranged a tab for us, so I guess that's dinner, if anyone's interested."

We repaired to the establishment in question, which turned out to be the standard small town café. There was a lunch counter with stools made of stainless steel and red vinyl upholstery, as well as a row of booths, covered with the same vinyl. A neon clock on the wall sported a revolving advertisement display with things like "Boychuk Feed and Seed" and "Scona Electric Ltd." printed on them.

The waitress was fifty, fat and surly with a goiter the size of a golf ball on her neck. She took our orders on her pad with an air of indifference and returned with a half empty coffee pot, which she plonked down on the table and left. Pouring was apparently not part of the service.

We helped ourselves and sat waiting for our food to arrive, uncharacteristically quiet. Everybody was worn out from the long drive and the labor of setting up. We all just wanted some food and a little time to get ready to play.

No one was surprised when our orders came and the food was crappy. The roast beef was stringy, the cutlets were tough, the instant potatoes were watery and the canned brown gravy that covered everything was cold. We ate what we could and washed it down with the luke-warm coffee.

"Hey, there's pie," Percy remarked optimistically.

Following his gaze, I saw the glass display on the counter. There were a couple of fruit pies and a selection of suspiciously colored cream pies as well.

Suddenly, the thought of a nice, cold slice of apple pie somehow appealed to me. I no sooner thought of it than a memory came to mind-of my aunt Marge dishing out slabs of her miraculous three inch deep, home-made apple pie with thick slices of sharp cheddar cheese on the side. Just the thing, I reckoned, to ease the homesick melancholy that had been dogging my heels.

"How's the pie?" I asked when the waitress returned.

"It ain't bad, if you don't mind chewin' on the crust awhile," she replied.

The waitress looked at me oddly when I asked for the cheese. Perhaps that particular tradition was not common in these parts, I mused. I was therefore unprepared for the arrival of my pie.

It was not cold-on the contrary, it seemed that our waitress had taken a moment to heat it under the lamp after putting the slice of processed sandwich cheese on top, assuming, I guess, that I would want the cheese melted.

With a sigh, I picked up my fork and poked despondently at the thing a few times before giving up. It was not what I had wanted.

"We'd better get moving if we want to freshen up before stage time," said Gary, "We don't want to be late for the first night."

As it turned out, we didn't have to worry about it, because nobody came to the gig. Five nobodys, to be exact; three male, one obviously female and one of no discernable gender. They did not dance, nor did anyone approach the band. At no time did any of them show any sign of awareness that there was, in fact, a band playing in the room.

There are few things more difficult in the life of a professional musician than playing to an empty room. It is boring, demoralizing and downright embarrassing. Even the staff is embarrassed and the unspoken implication is that it's somehow the bands' fault that nobody came.

Never mind that the hotel failed to advertise either the name of the band or even the fact that there would be one. Never mind that the manager had failed to take into consideration that the other hotel in town had brought in strippers that week, or put in a giant screen for the hockey play-offs.

No, no; somehow the people in town were supposed to have magically come to know that there would be live rock and roll; if they didn't show up in numbers, it was because the band was no good.

Still, a contract had been signed and the gig needed to be played, so you get downstairs on time, go through the motions of welcoming the few anonymous bar flies that would have been there anyways, as long as the beer held out, and you played.

Of course, the flip side of an empty, or at least a semi-empty room was that it was more intimate than with a crowd. We got to know the staff and the few regulars that did come in on a more personal level. Sometimes this could be a good thing or sometimes, as in the case of the Dallas, not so much.

Every bar had one regular who had been drinking there so long that he'd come to feel like he owned the place. In the Dallas, this was a shared role, co-occupied by a diminutive consumptive gent named Clyde and a similarly shabby individual that referred to himself as "Dutch."

Clyde was a man in his sixties with remarkable body odor issues and a thick eastern European accent. He wore a pair of ancient coveralls and a train conductors' checkered cap. He wasn't a bit shy about cadging a beer off someone. If you ordered more than one draft to the table, Clyde just took it as written that the extra was for him. Having availed himself of your surplus beverages, he felt obliged to join you at your table and fill you in on local lore.

Dutch, on the other hand, was a tad more retiring; shy, even-possibly owing to the fact that he suffered from a disfiguring skin condition on his face and hands that presented as red, weeping clusters of pustules not unlike historical descriptions I've read of the "red death."

He was therefore reluctant to draw too close to us, although the lure of free beer held him in orbit a few tables away. He would sit and watch Clyde enjoying his ill-earned glass, occasionally calling across the intervening space at him, admonishing him to leave us alone.

"Stop buggerin' them boys!" he would shout, "Dem boys don't want you around!"

Clyde would wisely ignore him and continue to drink our beer with a sage-like detachment, only occasionally moved to respond.

"Shut yer fookin yap, you!" he would hurl over his shoulder, "I'm havin' a chat wit' dem!"

Of course, what Clyde meant was, he was having a chat with *me*. Over the years it has become apparent to me that I have somehow been appointed official listener to the worlds' unfortunates. I don't know why this fate has befallen me, I only know that, wherever I am, the addled and unfortunate of the world seek me out and tell me their stories.

They seem to know that I'll listen. Why I do is something of a mystery to me as well, when I could just as easily invite them to buzz off and leave me alone; some weird combination of the manners that my parents imparted to me growing up, combined with a measure of prurient curiosity, I suppose.

As Clyde's focus narrowed and finally settled on me, like some great smelly insect whose instincts lead him to the easy victim, the other guys in the band, familiar with my affliction, recognized what was happening and one by one found somewhere else they had to be, leaving me to my fate.

As I sat there listening to his tales of woe, it occurred to me that there was nothing particularly unique about Clyde's story-nothing I hadn't heard before. It was his way of telling it that set it apart and made listening to him at least somewhat interesting. He had a habit of trailing off and spending long moments not speaking at all, until I began to think (hope?) that he was done and I might get away. Then he'd erupt with some explosive expletive, by way of launching into a new story.

"Bastard!" he'd say suddenly, "What kinds of brother is that, eh? Sleeps with yer wife and steals yer goat, next thing, he's at yer door, asking can he borrow yer tractor?"

"Bummer," I'd offer, knowing that my participation in the conversation was optional. I just threw in the odd commiseration in hopes of moving things along.

"I knew I shouldn't do it. I knew it! Borrow that guy yer tractor, you never see it again, les' ya go and get it, where the son-of-a-bitch has it hid."

And so on, for long, long minutes until it was time for me to get back to playing. I didn't need to worry, though; now that he'd found me, I knew Clyde would be back each night for the duration of the gig, eager to pick up where he'd left off the night before. If I didn't want to spend the entire week hiding in my room over the breaks, I was going to be treated to the complete, unabridged story of Clyde.

"Son of a Bitch!" cries Clyde, commencing a new chapter.

It all made for a small distraction from the oppressive boredom. Like most bands, we tried to think of it as extra practice time, and used the dead room to introduce new material that might have been too rough for a good crowd. That used up about ten minutes, then the tedium started up again.

Forty minutes on, twenty off and nothing to do all day long but wait to do it all over again that night. Bored to the extremes of human tolerance, band members had been known to resort to some fairly bizarre devices in order to preserve their sanity.

Percy was famous for coming up with ways to break the monotony. Once, he purchased a novelty FM transmitting microphone and placed it over the mirror in the Ladies room, with an FM radio/recorder as a receiver upstairs in his room, recording the conversations that took place there.

He would run upstairs on the breaks and listen to the tape, trying to then figure out which audience member had said what. The idea was to pick up any girl-talk about the band. If any of the women in the room talked to their girlfriends about liking any of the band members, all we had to do was figure out who was who and maybe score with a big advantage. At least, that was the theory.

One evening, he came back down looking distracted. Nervously surveying the crowd, he addressed the band.

"You guys ought to come up and listen to the tape," he said.

One look at his face and we all complied without any further ado. We crowded into Percy's room and hovered about the recorder, hushing one another in order to hear the tape. There was the usual garbled babble for a few minutes, then a voice came out quite clearly.

"So, are you really going to do it?"

"Damn right I am," came a second, equally clear voice.

"You're going to kidnap the guitar player and rape his ass?"

"That's the plan, girl. Got it all laid out. The second he steps outside, my boys are going to grab him for me and take him out to the old farmhouse. I'm going to tie him up and play with his little body until he squeals for mercy.

"The blonde one, right, with the funny name?"

"Percy. That's the one."

We looked at each other, then at Percy.

"Holy shit, Percy; any idea which one it is?"

"Haven't a fucking clue, man."

"Well, don't go outside until you do, man. She might be hideous."

It turned out, of course, that the whole thing was a prank. The girls who worked at the bar had found the microphone and decided to serve us a lesson. After they let Percy sweat it out all evening, they presented his mike to him. Everybody had a big laugh.

Then there was the time Percy brought an inflatable sex doll along on a road trip. This was the latest in the on-going fantasy about what went on in the room he shared with Doug. He brought it out and inflated it, leaving it sitting in a chair by the window, obscene plastic mouth agape, much to the disapproval of the cleaning staff. One of the maids complained to the manager, who had a quiet word with our manager. We were asked to remove it from the room, so we complied.

He didn't, however, say anything about putting her on the stage.

Once the idea caught on, we all got into the spirit of the thing. The band went on a shopping trip to the Kresgie's store in town and came up with a little outfit for her to wear.

Somebody found a pair of used cowboy boots in the pawn shop next to the hotel, along with an old oscillating fan. A can of hot pink spray paint was found at the local hardware.

That night there was a new addition to the band on stage; a go-go girl named "Breezy", who shimmied and shook by the speaker stack in her bright pink boots and gold lame mini-skirt, her blonde hair wafting about as she moved. Some got it, some not so much. One old farmer, sitting by the front of the stage, watched her for a while and then commented to Gary;

"For a gal whose mouth is always open, she don't say much, does she?"

But she did.

Such were the lengths we went to, in order relieve the tedium and to preserve our sanity on the road. It was a paradox of the first order; the more creative our attempts to keep from going crazy between shows, the crazier the things we did became.

Our trip to Yellowknife was a classic case. Kept indoors for weeks on end by the harsh northern climate, imaginations went into high gear. Somebody finally braved the -40 weather to make a trip to the dime store and came back with a bean gun.

There were a lot of plastic toy guns available in the days before a more moderate sensibility prevailed in the toy makers' convention. There were the cap guns and the water pistols, the Nerf guns and the ones that fired ping-pong balls but, with the possible exception of the spud gun, never was a toy gun invented that was more practical or fun as the bean gun.

These were spring-loaded pistols, manufactured by the Hodendods Company out of Finland under the name "Sekidens". They were modeled after the Walther P-38 automatic that James Bond made famous as his pistol of choice. The guns came with a pho-hardwood grip and a non-functioning hammer, but the great thing was the ammunition they used; plain navy beans-and the way they loaded twenty or thirty at a time. (To be fair, the spud gun, wonderful as it was, was a single shot weapon.) This meant long, uninterrupted gun battles without having to stop to reload. Navy beans were cheap to buy in the one-pound bag and, believe me; there's a lot of shootin' in a pound of beans.

Propelled by the spring mechanism in the gun, the beans actually fired from under the "barrel" of the pistol, as the cook at the Yellowknife Inn proceeded to find out by shooting himself in the eye, trying to shoot himself in the forehead. Barring that kind of stupidity, the bean guns weren't actually dangerous. They stung just enough at close range to make the game interesting.

In no time flat, we were all outfitted with Sekidens of our own and had made heavy inroads on the local supply of navy beans. Gun battles raged up and down the halls of the hotel and none of us gave too much thought to the amount of beans that were left on the carpet until some of the cleaning ladies complained to the management about having to vacuum them up.

The real fun came on the way home, however when, after two months of cabin fever, we found ourselves set loose in the roomy "Arrivals" area of the Edmonton International Airport.

Possessed of a little time to kill, we decided that this was the perfect time to get out the Sekidens and have a rousing game of shoot-em-up, running from cover to cover, firearms in hand.

The airport cops didn't know what the hell they were dealing with, at first. When various reports came in of a group of men with pistols running around the building, they must have wondered if they needed to call the SWAT teams in.

God help us if we tried that today. We'd likely all be shot by the over-hyped, post- 9/11 security people.

As it was, we were apprehended by the RCMP and herded into a back room for a stern talking-to about airport etiquette. They didn't get it. Unaware that they were dealing with people who had left the world of normal behavior far behind in the frozen North, the policemen couldn't understand why the boys in the band seemed so oblivious to the seriousness of the situation.

Not that we didn't try more normal diversions. A lot of the little towns we played in had one or more places besides the tavern where a guy could while away the time.

There was often a pool hall. Percy's dad had a table at home, so he'd gotten pretty good at snooker, the game of choice for most prairie town tables. We had to be careful not to monopolize the tables, though. For some of the townies, it was their only source of social interaction and they didn't take it kindly when some bunch of city guys moved in and took over.

Sometimes there was a bowling alley in town; always the Canadian five-pin version. A person can easily lose an afternoon bowling a few frames and we always took advantage of the opportunity.

Of course, the thing that both these places often had in common was the addition of a pinball machine or two. Even in a town that lacked all other amenities, life could carry on and sanity prevail, if only there was good pinball machine somewhere.

Few travelling musicians were immune to the siren call of the silver ball. Most players I've known were also pinball fanatics but for me the affair began early.

When I was growing up in Edmonton in the sixties I had a paper route, probably the best one on the entire south side. It was better than most for several reasons; firstly, it started about one block from the "shack," where all the paperboys picked up their newspapers each morning, so only minimum time was wasted getting on the route. Number two, the route was made up entirely of apartment buildings.

There were three three-story walkups that afforded easy and fast delivery, not to mention being indoors and out of the weather, and two apartment towers, situated side by side. I could get my papers counted and ready, hit the elevator and press the button for each floor on which I had deliveries. As the elevator shafts were located right in the middle of the buildings with a circular hall that led back to the lift, I could exit to the right and deal the papers out like cards at a fast walk, getting back to the elevator just before the door closed and get ready to do the next floor on the way up to it.

Maybe the best part about my paper route, though, was that it ended at the Rex Bowl. After I got my bag of fresh popped popcorn, I would count my change up and make my way to the pinball game.

The Rex Bowl had one of the last old-time analog pinball games and it was a classic. "Baseball" by the Williams Co. featured a real miniature baseball diamond with tin players that popped up and ran the bases in a slot track as your accuracy with the silver ball hit targets labeled "single," "double," "triple" or, if you could hit the ski-jump down the center and send the ball up to score a "home-run" you were rewarded by the solid 'THOK' of a free game. I spent hours and most of my paper route money on that game, patiently racking up new top scores and acquiring pinball skills that are with me today.

Failing the availability of either a pool hall or a bowling alley, the next best way to kill time in small town Alberta was shopping. In the '70's, many of the towns we played had only one major store, usually one of the home-grown chains that once flourished across the prairies; Kresgies, the Met, Saan Stores or Co-op.

These were 'department stores' which carried a wide variety of things. There would be a clothing department, divided into Men's, Women's and children's areas, a shoe department, a toy department and a "house wares" department. If the town lacked an independent hardware store, there would likely be a small offering of tools, paints and nuts & bolts in the department store as well.

The larger stores typically had a lunch counter. When they did, it was a sure bet to have the best deals, if not the best meals, in town. They served your traditional café fare; bacon, sausage or ham and eggs and a choice of omelets until 10:00, the burgers and fries, grilled cheese and soup & sandwich selection for lunch, with dinners like open-faced turkey, roast beef or hamburger steak sandwiches slathered with canned brown "gravy," or breaded veal cutlets, all served with instant "mashed" potatoes and kernel corn. Milk shakes were made in stainless steel containers with a little green enamel 'Warring' brand mixer on the back counter and then poured into a wax paper insert to serve. The coffee came in thick walled porcelain cups with a single red stripe around the side.

Some of these places had menus that dated back to the depression, with items like sardines on crackers for seventy-five cents, or beans on toast for a buck.

Everything was the same predictable quality and everything was dirt cheap. If there was a lunch counter in the department store, that's where you'd find the band at mealtime.

One of the things that made these places interesting to shop in was the fact that, perhaps owing to the growing habit of farm families to drive into the nearest city to do their shopping, they didn't change their stock often, or ever, actually. So it was entirely possible to find items that hadn't been available in the city for years, decades, even, still on the shelves.

I remember my joy in coming upon a shelf full of H.O. scale plastic "army men" in the toy department of a Met store somewhere. I had been an avid collector of these toys as a boy but I hadn't seen them in the city for years. At ninety-nine cents for a box containing a complete set, they were a bargain. I bought out the entire stock and spent a happy week setting up tiny battleground scenes on the bed in my hotel room.

These places were also reliable sources of "gimmick" products, like those produced by the K-Tel company who, when they weren't busy putting together vinyl LP collections of every kind of music ever recorded, advertised things like the "Kitchen Magician" on television.

For years after they had disappeared forever from the TV screens and discount stores in the city, you could still find things like the "Patty Stacker," a device for forming hamburger meat into perfect patties with a plastic plunger-like thing (in case you'd lost the use of your hands). Or the Dial-o-matic, which was just an overly complex plastic version of the classic mandolin slicer, one of a family of products that included the "Brush-o-Matic," the "Veg-o-Matic," the "Stitch-o-Matic," and my personal favourite, the aggressively named "Blitzhacker."

One time I got excited enough to purchase a "Bopeel's Pocket Fisherman," with some wild scheme in mind about spending my days ice fishing, only to learn that there wasn't a lake with fish in it for a hundred miles.

Gary, who was something of a YO-YO expert, once found a rare and out of date YO-YO gathering dust in a SAAN store. The same item, if found today would fetch thousands in the collector market.

And then there were the antique stores. They often doubled as pawn shops, where folks would bring old things that had outlived their usefulness on the farm and get a couple of bucks for them.

These stores often sprang up as the local businesses died and left vacancies for lease on main street at bargain rates. They usually had corny names like "Ma's Spot," or "Grandma's Corner." There was no telling what you might find in a place like that. I once saw a Victoria Cross in one. There was an unsubstantiated rumor that somebody had purchased a violin in one of these emporiums that actually turned out to be a real Stradivarius.

A guy I knew once found an early model Fender Stratocaster guitar in a small town pawn shop, priced so low as to be irresistible. He had to get an advance on his next two gigs wages to buy it but it was just too good a deal to pass up.

I remember coming across some clothing in the back of a dimly lit store that was full of kerosene lanterns and flat irons and row after row of green glass bottles.

There was an unusual Tweed cloth cap, with earflaps that tied up on top, which the label said was a "Galamorra," and assured the wearer that it had been "made by me, in my cottage by the sea," with a tiny picture of an old, presumably Irish person. Beside it was hanging a complete three-piece herring-bone tweed suit, made for someone about three foot six. The label said; "Clothes for lads, cut like Dad's."

Of course, these pastimes were limited by the size of the town and one soon exhausted the possibilities, so we were always on the lookout for other ways to fill our idle days.

It wasn't so bad in the summer, when one could just get out for a walk or trek out to some local site. There was often a park in town, sometimes a ballpark or some hoops. Even a vacant lot, of which there was an increasing supply, could serve as an impromptu court for a Frisbee match.

Allow me to take a moment here, just to say; thank God for the Frisbee.

Well, actually, thank He and Mr. Fred Morrison. Had Fred Morrison not pursued his invention so zealously as he did, finally (in 1958) receiving U.S. patent #183,626 for his "Flyin' Saucer" before selling distribution rights to the Wham-O Corporation, entire generations of bored kids would have suffered. The Frisbee saved us from those long summers full of empty days that stretched out ahead so that they seemed to go on forever.

As long as somebody had a Frisbee, there was something to do. It is my considered opinion that Mr. Morrison should be awarded the Nobel Prize, possibly the Peace Prize, for his invention, for, who knows what manner of dastardly plots might have been hatched over the years by the over heated brains of young people, bored out of all reason, if they hadn't had a Frisbee to throw?

Entire civilizations have come and gone and contributed less to the overall well being of mankind than did the Frisbee. Thank you, Mr. Morrison.

Anyways, it beat hell out of golfing on sand greens.

Few things reveal the desperate measures to which rural people will go, in order to relieve the tedium in their lives and find something, *anything* to do, like the sand golf green.

These hideous things are thankfully more or less extinct on the prairie now, but in the 1970's, if you went out for nine holes at your local country course, the chances were pretty good you'd come to the end of the fairway and find, not grass, nor even Astroturf, but ugly, brown *sand* surrounding the hole.

OK, I get it-the cost of maintaining proper golf greens, especially up north, is prohibitive. I imagine it's quite out of the reach of your average small town club, who would have to come up with *some* kind of affordable alternative, but *sand*? Really?

I mean, why not just let the clover take over and then mow it close? Or keep goats or sheep to crop the native grasses as they are so willing to do? Even the less attractive option of fake grass would at least allow the ball to *roll.*

Any sane player, or more accurately, any that would keep his sanity, just took two strokes and walked on, anyways, so what was the point? Some places even *oiled* the stuff, in a lame attempt to make it more serviceable. There were courses that provided a roller, by which means a player could flatten the sand out in a nice swath from his ball to the hole, before taking his putt. It made no difference.

The ball would advance a few inches and, naturally, come to a stop, having dug itself a little furrow in the sand. It was like having a final, unavoidable sand trap at the end of every hole.

Like so many things on the western prairie-the lunch counters, the grain elevators, the family farms, the "Ladies and Escorts" signs over the tavern doors and the habit of being civil to a stranger, the sand green is a thing of the past. Unlike many things, it will not be missed.

Something that will be missed is the small town theater.

If we were very lucky, there might be a cinema in town. If we'd been good all year, there might even be weekday matinees. One thing for sure, there would be popcorn. Small town movie houses were slow to come to the realization that they could realize a better bottom line by charging extortionist prices for the treats.

For a few years, when a little bag of day-old, pre-popped corn with a dab of simulated cholesterol sauce on top might run you five bucks or more in town, lots of little theatres in the sticks would give you a big family-sized bag of hot, freshly popped corn with as much real melted butter as you wanted for some ridiculously out-dated price like fifty cents.

For semi-starving musicians on the road, it was a great way to supplement one's diet, and with the added bonus of catching up on all the two-year-old movies you'd missed while you were travelling.

I will never forget seeing the original "Superman" movie in a theatre in southern Alberta. We got there a bit late, so we ended up sitting in the very front row, craning our necks up at the full-sized "Technicolor" screen. This turned out to be the best seating in the house for that particular film.

When Christopher Reeve suddenly appeared, swooping through the air to catch a terrified Margot Kidder in mid flight and save her from going 'splat' on the pavement in front of the Daily Planet building, we went bananas.

"HURRAY, SUPERMAN!" we yelled, pumping fists and laughing with joy, much to the consternation and amusement of the townsfolk behind us. That night the tavern was especially busy, perhaps filled with movie goers who wanted to see if our enthusiasm translated to a good musical show, as well.

We did our best to make use of our time in those towns. We held rehearsals before the tavern opened in the morning, or acoustic and vocal rehearsals up in the rooms. We practiced our own instruments alone, learning or improving our parts. Several hours a day could be put to use in this way, but we were still left with a lot of dead time on our hands at the best of gigs.

The tough ones were when we got booked for two or three weeks in a place, which happened more often as we earned a reputation for good music.

We would generally exhaust the various avenues of distraction the first week, repeat everything the second week until we couldn't bear to play any more pool, or heft another bowling ball. Even the best pinball machine sooner or later became too easy to beat.

By the end of our second week in any small town, we were bored, bored, bored, bored, bored, bored, bored, bored, bored, bored.

On a long road trip, one where we might play three or more gigs in a row for a week each or more, life could get truly tedious. When there wasn't even an audience, it could be pretty hard to find the energy just to get up on stage.

Now, faced with another week playing in a town that showed no promise at all, I was feeling despondent to the verge of depression.

The thought of five more nights like this was just too much for me to bear. Lying in my sway-back hotel bed after the last set, listening to the guy in the next room dying of emphysema, I tried to think of something that would make it worth continuing to do this.

I told myself that there had to be something, somewhere along the line that had been left behind, or forgotten; that, if I could only remember what it was that had made this life so appealing in the first place, maybe I could find a way to go on.

"Where to begin?" I asked myself.

"Well, at the beginning, I guess."

THE FOREGONE

When I was a little kid I could sing like an angel. It was easy. I just opened my mouth and music came out. I never had to think about it. All I had to do was hear a song once or twice and I could sing it.

Once I had sung a song all the way through, it was mine. The melodies made sense to me and somehow illuminated the lyrics, so that the words became locked into my memory, impossible to forget.

I can still sing songs that I learned fifty years ago and never fear dropping a word or forgetting how the melody went, although there are days I can't remember my own address. It wasn't like some bit of prose that you memorized. That's not the way it worked. It wasn't some kind of mechanical process that could fail without maintenance-it was simpler than that and more complex, too.

I had a set of tools that allowed me to learn music by ear and once learned, it became a part of me. By the time I was six years old I had a solid repertoire of twenty or more songs.

I don't know why I had this ability. No one else in my family seemed to. I don't remember when I first became aware of it. From my earliest memory I was able to connect with music in this way. And, along with this affinity for learning and retaining music, I was gifted with an extraordinary singing voice.

I was a boy soprano. My singing voice was clear and strong, tonally accurate and with a sweet timbre that made heads turn and brought tears to the eyes of women. My vocal range allowed me to reach the highest notes in any popular song easily. There was no effort involved.

I knew when I was singing right, or perhaps more accurately, I was acutely aware when I sang off pitch. It hurt. My ears would feel like someone was dragging their fingernails over a chalkboard if my voice wasn't right on.

It is difficult to describe the feeling I had when I sang. There was an element of ecstasy involved. It was blissfully overwhelming, intensely subjective. I felt as though my voice was a bird on which my trembling young soul could soar aloft, transported to a higher realm on wings four octaves wide.

When I sang, I was completely unaware of my surroundings and when the song came to an end I found myself looking about me as if returning from another realm, blinking as mundane reality once again asserted itself.

As a child I sang all day. When kindergarten groups did sing-a-longs, I sang with complete abandon, unaware of the effect my voice had on the others. I was as shy as most when schooldays came, except when it came time to sing. There was never any question of holding back or keeping it quiet. When I sang, it was with my whole heart and in my full voice.

When I sang something I had heard, whether on a recording or elsewhere, I sang it exactly as I had heard it, in the same key. When I sang in a group, I always waited a second to see what common key the group would begin on, then I chimed in above everyone else, instinctively singing the octave above the strongest singer in the group. It was not uncommon for me to start off with everyone else, singing "Happy Birthday," only to arrive at the end singing alone with a circle of startled faces around the table.

I saw no reason not to sing at the best of my ability. In those innocent days of childhood, before life became an endless competition and something like the sound of a persons' voice could become grounds for ridicule, my friends all looked on my singing as a thing to admire. They even told their parents about it.

In grade three we had "Singing Class." One of the teachers at the elementary had some experience in voice training and aspired to form a choir. Mrs. Brandon had quite a nice singing voice and, more importantly, a music degree, majoring in vocal studies.

The first day, she had us come up to the front of the class one by one and sing a song of our choice, no doubt in order to assess what she had to work with.

What a cruel thing to do to nine-year-olds. The boys, especially, went through their own private little hells, screwing up their courage to get a song out, all alone in front of everyone.

Not me. I could hardly wait for my turn.

The children went up by alphabetical order (which put me almost last) and did their best, with predictably varying results. Mrs. B. accompanied on piano, listening closely to each performance and making notes in a big new binder as we progressed through the roster.

When it came my turn, I stated my song of choice; "Kookaburro Sits in the Old Gum Tree."

Mrs. B. began to look through her sheet music but I stopped her. I was confident in my ability to perform the song unaccompanied. It was a favourite of mine that I had learned from one of my mother's LP records, a collection of popular music sung by opera stars of the time. I had learned it note for note from the version sung by the great Roberta Peters, in the original key.

"It's OK, ma'am, I can do it without music."

"Are you sure, Neil? Very well, whenever you are ready."

I took my place at the center of the little stage there, closed my eyes and let 'er rip.

"Kookaburro sits in the old gum tree,
Merry, merry King of the woods is he,
Laugh, Kookaburro, laugh Kookaburro,
Save some gums for me."

As usual, the singing was effortless for me and I was oblivious while I was doing it. When I returned to Earth after three verses, it was to a classroom gone still and silent. Rows of shocked, staring faces came into focus. A glance to the side showed Mrs. Brandon similarly stricken, her eyebrows raised in an expression of surprise and disbelief.

The spell was broken by a clattering sound by the piano. Mrs. B. had dropped her pen. She shook her head a bit.

"Neil, would you mind terribly doing that again? I wasn't quite… prepared that time."

I obliged.

This time there were murmurs and stirring when I opened my eyes.

"Well, that's fine, Neil," Mrs. B. said, "Children, I hope you were listening. *That* was singing."

Mrs. B. asked me to stay after class that day and gave my voice a thorough going over. With her sitting at the piano and me standing beside her, singing the notes she played, we discovered that my range was just over four octaves, well into the soprano end of the keyboard. Mrs. B. was clearly excited.

"You have a rare gift, Neil," she said, "not three boys in a thousand can sing like you do. Your range is extraordinary. It's rare enough to find someone who can sing a range like that but you have a lovely voice, as well. Your ability to sing on pitch as you do is a rare thing, as well. I believe you may have perfect pitch, which can be both a blessing and a curse."

I didn't understand half of what she was saying but I was a little boy and she was talking about me and obviously pleased, so I was happy to hear her out.

The gist of it was, she wanted to tutor me in the finer points of classical singing, with an eye on having me try out for one of the major choral groups in town. My parents agreed and it was decided, much to my displeasure, that I would spend two of my lunch hours per week and a spare period in the music room, learning to sing "properly."

I was not happy. While I'd never had any great ambition for my vocal talents, I certainly had never expected to be punished for them.

The day had not yet dawned when my peers would begin to single me out and view my voice as an oddity, although I suspect some of the other boys were a tad jealous of the extra attention that my singing afforded me. When word got out that I was to receive special tutoring after class, Terry McGuire took exception.

"What a freak, Martin," he said.

I went and I learned what Mrs. Brandon had to teach me, mostly about breathing at the right time and proper "placement" of the voice in what is known as "the mask"- the various parts of the head and torso from which the voice resonates in different registers. These technical aspects to the singer's craft were mostly above my head when she described them to me but I learned to experiment until I hit on the sound she wanted and then just memorize the feeling so as to reproduce it on request.

At some point, about midway through the year, Mrs. B. decided it was time for me to make my first appearance in public as a soloist.

There was to be a Christmas pageant and talent show at the local high school that year. Our singing class had already been working on learning a couple of numbers for our own elementary schools' Christmas party. This would serve as a dress rehearsal for the big show. We would just have to step it up a notch for the larger venue.

I was given a song to sing, called "The Wee Piper of Fife," a Scots folk song with lyrics that, if sung today, would bring legions of torch-wielding suffragettes to the streets in protest;

"There was a wee piper that lived in Fife,

(nickittey-nackety-noo-noo-noo)

Who always used to beat his wife,

(hey, willy-wallecky, ho, John Dougal, away Maclafferty noo-noo-noo.}"

I was to portray the role as well as sing it, pretending to beat one of the girls about the head and ears with a red plastic baseball bat. Somehow, the prop department found an unusually comic looking bat for me to wield. It wasn't even a realistic baseball bat but one of those shorter, fatter versions made for toddlers. It had the words "BAM-BAM" molded into the fake wood grain.

I hadn't minded the idea of performing in front of a big audience. In fact, the idea rather excited me at first but as I realized how silly I was going to look carrying this ridiculous thing on stage, I began to have some doubts.

When talk turned to the procuring of costumes for us I really started to get nervous but it wasn't until my mom volunteered to make me a kilt that things went seriously south.

My mother was well meaning. She was, after all, an experienced professional seamstress and had been supplementing our household income for years by designing and making costumes. She did period wear for the annual "Klondike Days" celebrations, St. Patrick's Day get-ups and Halloween costumes galore. A kilt would by no means challenge her skills.

She took me into her sewing room and measured me up and down, recording everything with a worn nub of a pencil, in a black notebook with an elastic band on it to keep it closed. She talked about finding some plaid sox to go with the kilt. The next thing I knew she'd decided that I would need a sporran to make the outfit realistic and that I should make the thing myself. The sporran is that little purse-like thingy that wearers of the kilt have suspended from their belts, often decorated with fur and silver clasps. It serves as sort of fanny pack, as the kilt has no pockets.

It seemed unfair to me that I should be expected to take part in the making of my own costume when, after all, was I not to bear the heaviest labor of all by wearing the thing? Such arguments bore no weight with Mom, though in the end she pretty much constructed the sporran herself and let me glue the thing together.

The real problem came when she went out to buy material for the kilt itself. There were few places to buy cloth from the bolt in those days and only one carried material of the right weight in plaid.

Unfortunately, they had been called upon to supply the local pipe and drum brigade with fabric for their recent induction of new recruits and hadn't replenished their stock. They were out of every plaid except a horrid green-on-green called "Clan Gunn," of which they were short of having what Mom needed by about two inches.

Having promised to supply a kilt, mother felt honor-bound to do so, even if it meant making me wear one that clearly wasn't the right cut.

A proper highlands kilt covers the wearer from the "natural waist"-midway between the lowest rib and the hip-to mid knee. Under no circumstance is it considered decent to wear the kilt hemmed above the knee.

As I stood in front of the full-length mirror in my mom's sewing room for the final fitting, even I could see that my kilt had some serious shortcomings. Tug on the waistband as she might, my mother couldn't get the hem close to my knees. It was a good three inches above them, which is more than it sounds like when you are only four feet tall.

I cried and pleaded with my mom to no avail. She pooh-poohed my concerns, insisting that no one would know any better.

There was no way out. I was doomed.

In a few days, I would be standing at center stage in front of an audience of everyone I knew, not to mention six hundred strangers, wearing a plaid mini skirt. My life as I knew it would be over.

I talked it over with Myles, my best buddy. He thought I should hop a freight train the night before the performance and head for the coast. It sounded great, except that I had no idea where I might find a freight train and no way to find out.

There was, I concluded, no hope. I resigned myself to my fate, convinced that my standing in the community was about to be reduced forever to that of the local clown.

As the day of the talent show approached, I felt no excitement. There were no butterflies in my stomach, just a sick, sinking feeling of hopelessness and despair.

Mrs. B. noticed my lack of enthusiasm at the dress rehearsal. She thought it was just pre-performance angst.

"Now, remember the things I taught you about breath, Neil. You must support your voice on a column of air. You must portray vitality in your voice. You are sounding like you have no vitality at all. Don't think about the audience. Just think about the voice. Focus on the voice."

She might as well have been talking in another language.

The day drew nigh, and then it was here. We were bused over to the high school with an hour to spare and given a couple of rooms in which to change. I didn't even glance into the mirror after I put my costume on. I knew what I looked like. Picking up BAM-BAM, I made my way vacantly to the side of the stage. I tried not to think about what was to come as I watched the other performances through a fog from the wings.

And then it came. The M.C., who was also the principal of the high school, introduced us. The lights went down. I followed the little girl who was to be my "wife," whose name I cannot recall, out onto the stage and we took our marks. The lights went up as Mrs. B. played the opening bars of the melody from the pit.

I began to sing, clutching my bright red club in my hand, acutely aware of the smattering of laughter coming from the front rows. Were they only amused at the sight of a boy wearing a kilt? At the size and shape of the bat? Or had they perceived the length of my kilt to be somewhat less than proper?

Whatever it was, it was enough to distract me from the task at hand. The plan was that I should sing the first line, then advance a step to be within clubbing range of my "wife's" head, so that as I sang the second line-the one about beating her-I could pretend to hit her over the head with the bat in time to the beat. That's what we'd rehearsed.

"There was a wee piper who lived in Fife'
Nickety-nackety, noo-noo noo..."

Whether it was just nerves, or the tittering from the crowd, or my self consciousness about the kilt, I flubbed it up.

"Who always used to beat his wife,
Hey, Willie Walleckey, Ho, John Dougal, away..."

I got no further.

Instead of *pretending* to bop the girl on the noggin as planned, I reached out and actually rapped her solidly on the back of the head. Bam-bam, being more of a hard plastic balloon than a bat, emitted a cartoonish "pong" on impact, which was picked up and amplified by the lone microphone on the stage and elicited a hearty roar of laughter from the audience.

My stage-wife reacted as any nine-year-old girl would who's just been beaned on the nut by a boy. She turned around and kicked me.

No doubt she meant to give me a boot to the shin or the kneecap, as was usual on the playground, but the stage fright or the stage lights affected her aim, too. Her hard-surfaced little dress shoe missed my sporran by an inch and disappeared up my kilt, making solid contact with my unprotected scrotum.

There was a sound then that I'll never forget. Immediately upon contact of her foot with my testicles, every male in the audience said;

"OOOoo..." in an involuntary and empathetic tone that is only used by men on witnessing another man getting kicked in the balls.

I collapsed on the stage, holding the pain in both hands. The lights went down as teachers rushed to my aid. My debut as a boy soprano was over.

As fate would have it, so was my time as a soprano singer.

A few weeks later, in voice class, while attempting to sing a particularly tricky passage in something by Verde, my voice broke. I don't mean as in a little break, or a warble like boys voices make when they start to enter puberty.

I had been putting such a strain on my vocal chords that one or more of them ripped, like an athlete tearing a ligament.

There was blood. It hurt.

I went to see a doctor, a specialist, who made a lot of disapproving noises about pushing things too far too early and advised me not to try talking, let alone singing, for three weeks. That was fine with me because, at that point, any attempt to speak was painful.

I stayed completely silent for a month, patiently waiting for the day that I could start to sing again. When I went back to the specialist, he examined my throat and then asked me to say a few words, quietly. I did, and was completely taken aback by the sound of my own voice.

The voice that came out of my mouth was that of an older person. It was 'way too low and had a rough, whiskeyed rasp to it. It had no business coming out of the mouth of a ten-year-old boy.

"As I thought, you've lost the higher range of your voice, but the lower chords seem to be compensating nicely. You are just going to have a lower voice than most of your friends for a while. Don't worry-they'll catch up."

"What about singing, though?" I croaked.

"Oh, I wouldn't recommend it, at least for a while. Give yourself time to heal up completely, say a couple more months. Then start slow. You'll have to see what you have to work with."

See what I had to work with?! I couldn't believe my ears.

"You mean I lost my voice? I won't ever be able to sing again?"

"I wouldn't say that. You'll just have to learn to sing a bit lower, that's all."

A little bit lower turned out to be a lot lower. Over the next few months, working with Mrs. B. after class, I discovered that my singing voice had abandoned the stratospheric realm of the soprano to take up residence in the baritone, with the upper limits of my new, almost-two-octave range just slipping into the low tenor. And it wasn't just my singing voice that was affected.

My speaking voice had finally settled down and lost its' raspy quality but it sounded like it should belong to someone twice my size. At ten years of age I had the voice of a twenty-five year old lumberjack.

Once again my voice shocked people but in a new way. When I spoke, people did a double-take, wondering where the man was. I was sad to have lost my beautiful singing voice but I tried to look on the bright side.

Myles thought it was cool.

"You sound just like Ben Cartwright on "Bonanza," he said.

It was great for phone pranks and it certainly put an end to any speculation that, after the kilt incident, I might be a "permanent soprano." Indeed, my new speaking voice seemed to instill a sort of unconscious respect in most of the other kids, with the notable exception of Terry McGuire.

"You're still a freak, Martin," he assured me.

I grieved the loss of my singing ability for years, even as I worked to learn how to use my lower range. The love of music hadn't left me and I was determined to find a way to feel again the way I had when I sang.

The best thing about my new singing voice was that it was far better suited to the singing of pop and rock n' roll. The fads of the times were leaning that way. Dylan had appeared at Newport with an electric guitar and the Band in tow. The Beatles were commanding the pop charts with hit after hit. The future was rockin', so anyone who wanted to be cool had better rock, too and I was far better prepared to sing rock than I had been.

Of course, if you want to sing rock n roll, you need a rock n roll band. Lots of the kids at school were learning instruments. After the Beatles first appearance on Ed Sullivan, everybody wanted to play guitar. For me, though, the drums were the obvious choice.

I had been playing beats on any surface available since I was able. It came easy to me. Not as easy as singing had before my injury, but I had a talent there to pursue and pursue it I did. I took lessons at the local school until I was able to play three or four of the more common rock n roll beats, then I set about teaching myself to sing while I played.

When I thought I was ready, I went out looking for a band that needed a drummer. It might have been a tad premature, owing to the fact that I didn't actually own any drums, but where there's a will, there's a way and what I did have was something that proved far more important-I believed that I was a drummer. As far as I was concerned, the rest would come in good time.

My conviction was so strong in this regard that I was able to convince other musicians, too. In no time I was in Randy Nichols' parents' basement, learning songs with Randy playing guitar and his buddy Roger on bass, while I used an old tin cookie can for a snare drum and one of my mom's pewter pie plates for a cymbal, turned upside down with a hole drilled in the center so I could mount it on a music stand.

I got a real snare drum for Christmas, and it wasn't long before my Dad bought me a cheap but complete set of drums on the understanding that my birthday presents were going to be pretty modest for a couple of years.

By this time, our little ensemble had managed to put together a half-dozen songs and even found a microphone for me to sing through, though it was a while before I could afford a mike stand, so I had to improvise with a coat hanger. We played at parties and down at the neighborhood drop-in center, where one of the teachers on supervision heard us and hired us to play the Christmas dance at the school.

We were hardly ready but we knew we couldn't miss the opportunity. We learned a bunch of new songs as fast as we could and, with time in short supply, we began planning for our stage set.

It was a simple thing to borrow the overhead projector from the Art department and assign a friend to manipulate two plates with colored oil between them, throwing psychedelic images onto the back curtain on the stage. What we really wanted to have was a strobe light. The real thing was hellishly expensive, so we made do with a design out of an arts and craft magazine. Dwayne borrowed his Mom's mixer and fixed it into a crate. Then he cut a cardboard disc about a foot in diameter and made a V shaped notch in it, which he covered with colored plastic. The disc was holed in the center and attached to the shaft of the beater with a generous application of duct tape and a spotlight was affixed behind.

Setting this contraption on a chair at the side of the stage, Dwayne set the mixer on 'High', and as the disc got up to speed, the light began to 'strobe. It was almost as good as the real thing, and it worked almost all the way through our second set, when the tape let go and the disc came loose, rolling comically across the front of the stage as we were bathed in the uninterrupted glare of the naked spotlight.

We were a smash hit and our street-cred went up whole points that night.

Meanwhile, time was marching on and likewise school. It was time to go to junior high.

The transition was not going to be a smooth one. The baby boom had caught the education system unprepared. The province was building schools as fast as they could afford to but, try as they might, they couldn't hope to keep up with the demand for teachers.

There was such a deficit that the school boards put out the call to those who had retired. People in their seventies and older were put back to work in classrooms swollen to thirty-five or forty kids.

We had the dubious honor of being given over to the care of a seventy-three year old math teacher by the unfortunate name of Mr. Christy, which was immediately changed to Mr. Crusty by the kids.

Although he must have been a tall man in his prime, Mr. Christy was stooped with age and shaky of hand. His eyesight was none too acute and his hearing needed testing. He was, in short, the perfect victim for classroom pranks.

Mr. Christy's infirmities alone guaranteed the class would turn into a zoo but he came to us blissfully unaware of how classroom discipline had suffered at the hands of the baby boomers.

He paid no attention to seating arrangements and allowed the worst behavior cases in the class to form a tight group at the center rear of the room. His indifference to the consequences of this, combined with his inability to perceive the antics that resulted, made math class, for the first time ever, our favorite.

At the center of the group was Brent Nolan, master prankster and owner of the most impressive private menagerie of pets in the known world. Brent lived in a huge mansion in the swankiest part of the suburbs, overlooking the river. To say that his parents were well off was an understatement. Brent always had the newest toys or gadgets, sometimes even before they came on the general market but where his folks really went all out to indulge him was with the pets they gave him.

It had started out normally enough; at five or six, Brent asked for a hamster and was given one. We all asked for hamsters after that, with varying success. Next year we all wanted turtles when the local department store put on a display of them. These were the standard, tiny little green guys and most of our parents indulged us. Brent got a snapping turtle about six inches across.

When we got up into grade five and six, some of us started aquariums, usually just a couple of guppies in a modest one-gallon affair with the obligatory air pump and colored gravel bottoms.

Brent asked for and received a two hundred gallon salt-water aquarium with a living coral reef, inhabited by a nine-inch leopard shark, a puffer fish and a pack of little lobsters.

When some of us got dogs, Brent got a spider monkey, a wonderfully disgusting creature who liked to terrorize house guests by pelting them with feces, or laying in wait at the top of the stairwell to leap on the unwary head.

The basement of their house was finally given over entirely to Brent's collection, which grew to include chameleons, rat snakes, tarantulas, a six-foot boa constrictor, two ferrets named Heckle and Jeckle, a Ring-necked Parakeet called Marty and a host of other pets too numerous to name.

Brent loved to bring his pets to school and usually had one with him, whether a gerbil in his pocket or a rat snake coiled up under his shirt. On one memorable occasion, he decided to bring his most recent acquisition, a four-foot iguana named "Melvin", who liked to ride on Brent's back, hanging from his shoulders. The effect of Melvin's tail protruding from under Brent's jacket as he walked down the hall turned his passage from Art class to the lunchroom into a joyous parade the length of the hallway and resulted in Brent being called to the office, where he was asked to take Melvin home for the rest of the day, with mild admonishments to leave his animals at home in the future.

It wasn't until the following year that they really lowered the boom after what has come to be known as "the budgie incident".

Besides Marty the parakeet, Brent owned a large variety of birds, from finches and lovebirds to an African parrot and several mackaws. His collection culminated with a handsome Merlin that he'd rescued from an abandoned nest near his house and raised by hand for several years.

I loved to go over to his place, even braving assaults by the monkey to sit and watch the Merlin, whose name was "Sir Beak." The beauty of his plumage and the utter wildness of his stare thrilled me in a way none of Brent's other charges could. But it wasn't Sir Beak that caused the school to ban all pets from the property.

When Brent brought "Tweety," his green and yellow budgerigar, to grade seven, he meant no harm. Tweety being such a docile little fellow, Brent had no second thought placing him in his side pocket for a day at school.

The two of them attended home room in the morning without incident and a couple of us noticed when Brent took Tweety out for second, so the trip from home room to English was filled with kids pleading with Brent to take the budgie out again so they could see him.

Those of us who didn't get close enough and missed the brief chance in the hall pestered Brent once in class until he relented and brought his feathered friend out once more.

The English teacher, Mr. Cowan, was a nice looking younger man we generally agreed was of the cooler types as far as teachers went. None of us had any way of knowing that he suffered from a morbid fear of birds so potent that he'd been years in therapy for it.

He'd apparently been attacked by crows as a baby, in an incident that had burned itself onto his psyche so that the merest hint of a rustle of feathers was enough to give him flop sweats, while knowledge of the actual presence of a bird-any bird, large or small-in his immediate vicinity rendered the poor man a gibbering wreck.

Noticing the commotion around Brent's desk, Mr. Cowan assumed there were candies being passed out and strode straight over to confiscate the offending stuff. When he confronted Brent and demanded that he open his hand, Brent did as he was told, thrusting Tweety up directly into the teachers face, with instructive results.

The instant he realized what he was looking at, Mr. Cowan emitted a sound unlike anything we'd ever heard a human being make. Simultaneously, he threw his arms up over his head and ran back to his desk, which he leapt upon in an unexpected display of athletic ability. There he stood, emitting little bleating noises and shaking like a leaf, while the entire class stared in mute astonishment.

It was one of the girls that finally decided to take control of the situation. After trying unsuccessfully to communicate with Mr. Cowan, she ordered Brent to take the now frightened bird out of the room and used the intercom to contact the office.

At first they didn't get it.

"Where is Mr. Cowan?" the secretary asked her.

"He's, um...standing on his desk," the girl replied.

"ieybah, ieybah," said Mr. Cowan, towards the speaker.

"What in the world was that?"

"That was Mr. Cowan," the student replied.

"Good Lord!"

The English room was only a few steps from the office and the secretary lost no time getting there. The principal was called and the classroom cleared. Poor Mr. Cowan was led to the staff room and ministered to by the nurse, while we were herded to the cafeteria for a free period.

After that, Brent was banned from bringing pets to school in no uncertain terms, but that didn't stop him being the source of much amusement. He was one of those kids that had an enormous wealth of humor, always grinning and laughing, usually at someone else's expense. Brent spent a lot of time searching for new things to do in order to escape doing schoolwork. He scoured the backs of comic books for things he could send away for. We'd all had our turns ordering the chattering teeth or the x-ray specs and we'd all shared the same disappointment when they'd arrived, sad imitations of the versions we'd held in our minds.

Brent, however, never lost faith. He had sent away for them all and used them in rotation, never without a pocket full of onion gum or a palm zapper in his hand.

He was always on the lookout for a new gag. He owned books on balsa airplane design and model rocketry. He ran experiments using different chemical concoctions as fuel for his home made missiles and stink grenades and kept an arsenal of them in his locker, ready for use.

When technology failed him, however, Brent was not above improvising. On a day when his more ingenious distractions had failed to pass the time, to start chewing paper wads and fashioning little silver foil spear cups from gum wrappers with which to hurl the soggy paper balls up to the ceiling of the classroom, one by one until, by the end of the period he'd left a tiny forest of shiny stalactites hanging above his desk.

Next math period, all the kids in the group had their pockets stuffed with gum wrappers and were soon chewing industriously away, hard at work on their own ceiling displays.

Before long, the entire center third of the room was over-shadowed by what must have been hundreds of spitballs with their foil tails hanging down. It probably hadn't occurred to any of the kids just what an incriminating act it was, when the only way to get a spitball to adhere to the ceiling tiles was by throwing it straight upwards. Even a slight angle would rob the missile of enough energy to stick, causing it to fail on contact and fall back to the ground, onto someone else's desk, or if you were really lucky, onto the hair of a girl in class. Only those that were thrown straight up and true would stick, which meant, of course, that the perpetrator of each and every successful installation was clearly indicated by the position of the object itself.

The fact that Mr. Christy never noticed the ever-growing patch of foil on the ceiling was testament to just how oblivious the old boy was to the goings on in his class. We never truly appreciated the depth of his unawareness, though, until Brent came up with the megadart.

The megadart was the latest in a long line of increasingly dangerous home-made throwing darts that Brent had started out designing in grade seven. The first ones were tiny, made out of toothpicks and pins. These little toys were fine for chucking across the aisle when the teacher wasn't looking, hopefully to stick into someone's notebook or, better yet, their forearm.

As his early successes gave him more confidence, Brent began to improve on the design of his missiles, with an eye on increasing both range and destructive power. Over time the designs called for sturdier materials to withstand the velocity and shock of impact over distance. Toothpicks gave way to matchsticks, pins to needles.

Brent found he could build darts that would easily soar he length of the classroom and had enough penetrating power to get through layers of clothing and stick into the targets' skin a good quarter inch. He was acknowledged throughout the school as the master dart maker.

It must have been a slow day for Brent when he found the time to build the megadart. Maybe the idea had been floating around in his head for a while and all he needed was to go ahead with the manufacturing. History will never know for sure, as Brent has not been forthcoming with the facts.

All we can say for certain is that, one day he went to his locker before math class and produced the most formidable weapon in the history of dart making; a projectile so large as to be classified as lethal.

The megadart was made of five wooden chopsticks that surrounded a piece of coat hanger wire about twelve inches long. The rear of the thing had four cardboard feathers, each one nearly three inches at the back and tapering to an inch in the front for stability and speed. The business end was sharpened to as keen a point as could be produced on the grinder in shop class. Held together with big rubber bands fore and aft, with extra ones at the front for weight, it looked as rugged as it did deadly.

Brent had shown a few of us the megadart on the way to math and explained that he'd made it with the intention of seeing if he could throw it hard enough to penetrate the blackboard surface and stay. It was a breathtaking goal. We all knew how hard the surface of the blackboard was. Nothing had ever been invented that would penetrate that slick, green barrier.

We were honored to be present to witness such a monumental attempt. We couldn't have been more excited if we'd been asked to watch Chuck Yeager try to break the sound barrier in the X-15. Well, maybe a bit.

Of course, in order to qualify as a truly daring feat, the attempt had to be made in class, with Mr. Christy present. The trick would be to choose the moment when he had his back turned and was standing off to one side, presenting enough empty blackboard to target safely, stand up to get a good throw and then, having done so, sitting down and looking normal by the time the teacher reacted and turned around.

Mr. Christy started the class as usual, with a brief lecture on the subject at hand, which he then began to illustrate on the board.

We held our breath and watched Brent. He was playing it cool, keeping his head down and watching, waiting for his moment. Twice he started to move, only to have Mr. Christy turn around unexpectedly to stress some point. Then, the time was right.

Brent stepped smoothly and silently into the aisle, standing and bringing his throwing arm back in one fluid motion. Without hesitation, he hurled the dart with all his strength.

Unaccountably, at the exact same second, Mr. Christy suddenly took a step to the side. Perhaps he meant to point out something he'd already written on that part of the board. We'll never know for sure what it was that made him step, with exquisite timing, directly into the path of the speeding missile. There was a collective gasp as it struck him in the back of the neck.

Mr. Christie whirled about to see what we were all so shocked about, only to find the entire class staring at him in horror. The dart was protruding from the back of his neck, like some bizarre feathered ornament.

After surveying the room with a puzzled expression, he turned back to the blackboard and continued his lesson, apparently totally unaware of the offending object, now bobbing up and down with the movements of his shoulder as he wrote.

We gradually became aware that the megadart had miraculously penetrated only the collar of his suit jacket, piercing both it and his shirt collar but narrowly missing his flesh by what must have been mere millimeters. Lodged there solidly, it continued to flop around comically as he moved about, oblivious.

One by one, we got over our initial shock and began to appreciate the humorous aspects of the situation. Some of the girls began to giggle. The boys were hysterical.

Mr. Christy turned around once more and spent a moment silently regarding us all. He took his glasses off and cleaned them with his handkerchief, then replaced both. He must have thought we were just being unusually boisterous for some reason and after another moment of pondering what in the world it might be that had got us all so twitter-pated, he returned to his task at the blackboard. It wasn't until the period ended and Mr. Christy made his way down the hall to the office that the prank came to light.

There was an ear-piercing scream from one of the secretaries who, spying the thing sticking out of the old man's neck, had assumed the worst.

The next math period, the principal was there, waiting when we entered the room. He waited, calmly observing the class, until everyone was present and seated, then stood and began to address the class.

"You people," he began, looking down at the floor and hooking his thumbs under his suspenders, "have no idea the trouble you could be in."

Strolling casually to the front of the class, he turned and started down the center aisle as he went on.

The principal stopped directly under the densest concentration of spitball darts; right beside Brent's desk. Brent had his head down concentrating intently on something in his binder.

"Indeed," he continued, his voice rising in tempo and volume, "had this diabolical weapon, which had no business being brought into my school in the first place, actually done the harm that it was so obviously capable of doing...I would not be standing here. You would find yourselves instead being addressed by a member of the Police force, who would be investigating a case of ASSAULT WITH A DEADLY WEAPON!"

He succeeded in getting the message across and there were no further incidents of dart throwing for the remainder of the term.

Mr. Christy decided, perhaps in part because of the mega dart affair, to return to retirement the following year and was replaced by a younger man, named Mr. Zucherman. He was given both the grade eight and nine math duties, which meant our class which, in a testament to how few resources the school really had, remained more or less the same into the new school year.

For me though, it was still all about the music.

My band, "The Forgone Conclusion" had broken up that year when the guitar guy's parents had told him he needed to improve his grades, leaving me without a venue for my music.

Lyle Doonan, the guy who had been acting as the band's manager, was of the opinion that I was a better singer than I was a drummer, and had asked me if I wanted to front a band. I had said yes at the time, without thinking much about the possible consequences. No one was more surprised than I was when he called me up to tell me that he'd found a band for me to sing with.

He'd arranged for an audition in the basement of the church near my place. To my enduring surprise, I found that he'd actually found a real band. I don't know what I had expected but these guys were the real deal-a tight four-piece group, complete with a guy named 'Fang' on Hammond organ. They were good, 'way better than my band had been. They were just in need of a singer.

I never found out if the band was supposed to be auditioning me, or the other way around, but it was a moot point as we all liked the way things sounded and agreed to start rehearsals right away.

I had a list of tunes I wanted to sing, headed up by a selection of rhythm and blues songs that had made it onto the pop charts; "The Letter," by the Boxtops (a number one hit in 1967, long before Joe Cocker put out his excellent version on the "Mad Dogs and 'Englishmen" album), "In the Midnight Hour" by the great Wilson Pickett, "Sittin' On the Dock of the Bay," by Otis Redding, "Soul Man" by Sam & Dave. There were a couple of tunes by Three Dog Night, arguably still in the R&B genre and a pair from The Band. A smattering of Beatles tunes and random male vocal hits rounded out the list and made for a set of music that would feature the singer, for better or worse.

Looking back, I realize the list of songs I chose to do that night was heavily weighted in rhythm & blues and yet, at the time I had no real awareness of that genre of music. I had always loved the Motown sound and had leaned in that direction when it came to suggestions for my bands' repertoire but it would be years before I put the thing together and realized what all these songs had in common.

A week or two into rehearsals, I started to wonder if I had bit off more than I could reasonably expect to chew alone, so I enlisted the aid of my buddy Rob, whose older brother was lead singer for a band in town.

Naturally Rob, possessed of a decent, if untested set of pipes himself, yearned to sing with a band as well.

We learned the two part songs together and worked hard on getting the harmonies right. We even worked out some rudimentary choreography, moving in and out of the spotlight as our vocal parts traded prominence.

By the time performance night came, we were feeling pretty good about our set. We planned our premiere show in the same church basement we had been rehearsing in. Lyle had posters printed up and distributed them around the neighborhood. Word of mouth took care of the rest.

On gig night there were a hundred and fifty kids sitting on the floor of the church basement, waiting for the show to begin. The problem was, I wasn't there.

My parents, in a display of lousy timing, had finally decided to do something decisive about my failing grades, which they correctly blamed on the amount of time spent at rehearsals. The night of the gig, they grounded me.

They made it clear that I was not to leave the house for a week on pain of dire consequences, then they went out for the evening. I still don't know if they actually had expected me to stay in and miss my debut as a front man in my own band but the instant dad's car lights rounded the corner at the end of the block, I was out the door and gone.

It took me five minutes to run to the church and another five to catch my breath well enough to do the opening number. The rest of the evening went by in a blur. Rob and I went through the song list, sang our hearts out and did well enough to get a healthy applause after every tune.

Perhaps most importantly, the foxiest girls in the neighborhood were all there in the front row, watching us in rapt attention.

And that was that.

To this day, I do not know what happened after that. We played the one gig, which went over very well according to everyone who was there, and then...nothing. No more rehearsals, no more gigs. That was that only time we ever played.

Once more, I found myself with no outlet for my musical ambitions. I tried to pretend there was something of interest there but it soon became painfully obvious that formal education and I were about done with one another. The school remained a recruiting ground for musicians, though.

I met a keyboard player named Dwayne, whose parents didn't mind us holding rehearsals in their basement. We put a band together and began working up a song list. After a few weeks we had learned ten or twelve tunes and it wasn't sounding bad but there was something missing. . The guitar guy was good enough, learned the solos well enough and was willing to do harmonies when called upon. The bass player had the proper equipment and was competent on his instrument. We added a second guitar with hopes of solving the riddle and Percy's excellent rhythm certainly filled out the band's sound, but there was still something more needed.

I think we all felt it-there was just no magic. There was also, perhaps therefore, a lack of direction. We continued to practice together for a few more weeks and then, one by one, the players found other things to do. The band just dissolved.

It was about this time that Percy's dad and him came to loggerheads about the amount of time Percy was spending on the band, as opposed to his school work. Percy senior gave Percy Jr. an ultimatum and found he had to back it up; he took away Percy's guitar and amp.

Percy reacted by running away from home. He took his camping gear and set up residence in the river valley, a handy distance from the school. We thought it was the best thing since sliced bread and spent all our spare time down there, hanging around the campsite.

Percy's mom was worried sick about him and, having shamed the location of her son out of one of his friends, could be seen standing at the top of the ravine, calling out to him that she'd brought "a few things" which she proceeded to toss down the hill in a bag. It turned out to contain some toiletry items and food, including some packages of steaks from their freezer.

Percy invited everyone to barbeque at his camp and we ended staying all night. The fact that it was a week night didn't occur to me until I went home to change and realized I'd missed school that day.

Next day, when I got back to school, there was a new guy in the class. John Tate was a tough kid from the mean streets of Glasgow whose parents had finally had enough of the failing economy in Scotland and decided to emigrate to Canada. He was a couple of years older than the average, partly because he'd not been doing so well academically in the British school system and because the standards there hadn't compared favorably with ours.

John had a whole different take on things. Growing up in the British version of the "projects" of America; badly conceived housing areas for the poor and under privileged, where drugs and violence ran rampant and teenage sex was a given, he immediately became something of a hero among us mild mannered Canadian teens.

His vocabulary, when you could understand it through his thick Glasgowegian burr, was peppered with liberal use of swear words with a wonderful disregard for local norms. We listened in awe as he recounted tales of his life over there, talking about how "some cunt glassed a lass in the pub and got slit up a treat for it," or some such colorful thing.

To hear him tell it, he had been obliged to fight every day at school and considered himself better than average with his fists. He didn't look that strong, with his scrawny arms and thin build but he exuded a confidence that belied his appearance. None of us cared to try him, anyways.

John's take on Mr. Z was immediate distain bordering on loathing.

"The guy's a cream puff," he said one day, hanging out at the Videl Café after school.

"A what?" someone inquired.

"He's a poofty Casper milktoast," John replied.

"Oh," we said, as if that had explained.

For his part, Mr. Z. didn't seem to know what to make of John. He seemed to sense there was something in the hint of a smile that was always on John's face that spelled "handle with care," so he pretty much left him alone.

One day, that all changed. Mr. Z. was in a foul mood over something from the moment he walked in the classroom. He was looking for somebody to take it out on and I guess he decided that was the day to finally put the new kid in his place.

John was minding his own business as usual, chatting with the girl who sat behind him, twisted about in his desk so he could give her the benefit of his rakish grin, when the teacher addressed him.

"Turn around and face front, please John."

John declined to react.

"John-I asked you to turn around. Now."

"Wha'?" John's voice was dripping with scorn.

"Don't use that tone with me, mister. Turn around and sit properly."

"Feck you."

Absolute, complete, stunned silence ensued. No one had ever heard a kid tell a teacher to fuck off. Five stunned seconds passed that seemed like whole minutes.

"What did you say to me?"

"I sayd Feck off, ye poxy cunt."

Mr. Z. advanced threateningly towards John's desk. His face had turned an interesting shade of purple while the veins in his neck looked ready to pop. He was at least six inches taller than the lad and out weighed him by a hundred pounds or more of solid muscle. We all thought John was going to get dragged bodily out of his desk and down to the office but that's not what happened.

As the muscular teacher approached him, John attempted to stand up but waited a second too long. Mr. Z. got a hold of his collar and propelled him towards the front of the class.

Caught off balance and skidding on the slick classroom floor, it took John a few seconds to recover his balance. It was all he needed.

"Put yer hands on me, ye berk? Okee, come an' get et."

A more experienced fighter would have recognized the way John went into a crouch, at the same time going up on the balls of his feet and turning to present his left side to his opponent, hands raised only to waist level but ready.

Mr. Z. missed the warning signs and blundered straight at him with his arms outstretched as if to engulf John in a bear hug. He probably had no clear idea of what he was intending to do once he got a hold of the boy but he didn't get a chance to see.

John ducked under the encircling arms and came up inside them, twisting at the waist with his wrist, elbow and shoulder locked and his legs driving him up to deliver every ounce of his weight, all one hundred and five pounds of it, into his fist and onto the very point of Mr. Z.'s chin.

The teachers' mouth snapped shut with a percussive "pop" as the breath left his body and he collapsed on the floor, out, as they say, like a light. We couldn't believe our eyes.

Then John wound up and delivered a solid kick to the unconscious man's crotch that lifted him off the floor.

"And there's somethin' to wake up to, ye cloth-eared git."

He turned on his heel and walked out the door.

That was the last we saw of John. He never returned to the school but he left a lasting legacy behind. Every one of us felt it. It was as if his one act of ultimate defiance to the tyranny of that man somehow freed all of us.

The knowledge that a student could stand up to a bully, even one who had the authority of the school system behind him made us all aware of our own personal power to choose. We walked a little taller, laughed a little louder. We looked the teachers in the eye after that and found, to our surprise, that they mostly looked away.

For me, the incident fed a growing awareness in me that school was not where I belonged. High school began. I stopped feeling that I should try to get better grades and began to focus on the things that were really important, like music.

I was still struggling with the problem of personnel. Dwayne, Percy and myself were left looking for a singer and a bass player to round out the roster. We held auditions for singers, inviting hopeful candidates down to the basement to try out.

There were a few that had decent voices but sang in styles that didn't fit. Others were in denial about the level of talent they possessed. The sixth or seventh person we interviewed was a guy named Doug, who Percy and I knew slightly from school.

The first time I'd seen Doug, he'd come swooping down the hall towards me, flapping his arms in an uncannily realistic impression of a large bird.

"Seagull?" I ventured.

"Vulture," Doug corrected, as he came in for a landing nearby.

"Ok, so you're a Vulture. Cool."

"I hear you're looking for a singer."

"Yup."

"I want to try out."

"OK, be at this address at six."

"See you there," he said and, spreading his ungainly wings, flapped off down the hall.

Doug was very surprised when we told him we didn't think he was that good a singer. He could sing but, like a lot of people, his opinion of his own singing voice was based on his performance in the shower and bolstered by compliments from his parents and others who were, perhaps overly kind. If you love someone who has an average singing voice, don't tell them they are better than they are. They might go out and try out for a band and have their feelings hurt.

Having failed to find the perfect voice to front our band, we decided to move on to interviewing for the bass player seat in the band. After all, once we had a bass man, we could start rehearsing the full rhythm section. A singer was bound to come along. We needed to get to work.

So, picture our collective surprise when the first person to show up with a bass guitar was Doug the vulture. When he turned out to be rather good at it, we were doubly bemused. He had a unique, melodic style on the bass, which impressed us over the more workmanlike approach of most players.

We did have a couple of other players to try out and one of them was something of a local celebrity. He'd been a member of an early Edmonton rock band that had really made a name, actually producing a record and getting airplay on local stations.

The reason he hadn't been active for the past few years was the topic of wide speculation, which had given rise to some stories that verged on urban legend. There were various versions of the story but they all revolved around the idea that he'd eaten an entire batch of acid and had never really come down again.

When he arrived and set up in the garage, we were encouraged to see his equipment was top-drawer stuff. He seemed a tad uncommunicative but otherwise all right, except for the fact that, once he got set up and turned his amp on, he seemed to only want to repeat one simple phrase; over and over again. We waited patiently for him to stop, trying to be polite. Then he turned his amp up to full and cranked the outputs on his bass wide open. As he returned to his pet phrase, the sound was annoyingly loud, even though it was just bass.

Before we could get his attention and ask him to stop, smoke started coming from the back of his amp. He'd overloaded his amplifier so much that the circuit boards had actually caught fire.

"Hey, man! You fried your amp!" Percy yelled through the din.

He was rewarded with a blank stare. The guy continued to play, with only distorted crackling and buzzing now coming from his ruined speakers.

It took us half an hour to convince him that the interview was over and help him pack up his now useless equipment. That was the end of that audition.

After a brief consultation, Doug became a part of the band. A pleasant, easy-going guy with an artistic approach to his playing as with his life, he fit right in.

My need to sing while I played put certain limitations on my drumming, resulting in a style that was more about holding down the tempo and the beat than playing flashy fills, which suited me fine. I'd always been more of a Ringo Starr/Charlie Watts fan, rather than the less musical, more showman-like playing of Keith Moon or John Bonham. Doug's melodic, meandering style on the bass went perfectly with it.

Percy was an excellent guitarist, a solid rhythm player who understood the function of that role in the band, as well as a tireless pursuer of the right sound for his solos. Percy would spend hours learning a riff and more time finding the combination of settings to produce the exact sound on the recording. If his present setup wouldn't give him the right sound, he would find - or build – an effects pedal that would.

Dwayne was pretty good as a keyboard player. He knew his scales and chords and brought a certain level of showmanship to the gigs with his signature move of getting down under his electronic organ during a solo and then, supporting the thing on his back, continuing to solo while humping it around the stage like a wounded animal. It got the crowd's attention.

We got hired to play a weekend gig in the local high school hangout, the "Nighthawk" restaurant. They didn't have a stage but with a little rearranging they made room for us in the corner by the door. It paid very little but, hey - it was right across the street from our high school and all the girls we knew were there to see us. The owner was a big old Italian guy named Nick, who wanted to give us advice about "the show business."

"You musta looka nice for the people," he said, "notta serious likea this. You gotta smile for the crowd."

We ignored him, of course. He wouldn't be the last.

We decided to do some gigs in small towns for a while, to gain some experience performing. We started out by renting a local hall and putting up posters around the town and in the surrounding area.

The first one we did was in Castor, AB. Why there and not somewhere a bit closer to town is a mystery, lost to the intervening decades. We also decided to share the stage with another band, which would seem counter intuitive but then, it was all about the learning curve so, who knows what we might have been thinking. Safety in numbers, for one thing.

We had about ten musicians and two groups worth of gear to transport and no access to any one suitable vehicle, so we ended up taking three. It became apparent that one of the things we needed experience in would be logistics when Percy and me somehow got lost in the shuffle and left behind. His dad, in an act of good father-hood of the highest order, drove us the two hundred plus kilometers to the town in a blizzard, then, with nothing more than a "thanks, dad", turned around and drove home again.

The plan was to sleep in the hall, thus saving expenses. This provided Percy with a perfect venue for the beginning of what was to become an ongoing parade of pranks that would continue for the duration of the bands' life.

Two a.m. found us all lying awake in our sleeping bags on the cold, hard floor with the lights out. Suddenly, the light went on in the corner of the room to reveal Percy lying on top of Dwayne in his sleeping bag.

Waiting only until he knew he had everyone looking, he looked into Dwayne's eyes and said;

"This is your first time, isn't it, honey?"

General hilarity ensued.

What we did mostly in those days was rehearse. We never seemed to have enough good songs in our list to do a whole night without repeating something and it seemed in those early days that, for every song we learned, there was one that we dropped from the list because it wasn't sounding right. I guess one of the things we were learning was how to pick songs that fit us.

We needed a place to practice. Most of our folks were good about letting us use their basements, but even the most patient and loving parents could stand a full fledged rock band for only so long, then it was time to move on.

We rehearsed for a while in Dwayne's parent's basement.

Dwayne had an interest in chemistry, which combined nicely with a fondness for getting high.

It was by no means easy to build a reputation for being hard-core dopers in 1970 Edmonton. Real drugs were hard to find in those days, except for pot and, when available, hash. There weren't a whole lot of alternatives. The big drug dealers in the south had yet to become interested in the tiny market north of 49, so we were left with what-ever the local pushers could come up with. This led to a rash of underhanded schemes with people selling dime bags of parsley and oregano to unwary youths. Once or twice a year, somebody brought in some acid but you had to move fast. There was occasionally an influx of one or other of the more common pharmaceutical drugs of the day-MDA, PCP and a variety of uppers and downers but that was about it.

Not good enough for Dwayne. He stated that he could and would produce his own drugs and set about doing so with a will. He bought up suspicious quantities of cough syrup from all the local stores and began to experiment in his bedroom. It was weeks before he claimed to have had any success, showing us a gummy black substance he claimed was "Bella Donna," and proceeded to serve as his own guinea pig by downing it. When nothing happened after a couple of hours, he admitted the formula must have been off. When he realized how much hash he could have bought with the money he'd wasted on cough syrup, the experiments ended.

We had some great times with Dwayne. His parents had a thing for travel and often left town for weeks at a time. Dwayne being an only child, this left us with a party house where we could stay all night and get really stoned.

It was there that the real indications of what would become Captain Nobody's prankster nature began to manifest.

On one occasion, at an all-night dope fest in Dwayne's parent's house, when Dwayne had disappeared into his bedroom with his girl-friend, Percy and Doug dressed up convincingly as Dwayne's parents in clothes from their room. Doug looked good as Mr. Doherty in one of his suits, complete with fedora and tie but Percy, having found one of Mrs. Doherty's blonde wigs to set of his dress and pearl necklace, really looked the part.

When the two of them made noises on the back landing as if they were coming home early and found the rest of us upstairs, then pro-ceeded down the stairs to Dwayne's room where they threw open the door and rushed towards the bed, they were lucky the lad had a normally healthy heart. I still swear I saw Dwayne actually climb up the wall *backwards*, and cower there for a moment suspended by his fingernails.

And thus was born another timeless tradition in the band; payback.

I have to hand it to Dwayne. He was able to bide his time, waiting or the perfect opportunity to take his revenge. He focused on Percy as the target because he knew it had to have been Percy who came up with the idea. He waited until another all-weekend party took place and if I remember, it was Dwayne who secured a quantity of particu-larly powerful acid for the occasion.

I can recall sitting on the living room floor listening to Chicago play "Twenty-five or Six to Four" about thirty times in a row, digging deeper into the horn arrangement with every repetition. I hadn't noticed that Percy had fallen asleep on the couch until I saw Dwayne come into the room holding the big, floor-length hallway mirror. He went over and, holding it face down, a foot above Percy's sleeping form, began to call his name.

"Percy…" he called softly, then a bit louder, "Percy, time to wake up, now."

He kept his voice sweet and low, only increasing a little in volume as one would, waking a sleeping child. He didn't want his victim waking up startled and ruining the reaction when he looked up and saw himself looking down.

"Percy…"

The sleeping form stirred, turned a bit.

"Wake up, Percy…"

Percy opened his eyes. He looked up at his own reflection and frowned. He blinked, looked again and then he invented a new word.

"Ngeeangafhwen!" he said, and so saying, somehow managed to slither bonelessly up, over the arm of the couch and land in a puddle of gibbering protoplasm on the rug. Dwayne had his laugh, the sound of which brought Percy back from the brink and restored his faith in reality.

A minute later, he was sitting cross-legged on the floor, twenty-five or six to four-ing, grinning in good-natured acceptance that he'd been re-paid in kind.

Dwayne was a good guy and a good player but he was severely handicapped by the limitations of the instrument he played. It was an odd brand of organ called Rheem, the only one like it I've ever seen. It was much more primitive in design than the first wave of portable synthesizers that were just then coming available. About the best thing it had going for it was it's portability, lacking the weight and bulk of, say, a Hammond but it wasn't designed to produce more than just a few useful sounds. The piano sound it made was not that great and the best organ setting was just a glorified Farfisa, which was a little dated.

Dwayne knew he needed new equipment but, like the rest of us, he was broke. The new generation electronic keyboards were thousands of dollars, and then you needed amps to run them through. His folks, like most, were doubtful about his pursuit of a career in music and therefore not much interested in loaning him the cash. It fell to Dwayne to quit school and get a job.

The only thing he could find was an entry level go-for position on the railroad, which required of him to help with the shunting of cars around the yard. It wasn't the type of job that went with a stoner life-style. There were evenings we would drop Dwayne off high as a kite at the train yards for an eight-hour shift, wondering if we would ever see him alive again.

With the time fast approaching that we would need to upgrade our equipment to really take a run at playing professionally, Dwayne knew that his keyboards were just not going to make the grade, but the railroad job was just too dangerous. He was forced to quit and couldn't find anything else. He was under increasing pressure from his folks to go back to school and on to university. In the end he had to quit the band and pursue an education.

There was a time, just for a little while, when it was just three of us; drums, bass and guitar; me, Doug and Percy-playing in Doug's parents' basement.

We didn't have an agenda. We had some idea that we'd need more players, at some point but just then we were fine with three. We had some ideas about songs we wanted to learn and we would listen to album cuts and then try to reproduce them.

It was obvious that we lacked the instrumentation to pull most of the music off but we were learning. We were young. We had all the time in the world to experiment and try to get it right.

So we jammed. We would start off on a theme, whether it was some song we had been working on or just a lick someone came up with, and just let it develop.

There was no audience. We had no recorders going. It was a thing of the moment, not meant to be reproduced or incorporated into a finished work. It was just a jam; a chance to stretch out and push the limits of what we knew about how to play together, trusting that we would be there for each other, that wherever one player went, the others would follow and, if we all ended up going out on a branch with no way back, that was OK, too.

We went to some crazy places, sometimes. There are a limited number of tools available to a three-piece ensemble but I think we managed to make the best of them all. We would usually begin slow

and easy, groovin' on some thing or another, letting the chord structure go where it naturally wanted, then throwing in some changes and
allowing the thing to grow, letting the dynamic range suit the mood;
usually coming to a crescendo at some point and then dropping off to
a whisper. There were no rules. If the tempo wanted to take off, well
then off it went and we'd just go with it and see where it landed.

There were times that our enthusiasm out-stripped our ability and
the odd jam got so far out there that there was no way back. It wasn't
uncommon to have a piece just dissolve in chaos as we dissolved in
laughter. There was lots of laughter.

God, it was fun.

We didn't know it but we were laying the foundation for a solid
rhythm section that would become the heart of our bands for years
to come. We taught each other in that little basement rumpus room
that we could trust each other. Years later, if somebody forgot a part,
or a key, or found himself out on a limb soloing, he knew that he could
count on the rest to see it through, cover for each other, whatever it
took to get the thing back on track and finish the tune.

Nobody told us and it didn't occur to any of us until much later on
that we were playing jazz. We didn't want to play jazz. We wanted to
be a rock band. If asked, we would probably have said that's what we
were playing-some sort of experimental "free-form" rock, but if the
definition of jazz is improvisation on a theme, we were playing jazz.

Even then, inexperienced and naïve about the entertainment business as we were, we knew we couldn't do the same stuff on a stage as
we did down there. If we wanted to get out of the rumpus room, we
needed to learn some songs.

We needed to build a repertoire. Logic dictated that, if we wanted
to entertain an audience over the course of an evening that lasted
three to four hours, forty minutes on and twenty off, even allowing
time for friendly banter and introductions, we would need to have at
least two hours worth of songs learned, rehearsed and ready to go.

Average length of a song in the sixties; two minutes odd, stretched
to three with a solo. That meant we needed to pick forty tunes that
were well enough known to our target demographic (being, of course,
people like us) that they would want to listen.

We made all the classic mistakes in choosing material-we learned songs that we really liked to listen to, regardless of whether they had any possibility of being reproduced with three or (hopefully, one day) four instruments. We chose songs that we really wanted to sing, even when the vocal requirements were outside our abilities. There were songs whose arrangements hinged on instrumentations we didn't have, or vocal harmony tracks we couldn't hope to copy.

We had yet to learn an important lesson every copy band needs to get; if there is one thing worse than playing obscure material, it is playing well-known material badly. Nothing is worse than sitting in an audience in any venue, listening to a tune that you love being massacred by some inept troupe that is unaware of it's own limitations.

We had time. We would learn.

We came up with a name, which was an indication of the confidence we felt that, this time, it was going to turn into something. Captain Nobody and the Forgotten Joyband was born.

I didn't feel I was a strong enough singer to do the all the leads. Percy wasn't comfortable with the fact that he would be called upon to provide all the guitar parts. On top of all that, we would be unable to do anything with organ or piano in it.

We started to audition players again. Percy brought Gary over one day and we clicked right away. He had a strong singing voice that was appreciably higher than mine, making for the possibility of harmony lines. When he came back the next rehearsal with a song he'd written about the band called "Captain Nobody," he was in like flint. Two guitars were better than one and Gary's flashy, rapid-fire solo style contrasted nicely with Percy's more melodic approach.

We still wanted to have a keyboard player, though, and Gary knew just the guy. He said he'd been walking past the music classroom one day at high school and heard the most amazing piano music emanating from within.

Peering into the room, he saw a skinny, geeky looking guy that he knew vaguely as one of the brains of the school, a straight "A" student with an acumen for math that was off the scale.

The guy was sitting at the old upright piano, ripping out riffs that Gary couldn't believe, just free-forming on a mish-mash of styles from jazz to classical to contemporary rock and back again.

He listened until the impromptu concert was over and introduced himself, thinking that, if he ever got this guy to play for a band he'd have what The Band had in Garth Hudson.

Bob was classically trained, having taken his Toronto Conservatory on, of all things, accordian. He possessed a knowledge of music, including chord structure and harmonic placement that could give us a real edge in arranging things.

Trouble was, as much as Bob wanted to play for a rock band, he had a deal with his father that he had to complete grade twelve or face dire consequences. He had six months to go.

He did, however, come down to our rehearsal and play with us one day, confirming Gary's conviction that he would be a game-changing addition to the group. We agreed to hold off hiring anyone else until Bob was free to come and play with us.

Besides the breadth and depth of musical knowledge that Bob brought to our rehearsals (Percy says; 'he knew chords with numbers after them!') his playing transformed our sound completely.

Bob's piano added a dimension to the group that elevated us from being just another rock band to something special. The five of us without him laid down a thoroughly presentable groove and there was no reason to think that anything was missing but, once we heard the same band with Bob's embellishments, like an inspired re-interpretation of the song layered on top, we knew we had hit on something unique.

Hanging out with Bob, you gradually became aware that you were in the presence of a brilliant mind. He'd grown up with the knowledge that he almost always came off sounding like the smartest (or, more accurately, most intellectual) person in the room.

This wasn't something that Bob consciously aspired to, nor did he need to. With the exception of a few very rare occasions, he *was* the smartest person in the room, usually by a long shot.

Bob had this habit of taking any conversation, no matter how banal, and somehow managing to lead it into esoteric realms of science and mathematics that few but he understood.

After experiencing one or two of these conversational sojourns, following Bob down some innocent sounding rabbit hole into the arcane world of sub-atomic particle theory or fractal calibration, most of us learned to grin and nod and to not show any sign of our total lack of comprehension, lest Bob decided to give us a condensed course on the subject matter, right there on the spot, which he was always more than happy to do. He wasn't showing off, it was just the way his mind worked.

For Bob, I suspect that joining Captain Nobody presented challenges more in the social sphere than musical. The group dynamics of the band had naturally given rise to a subculture all our own, with various ways of dealing with the wildly divergent personalities within.

By now, Captain Nobody's well-developed sense of prankster-ship that had started back in Dwayne's parents' basement had become a part of the bands' culture. Spearheaded by Percy, who loved nothing better than a good practical joke and would go to great lengths to perpetrate a gag on one of us, the things we did for a laugh never involved any real harm and were always carried out with fun as the central theme.

Doug was often the victim and it was only his great good nature that saw him through years of cigarette loads, "frenched" sheets, whoopee cushions and hand buzzers.

The jokes were a way to relieve the natural tensions that come with any creative collaboration and stood us all in good stead by breaking the tedium of road trips and hotel life over the years.

We'd all been raised on Monty Python's Flying Circus and the brand of humor we shared was one that pushed the envelope of good taste but never that of personal safety or mutual regard.

We all understood that there was a difference between putting a dead fish inside someone's guitar case and, say, eating someone's pet goldfish, in an effort to make oneself look edgy and cool.

We all expected to be the brunt of simple practical jokes from time to time and took our turns being in on them, as well.

There was the time that the entire band dressed up as Arabs for a Halloween gig without telling Doug, who alone appeared on stage in street clothes. Doug, who was Lebanese on his dad's side, was not amused.

There were more complicated gags, too-usually featuring Doug as the brunt of Percy's efforts. Messing with his amp settings just before the set, the hiding his guitar after a gig and the memorable time that Percy wrote away for something called a "Whiz-Bang," which was a fiendish device, designed to be placed in the air filter of a vehicle engine where it would react to attempts to start the engine with a drawn out "whizzing" sound, followed by a truly memorable "BANG", accompanied by a gout of black smoke that together accurately mimicked the ultimate demise of a motor, past repair.

The story of poor Doug's initial horrified panic when the thing went off under the hood of his milk-truck has been told many times over many beers.

My favorite part is the way Doug, standing there helplessly watching the gouts of smoke pouring from under the hood, suddenly noticed that he was the only one who was concerned about it.

Doug's face was normally an open book and, as he looked from face to face at our barely-contained hilarity his features read like a grade school primer as the slow dawning of realization that he'd once again been had by the mischievous Percy filtered through.

When his gaze finally fell on his antagonist, standing a respectful distance down the boulevard and poised as if ready to start running the five hundred, something snapped. Doug's normal easy-going nature had absorbed hundreds of these assaults over the years and even the deepest well had its limit.

"You," he said simply, in a tone heavy with implied threat.

Percy got it. He was half a block away before Doug got up to speed. They'd done this before, Doug chasing Percy half-heartedly around until they both were tired and out of breath but this time, it was different.

Doug, having finally reached his tether's end, chased Percy non-stop about the neighborhood for almost half an hour. The rest of us stood around laughing, chatting and generally enjoying ourselves as the chase wore on. I don't know what Doug might have done had he ever caught him but he didn't, and they ended up sitting on the curb, ten feet apart, trying to get their breath back. Then it was time to get to the gig.

Somewhere around this time, we decided to get a band house. We all were at an age to move out of our parents' homes and it made sense to move in together. We rented a little house in 'little Italy' with bedrooms for all and one left over for a practice space.

I remember the excitement I felt, moving away from my parents' place for the first time. My folks had been forced to take in borders to make ends meet, with the result that I'd never been given a room of my own. After years of sharing with my brother, I was overjoyed to roll my sleeping bag out on top of my foamy and hang my single backpack of possessions on the door.

So there we were, living the dream. We had a band and a band house.

The band had professional gear, everything we needed to play any indoor engagement we might be called upon to do. We had a place to rehearse and, perhaps equally important, to party.

We had a set list of 35 songs, or so, subject to constant tweaking but enough to play three sets of respectable length. All of us had "stage clothes"- being one set of duds that we wouldn't ordinarily wear anywhere else but on stage, at least not yet.

There were only two things missing to make the dream complete; we had no vehicle with which to transport our selves and equipment to and from gigs. We expected to deal with this by means of rental trucks when the time came.

The time, that is, when we actually had somewhere to play, which was the second missing component in our plan.

We had no work and not the foggiest idea of how to get any.

It was an odd kind of conundrum faced by many members of our generation who had bought into the dream. Sooner or later we all had to face the fact that, Woodstock and the Rock and Roll revolution,

Age of Aquarius and the Summer of Love notwithstanding, the music business was just that; a business. It was fine and well to believe that, philosophically, 'All you need is Love' but if you want to make a living as a musician, you also need work.

There we sat each night, after band practice, feeling as ready as we thought we'd ever get to share our thing with audiences, wherever they might be.

We tried renting halls and putting on our own dances, but nobody came, or at least no one outside our own circle of friends, of which there were rarely enough to pay the overhead.

Approaching the booking agencies, we were turned down every time when we had to answer the inevitable question; where have you played? Catch twenty-two. Of course we haven't played anywhere; we don't have an agent. Well, go out and play some gigs and we'll consider booking you. Well, give us some dates and we'll go play them. Can't give you any dates because you haven't played anywhere, blah, blah, blah...

No wonder we did drugs. Not that we needed to worry about that becoming a problem. Without gigs, we had no money. The only drugs we had access to were those brought over by friends, who liked to come to our band practices.

There was that, though; being in a band, especially one with a band house, gave us all street cred and brought a lot of people our age into our circle, especially girls. We may not have played anywhere, maybe never would play anywhere-but we were a band and we had a place of our own and that was good enough for a lot of girls we would never have met, otherwise.

There was another, more practical side to this; by having a constant stream of people coming over to see us rehearse, we were learning how to perform in front of an audience. Even if was only for twenty or thirty people, crowded into the living room while we showcased the last couple of tunes we'd learned; when two or three of them were hot chicks we needed to impress, we were learning how to deal with that kind of distraction and still play.

Besides, we were trying to put together a playlist that would go over in a bar full of just these kinds of people. There was no better focus group to help us with our song selections.

Still, we were in the doldrums. We were living on hope and unrealistic expectations. The girls would only stop by for so long, unless we started playing some real gigs.

Most of us were going home once or twice a week for a good meal and usually coming back with a ten or a twenty from Dad, to keep us in Vitamin K for another week, but the rent was falling further and further behind and we were constantly under threat of having the power cut off. We needed a break.

It came in the unlikely form of "Football Fever '73".

In the early '70's, the Edmonton Eskimos football club was having a hard time penetrating the small town market. Ticket sales in the surrounding communities were low, especially when compared to sales in the city. These were hockey towns. Clearly the team needed to come up with new ways to promote the game and get the rural football fan on board.

It was decided, rather than just continue trying to come up with ways to lure the small-town dollar into the city to the games, to put together a tour. If the mountain wouldn't come to Mohamed, the Eskimos would go on the road.

The idea was a sort of travelling medicine show to take the message out to these smaller centers. Only, instead of rainmaking and snake oil, this one would be selling season's tickets and memberships in the "Knothole Gang."

Labatts' Brewery was approached and generously agreed to donate the use of its' "mobile events stage"; a soundstage built into the back of a semi-trailer unit, complete with generator, lights and speaker system. You just roll up and park, drop one side of the trailer down on pylons and start playing; instant stage.

630 CHED, a local radio franchise, pitched in by providing the stations' 'events van,' which was actually a luxury 48ft. Winnebago, to transport the performers out to the gigs. Not wishing to be up-staged by this, Labatts stepped up again by agreeing to keep the fridge full of beer.

CHEDs' highest profile DJ, the witty and gregarious Wes Montgomery, was recruited for MC duties. The better known players on the football team were asked to make appearances on a rotating basis, starting with their star quarterback, Tom Wilkinson.

The officials were contacted in a number of towns within a certain driving range of the city. A schedule was drawn up, dates were fixed and posters were distributed. Football Fever '73 was ready to roll, except for one thing; they needed a band.

The ideal group for the job would be a country act, one with appeal to the small-town sensibility and lively enough to entertain while not detracting too much from the central message; buy football passes. This turned out to be a tall order for the booking people, especially given the erratic time schedule that was required. The limited budget no doubt made the selection of candidates tougher still.

Lucky for us, Gary's dad had been employed as a trainer by the Eskimos for some years. As the first date loomed near, the call for a band became a desperate one. Relying more on his instincts as a dad, who welcomed the chance to use his influence to further his son's career, and less on any realistic read on the suitability of our unpolished garage band to the event, Tom suggested us.

To our mutual disbelief, we got the job.

At a set fee of $500.00 for nine engagements over a five-week period we weren't exactly rolling in the dough. We weren't even making union rates, if any of us had been aware that there was such a thing at the time. None of that mattered the least to us.

We were being paid to play. In an odd sort of way the lengthy nature of the contract almost made it feel like steady work. And the perks were enormous.

There's no way of knowing what, if anything, the neighbors had thought of us before the gigantic luxury class motor home, all painted up in the radio stations' logo, rolled to a stop in front of our tiny, unkempt house to pick us up for the first Football Fever gig, but it's a fair bet they were all a bit impressed.

I know I was.

Climbing on board that first time to see both Wes Montgomery and Tom Wilkinson, who were minor celebrities even to those of us who didn't follow the Eskimos, already seated up front with drinks in hand, well - it felt just a little like we were finally getting somewhere.

Which turned out to be Stony Plain.

In 1973, Stony Plain was a sleepy little village just off highway 16A. They had a legion hall, a Co-op grocery and an RCMP detachment, along with the usual grain elevator and a café advertising "Chinese and Western Cuisine." There were 4H activities for the young farm kids and a hockey rink for the local junior league.

The Ladies' Auxilliary put on a Bingo for seniors and guests in the hall on Saturday evenings and offered catering services for weddings and funerals. And now, for visiting football team promotions.

For lack of a proper fair ground or arena, it had been arranged for us to use the hockey rink for the show, this being the largest clear space in town. The caretaker mowed the grass inside the rink enclosure and took down that section of the boards used to get the Zamboni in and out of the rink and we parked the soundstage down at one end zone.

Down went the stage and up went the lights. On went the generator and we were ready to go. A half dozen curious teenagers and a couple of town officials looked up at us, we back at them. A microphone started to feedback and was moved behind the speakers to stop it. Someone cleared his throat.

Wes Montgomery stepped up to the mike and officially welcomed the onlookers to Football Fever '73, turned to us and said;

"Crank it up, boys-we need to draw a crowd."

"Ladies and gentlemen, please welcome - Captain Nobody!"

We launched into "Jumpin' Jack Flash" and let 'er rip, followed by "Johnny Be Good" and then "Substitute" by the Who. We had planned to do another five tunes for the opening set but by the time we finished "Substitute" there were a couple dozen people in front of the stage and more coming all the time.

Wes hopped back up on stage and told us to take a break, he'd take it from there. We moved over to the sides of the soundstage and hung about, not sure if we should get too far away.

Montgomery addressed the crowd like a barker at a small-time circus, talking about the team and the town, mentioning local officials by name and cracking wise about current issues in the area. Talk about a pro. In five minutes he had a couple hundred people eating out of his hand.

By the time he introduced Tom Wilkinson to the stage, you'd think he was a long lost son. The two of them traded insults and generally hammed it up in a way that was to become famous in later years. They gave away some Eskimo paraphernalia and a pair of seasons' tickets.

After about a half an hour, Wes turned and gave us the nod to get ready for another set. The crowd he handed over to us was ready to boogie and the area directly in front of the stage became the dance floor by mutual accord. We finished up the rest of our first set and worked through our second with the crowd showing no sign of thinning.

With no sign of Wes or Tom, we had no choice but to go right ahead and start the third set. We'd been playing for the better part of an hour and needed a break but with nobody around to tell us otherwise, we just kept going in hopes that somebody would tell us when to quit.

About another half hour later, one of the Labbats crew appeared at the side of the stage and told us the show had moved indoors and we'd better finish up and get in 'cause dinner was about to be served. We did one more song and thanked everyone for coming.

The plan had been for us to play some more after we ate, so someone mentioned that over the p.a. but after the dinner it seemed everyone had forgotten the plan.

Montgomery, Wilkinson and the staff all climbed onto the motor home and we were left scrambling to secure our gear inside the semi for the trip home. When we finally got on board we got some dark looks from the driver, like it was our fault for holding things up.

And that was that. Our first Football Fever '73 gig was over. They dropped us off in front of our little house, drumsticks and guitars in hand, to await the next trip in a few days.

It wasn't until then that it occurred to me that, with my drums locked up in the sound truck at the brewery, I had no way to practice. The other guys had their guitars, even if they couldn't amplify them, but I had nothing to play. When the next rehearsal came we decided to try going over all our tunes acoustically. I beat time with drumsticks on an ottoman and the boys played their guitars sans amps.

The very first song, we found two bad chords. We had to go back to the record and re-learn the chorus of the second one.

We also discovered that Doug had been playing one Rolling Stone's tune entirely in the wrong key. After trying it correctly, we all decided we liked it better the old way and Doug went back to playing it the way he had been.

Most conspicuous were our back-up harmonies, which we had assumed were a good deal better than how they sounded now, without the electronic racket masking the sour notes. We spent our next three rehearsals correcting errant harmonies and assigning new parts to fill in where needed.

Over time this became a standard part of our bands' practice; acoustic rehearsal time. For a group that learned everything by ear, this was time well spent. It paid huge dividends in better vocal harmonies and more accurate chord arrangements and, perhaps most importantly, a better overall understanding of the structure of the music we played.

It was a great summer. The lack of amplifiers at the band house made for a quieter atmosphere. We slept in late, rolling out of bed mid morning, lingering over spartan breakfasts and slowly convening in the practice room, barefoot, yawning, cups of tea in hand.

Rehearsal took up most of the afternoons as we moved between learning new material and brushing up the songs we already knew, constantly seeking ways to improve the repertoire.

At times we would get to a place where one or another of us required some individual time to learn a part or memorize some words. Then we would retire to various parts of the little house; the kitchen, the basement, the front porch, to work alone and then returning to try out the newly learned bit in context.

We had a rotating schedule for chores like making supper, so sooner or later in the afternoon somebody would be in the kitchen, starting the water for rice or noodles-our staple diet.

After supper most of us would head out to listen to the other bands that were playing in the bars around town, looking for new material or just seeking to cop some licks. It didn't cost much, at twenty cents a glass, to sit and nurse a beer (if you could call the stuff they served in the taverns in Alberta in the '70's beer) while listening to one or other of our competition.

Often Percy or Gary would come home with some riff they'd heard someone play, pick up a guitar and start working on it and the next thing you know, we had another song to add to the list.

On the weekends there would be parties. We would invite people from whatever bar we were drinking in over to the house after closing time, bring your own off-sales and any extra girls you can find who wanted to be seen at the band house. It wasn't exactly the Sex, Drugs & Rock 'n Roll lifestyle we'd heard so much about but the general consensus was that it would do.

The second trip with the tour was to Wetaskiwin. Things were a little more relaxed with the older guys on the Winnebago, with a couple of new players who decided to come back and have a beer with the boys in the band. Somebody put a Jimmy Cliff tape on the sound system and we passed the time chatting amiably until we got to the fair grounds.

Wes repeated his first performance flawlessly and we did our whole first set this time, drawing quite a crowd. The Tom and Wes show took over while we waited in the wings for our cue and then we did our second set.

By now we were working out a few glitches with the sound system that had marred the first gig slightly and feeling more comfortable with the venue. On the way home, Wes came back to talk with us, encouraging us to learn a few country tunes for the next trip. We didn't bother and it didn't seem to matter much but Wes kept up the suggestions just the same.

He was right, of course; the demographic they were looking to attract to these things was one that would respond more favorably to some country and western style music than the pop-rock we were doing. The crowds we brought in were teenagers, who wouldn't be caught dead going to a football game, even if they could afford it.

We just weren't a country band. Still, we made lots of noise and brought people up to the stage and once our group came, the older set generally followed if only to see what their kids were up to. Wes and Tom appealed to all ages and the prizes and the hand-outs were universal.

It was, I think, on the fifth engagement that we went to the town of Vegreville. Tom Wilkinson had begged off the trip, citing family engagements and had been replaced by Charlie Turner, a popular defensive tackle and something of a legend on the team.

Charlie stood six foot seven in his socks and must have weighed about 350 lbs with not an ounce of fat on him. The man was built like Arnold Schwarzenegger (of whom no one outside the world of body building had yet to hear) and had a reputation as an eater of mythic proportions.

It was said that, whenever the team ate on the road, Charlie would order two of everything. If he was going to have a steak dinner, he got two complete steak dinners and ate them both, then went on to down two of whatever dessert was offered, all washed down with three to four quarts of cold milk. If there were no game that night he would apparently stock up on snack foods and continue eating until bedtime.

His breakfasts were even more legendary. Apparently the over-night hiatus in consumption left Charlie famished in the mornings. He was always the first into the restaurant and was often suspected of having eaten a big breakfast before any of the other players showed up, only to order another complete meal to have with his companions.

We found him friendly and outgoing, laughing at himself when he had to turn sideways to fit through the door of the camper. He sat back with us most of the way to the gig, making jokes about being in the "back of the bus" while putting a serious dent in the beer supply.

When show time rolled around, Charlie proved himself a natural comedian in front of a crowd. He had them laughing from the get-go, trading insults with Wes and pretending to threaten the diminutive DJ with physical violence if he got too smart. The show went off without a hitch and we all repaired to the local community hall for a dinner on the town.

Now, it was a well-known fact that the Ukrainian farmers who had settled the area around Vegreville liked their food. The cuisine of Ukraine was famous for it's perogies, kubasa, borscht and other rib-sticking, substantial dishes designed to keep hard-working farmers well fuelled for their long days in the field. This tradition had come down the generations to inform the catering practices there, as anyone could attest who'd attended a Ukrainian wedding or New Years' party at their halls.

The ladies of the Vegreville Community League knew how to feed hungry crowds and took pride in putting out monumental feasts. It was their unstated mission to ensure no one ever went wanting, no matter how many uninvited guests turned up.

As for Charlie, when we mentioned how we were all looking forward to some good Ukrainian food, he admitted that he'd never had it. Born somewhere in the southern States, Charlie was more familiar with Cajun sausage than Kubasa, and had never heard of a pyrogy in his life. He was in for a treat.

"They're like little dumplings, with cheese and stuff inside." I told him.

I had the good fortune of being seated right across the table from Charlie and was able to witness the whole thing first-hand. The first servers who brought trays of buns and bowls of potatoes looked admiringly at the huge man and it was obvious that word got passed in the kitchen.

The ladies began to appear at the kitchen door in ones and twos, wiping their hands on their aprons and vying to catch a glimpse of Charlie. They stared at him and spoke to each other in Ukrainian from the corners of heir mouths, giggling like schoolgirls and blushing.

When the food began coming out in earnest, they all seemed to want a turn at serving Charlie. There must have been ten or twelve different women bringing food to our table in the next few minutes, while the other tables seemed to have only one or two servers each.

And man, did they bring food.

There were the expected pyrogys, boiled or fried, swimming in melted butter and fried onions, accompanied by big bowls of bacon bits and sour cream. Real sour cream; like, fresh from a cow.

Unending baskets of great, fluffy fresh-baked rolls and mounds of boiled potatoes that tasted like they must have been in the ground that morning. Corn on the cob, buttered green beans, Brussel sprouts,

Harvard beets, steamed carrots drizzled with honey and orange zest rounded out the side dishes.

There were bowls of pickled onions the size of golf balls and sliced or baby beets, mounds of celery relish and mustard greens, creamed mushrooms and mashed turnip.

Then came the meats.

Whole roast barons of beef, sliced a half inch thick and served with big ceramic boats full of dark, peppery gravy. Fried chicken seasoned with paprika and a white gravy on the side, pork shoulder roasted with onions and apples, hams baked in maple syrup and cloves and last but certainly not least, big chunks of the local sausage, first boiled then fried and served with carmelized onion.

It was all so good. There seemed to be no end to the amounts of food the kitchen had prepared. No sooner was one platter emptied than another would take its place.

The table groaned under the load and we groaned along, as we all proceeded to eat far, far more than was good for us and still, it kept coming.

All through it, I couldn't help but watch Charlie eat. He started right off shoveling it down as though he hadn't had a square meal in days. As the platters were passed from hand to hand we found it necessary to start them on either side of Charlie, so that the others at the table got a chance at some of the choice offerings before they disappeared onto the mound on his plate.

I don't know how much he must have eaten before I started to keep count but after that I personally saw him consume two whole chickens, three heaping plates of ham with potatoes and veg., two more of roast beef and gravy and at least two entire rings of sausage. He kept his fork in one hand and a freshly buttered roll in the other.

Early on, Charlie had tried his first pyrogy and declared it the "best dumpling he ever tasted," to the delight of the servers and cooks. From that point on, they made sure he was never without a fresh platter of pyrogies slathered with the trimmings at his elbow.

I had a little bit of everything and seconds on the roast beef, which was superb even without the gravy but when the desserts started coming I had to admit defeat.

Not Charlie, however.

When the desserts started coming out of the kitchen it was as if he caught a second wind. Chocolate cake, blueberry and apple pies four inches high, pyrogies stuffed with sour cherries, rice pudding, brownies to die for with bowls of clotted cream and custard on the side all found their way on to Charlie's plate and thence, miraculously into his seemingly un-fillable belly.

As the servers completed their tasks at the other tables, they loitered around ours, watching as Charlie continued to consume helping after helping of their good food.

One old gal, after seeing the way Charlie washed everything down with milk, armed herself with a huge pitcher and stationed herself by his side, ready to top up his glass whenever he was otherwise occupied.

Some of the cooks came out of the kitchen and sat down with cups of coffee where they could see the show. Leaning on their elbows, they lit cigarettes and looked on with something approaching adulation in their faces as Charlie continued to eat.

These were farm girls and as such it was deep in their culture to take pleasure in watching the men of the farm eat well. Buried deep in their collective consciousness was the knowledge that, if the men ate well they would work hard and hard work meant lots of food production, which meant they all would do well. It was the farmwives' circle of life. They loved to watch a man eat and in Charlie they had found their ultimate ideal.

Charlie filled his plate a last time with a selection of jam tarts and squares, which he proceeded to dispatch with relish, smacking his lips and rolling his eyes for his audience at the pleasure of it all. He drank off a final tumbler of milk and pushed away from the table, patting his distended stomach and grinning at the ladies gathered around him.

"Man," he exclaimed, "tha's what I call a *meal.*"

They actually applauded him. Natural showman to the end, Charlie stood up and took a bow.

The story has been told many times since and, as stories often do, it has been known to grow a little with each telling. It may even be that I have allowed an embellishment or two into my version but one thing is for sure; the ladies of the Vegreville Community League did not soon forget the Football Fever '73 Tour and the grinning black giant who'd almost eaten them out of food.

Dinner had taken so long that there was no time for a second show, so we packed up and prepared to hit the road.

Just as Charlie was making his way back onto the motor home, finding it a tighter squeeze than he had before supper, one of the Ukrainian ladies came bustling across the parking lot and thrust a big plastic container of pyrogies into his hands.

No one else could look at them but all the way home we had to watch Charlie munching happily away.

"I ain't never had dumplin's like these," he said.

The Eskimos organization sent different personnel along with the show, usually players and support staff but, on a few trips, we were accompanied by a young broadcaster who was doing the live game commentary for the team. His name was Rod Phillips.

It would be a few months before Rod would accept the job calling games for the Edmonton Oilers, who were still a part of the fledgling World Hockey Association. If we'd known that the guy was destined to become the "Voice of the Oilers" for 37 years and go on to be inducted into the Hockey Hall of Fame, we probably would have treated him with more respect.

As it was, when he got into a heated debate with Pete Travis and appealed to us for support, we disappointed him. The argument was over the question of whether a professionally trained announcer could do a better job calling a sports game than a player might.

Ignorant to the amount of technical knowledge and research that a good announcer had to possess in order to do as good a job as Rod did, we sided with the player.

"Thanks a lot, guys," I remember him saying.

The summer rolled on like that, every few days it was onto the motor home and off to another small town. Each trip had its own peculiarities and any attempt to tell all the stories that came out of the tour would exceed the boundaries of good taste.

There was the beer-drinking contest in Millet, when our Labbats' driver squared off with the local legend and between them consumed three tables full of draft without pausing for breath, or the time that Charlie disappeared in the motor home with the mayors' wife for two hours, leaving us stranded and embarrassed in the town bar.

All good things must come to an end and when the tour was over, we celebrated by taking our girlfriends out to dinner at the Steak Loft, after which we repaired to the Old Bailey's lounge downstairs to drink an intemperate amount of expensive booze and listen to the house band.

The band, aptly named "The Jury," represented the cream of the jazz players in Edmonton at the time. It was Moe Marshall on guitar with Wes Henderson on bass and Tom Doran on drums.

These guys were the cream of the western Canadian jazz crop, each one of them a master of his instrument. The improvisations they laid down in their solos and support of each other were way, way over our heads. Even if we'd been sober we wouldn't have been capable of understanding what we were hearing but as the brandy flowed we became convinced that this was the new direction for our band.

Screw rock and roll; that was for kids. Never mind that we probably needed a dozen years of study to even approach this level of playing. Who cares if there were even fewer gigs for jazz bands? We weren't in it for the money, anyways. We were Artists, man. We would become jazz players!

As we arrived home, drunk as lords and filled with inspiration from the liquor and the music we'd been listening to, we immediately fired up the amps and commenced trying to emulate the superb trio at the lounge.

I was so drunk I could hardly hold my drumsticks. The sound we made must have sounded as ridiculous as we all probably looked but in our minds we were *improvising, man.* We had joined that great pantheon of players that had carried the institution of jazz down through the years. We were *cool.*

And then we were sick.

As the overabundance of rich food and expensive liquor combined in our bellies, one by one we succumbed. It was a good thing there were two toilets in the house but I think I remember someone still having to resort to using the bushes outside the back porch to throw up when both were busy.

We had, of course, completely lost touch with the time. We had closed down the lounge and dropped our girlfriends off at their homes on the way back to the band house. It must have been 2:30am when we started playing our brand of pseudo jazz, maybe 3:00 when the police arrived to find us in an advanced state of pukedness, with Percy loudly addressing the porcelain loudspeaker upstairs, while I was busy depositing about $150.00 worth of haute cuisine in the downstairs facility.

They shook their heads at our lifestyle and, after securing promises we would not continue the jazz concert tonight, left in disgust.

And that was the end of the Football Fever '73 Tour. We came away from the experience with a little more savvy about the road, an new respect for the role of the MC in the world of entertainment, as well as a more serious take on the music business in general. Before "Football Fever" we were a bunch of guys playing at being a band. In an odd way, the tour made us into a real band.

The trouble with being in a real band is that, besides all the instruments, you have to have a sound system and amplifiers.

In the seventies, before the printed circuit had wiped tube technology off the map, a decent P.A. system with enough power to play in your average high school gymnasium was a huge thing with speaker boxes three or four feet square and if you could afford it, high frequency horns on top of that, all connected through hundreds of feet of cable to some kind of mixer and big, heavy power amp.

You needed that kind of power to cut through the god-awful echoes that the cinderblock walls threw back at you in those gyms. When I set up my drums in a gymnasium stage, all I had to do was hit my bass drum once to fill the room with a dozen bass drum sounds, bouncing endlessly from one wall to the other. A simple 5-stroke roll would sound like a four bar solo. Get the whole band playing together without using a sound system, all you had was a cacophony.

A 2,000 or 3,000 watt system could compress all that sound to the back of the room pretty well but there was still a lot of random echo on stage. The bands' amplifiers for the instruments were placed at the back of the stage, so we heard ourselves playing OK, but the P.A. speakers had to go right at the front of the stage, with the mikes behind them so they wouldn't feed back. The result was that we couldn't hear ourselves sing on stage without the further addition of a good monitor speaker system, which meant more miles of cable and maybe a separate slave amp, as well.

It added up to a lot of gear. All this stuff had to be moved somehow from gig to gig. At first, we rented all the sound equipment and since we were only playing small venues we didn't need much. If somebody owned a pickup truck, we could get everything in the back.

Captain Nobody went through a bewildering variety of transport options in our first year or two, trying to get from one-nighter to one-nighter, relying on the generosity of friends and family. When we moved up to playing the school gyms, we found the U-haul trailer to be the answer to our needs. Then, when we began playing out of town for a week or two at a time, the U-haul rental option started to get expensive, owing to the charges we incurred by parking the trailer at the gig.

Sometimes, being forced to take more than one vehicle had its' pluses. It was, for example possible, when we had two vehicles, for the one carrying the equipment to be driven directly to the venue and unloaded while the other one could be driven into the town center for supplies, by which of course, I mean beer.

On one occasion we were cutting it pretty close time-wise and in such a hurry to get the beer and get back to the gig, which in this case was a junior high school, we ran a stop sign. As luck would have it, this heinous crime was witnessed by a member of the local RCMP detachment, who immediately took up the chase, siren and lights on.

Doug was driving his old VW station wagon and decided, in a model of poor judgement, that it would be better to ignore the pur-suing squad car and continue on the two blocks back to the school, where everything could be sorted out in the parking lot.

This, of course, triggered all the wrong responses in the officer, who turned out to be a rookie on his first post, three days on the job and a bit keen to make his mark. As far as he was concerned, he was now engaged in a vehicular chase behind God-knows-what kind of element, already guilty of evading arrest.

By the time we got back to the school this poor guy had worked himself up into such a paranoid state that, when Doug stopped and we all got out of the car, he pulled out his sidearm and pointed it at us.

This, of course, got everyone's attention right away-ours, the teachers that were good-naturedly helping to unload the U-haul and all the fifty or sixty junior high students who had gathered in the parking lot to watch the band arrive.

We were all treated to the spectacle of the poor, frazzled cop attempting to hold his suspects at gunpoint, call for backup on his radio, instruct us all to face the car and put our hands on the hood and put his hat on, all at the same time.

The one thing he forgot to do was to put his car in park when he got out of it, with the result that he nearly managed to simultaneously run himself over and shoot himself. It was a miracle he didn't shoot someone.

We managed to stay calm enough that after a minute he began to gain some measure of self-control. He insisted on searching everyone in the car, which was too bad, as Bob's friend Milo had been stupid enough to keep a lid of pot in his jeans. Milo was hauled off to the detachment, which luckily had no real consequence to the band. The kids had a good show to kick off the dance and no doubt left with the conviction that they had been entertained by a real bad bunch of rock n roll rebels that day.

Another time, running late for a dance in, after some delay on the road, we had skipped our supper to get to the gig and were all starving by the time we did. Doug and me were sent to town to see if we could find a bag of burgers before the dance began.

There was only place open in town. We missed it the first time past, because it didn't look like a restaurant at all. It was, in fact an old stucco bungalow with an addition built onto the front. The hand-painted sign over the door said "Thelma's Place" in lopsided red paint. In the window were further examples of amateurish sign writing, advertising "Sandwiches, Burgers and "Homemade Pie."

We hurried inside to find the lunch counter area empty and silent. The sound of a television came from somewhere deeper inside the abode.

"Hello?"

Sounds came from inside. An elderly woman of a certain girth appeared form the gloom and eyed us suspiciously.

"What can I do for you boys?" she asked.

"We'd like to get some burgers to go, please."

"To go?"

"Yes, we're kind of in a hurry, you see. We are in the band that's playing at the high school grad dance tonight and we are supposed to start in about a half hour."

"Oh! Well, we'd better get those burgers on, then. Two burgers?"

"Ah, actually, we need six. We need to take some back for the rest of the band, too."

"Six," she said. Something in her voice made us look at each other.

"Yes, ma'm, if it isn't too much bother."

It was exactly the right thing to have said. Her eyes softened in appreciation of the courtesy.

"It's no bother at all, fellows. I don't know when I made six burgers in thirty minutes, but I will do my best."

She then turned to the fridge that stood there-just a standard household fridge- and, opening the door, took out a big glass bowl of hamburger meat, an onion, a tomato and a head of lettuce. These she put on the counter beside the fridge, then went back in to retrieve a bottle of ketchup, one of mustard and another of relish. This operation proceeded at excruciatingly slow tempo. We again exchanged looks.

Thelma walked over to the corner of the room and opened a little closet that was there. She took out an apron, in a nice pink color, trimmed with lace. It took her about three minutes to put it on, age-numbed fingers fumbling with the strings until we felt moved to offer assistance.

"Well, that's very kind of you boys but, no-a body's got to keep doin' for a body, as they say."

Finally, she finished getting the apron on and turned to the counter, from under which she produced a big cast iron fry pan, which she carried over to the stove and put on a burner, which she then proceeded to light with a match, at some length. Leaving the skillet to heat, she turned back to the produce from the fridge. She took the onion and began to peel the skin away with a chef's knife that looked as though it had come off the Arc.

We sat, helplessly watching as the glacial process of Thelma cooking burgers continued, one laborious, tediously drawn out task at a time. Between us was the tacit understanding that we should not speak, for fear that, if we engaged Thelma in conversation, she might take her attention away from the tasks at hand.

When she went over to the sink and washed her hands religiously before returning and digging into the hamburger to get a good handful that she began to shape into a patty by hand, Doug hung his head and shrugged. He glanced at his watch, smiled at me and lit a smoke, visibly relaxing.

"So," he asked Thelma, who had begun to slice tomatoes, "when did you open the restaurant?"

"Oh, about six o'clock, I guess. I make breakfast for the boys coming on shift at the plant and the mayor always drops by for coffee at 6:30."

Not much in the way of follow-up to that, so we let it go and resumed watching as the slowest food ever produced took shape before our eyes.

It was twelve minutes after the hour by the time Thelma had assembled six hamburgers (cheeseburgers, actually, after she went to the fridge and brought out a massive block of cheddar, from which she proceeded to slice one thick slab at a time before applying each one oh-so-precisely unto the very centre of each frying hand-made patty), wrapped every one up tightly in wax paper, then placed it in it's own little paper bag, which she then placed all together in a big paper bag.

"That'll be fifteen dollars even," she said, placing the bag of burgers on the fomica counter top. Doug paid up, adding a two-buck tip.

"Now, you boys enjoy that food and don't eat it too fast. Folks are always in such a rush these days, they don't take the time to enjoy good food anymore."

"You're right. We'll make sure we take the time to enjoy this. Thanks very much."

"Think nothing of it. Come again, sometime."

And with that, we took our leave of Thelma's and raced back to the school, where a nervous-looking principal was hovering about, worried at having to keep his inmates waiting.

We sat down in the wings and unwrapped our burgers. The dance started an hour late, so we offered to play an extra hour. It was worth the trouble, just to sit and take our time and enjoy those hand-made hamburgers, savoring every bite.

Playing junior high schools meant trying to put on a show for the kids. They expected us to dress all sparkly and glammed up and the guitar players were expected to leap about the stage and do athletic things while playing. Gary and Percy did their best, developing some interesting moves, culminating in their double guitar solos, for which they would move out to the front of the stage and stand side by side, playing harmony lines.

Once, we were booked into Grande Praire in the middle of January and got there just in time for a record cold snap that dropped the temperature down to -38 in a couple of hours while we were trying to sleep in the van we had rented for the occasion.

We woke, shivering with frost in our beards, just in time to ward off hypothermia by driving to the nearest fleabag motel and spending every dime we had on a single room for the six of us.

It was pretty grim but it was heated. We flipped coins for the bed and ended up with four of us I on the queen mattress while two unfortunate souls did the best they could on the chair and a too-short sofa.

The door lacked a lock, which didn't worry us any until the drunk in the next room started crashing through it every twenty minutes, apparently to see if he could catch us in the throws of some homosexual fantasy orgy that his feeble-minded, booze soaked brain had conjured up.

Time and again we sank to the verge of much needed sleep, only to have the homo squad kick the door open with a bang! Finally, about the fifth time around, Gary, who was closest to the door jumped up and confronted the fool, screaming into his face to desist or he'd kill him.

That left about four hours to rest before we had to hit the road. We made the most of it, undisturbed at last.

Then there was the gig we couldn't get a van from the rental agency. All they had was a cube van, which would only seat three legally in the front, meaning three of us would have to ride in the back with the equipment. We had no choice, so off we drove to the gig, which was mercifully close to town.

Things went fine until we were returning down Whyte avenue on a busy Saturday morning and the three in the back decided it might be entertaining if they began shouting for help from inside the cargo box.

Every time we came to a red light, of which there is never any lack on Whyte ave., the passersby were alarmed to hear muffled calls from the truck, saying there had been a kidnapping and asking someone to call the police.

Which someone obligingly did.

The cops pulled us over right in front of the Princess Theater. The usual throng at the bus stop there were treated to the sight of two of Edmonton's finest, weapons drawn, taking up positions on either side of the back door of the van while one of the band members was instructed to open it.

The looks on the faces of those within were instructive. When the accordion lift gate rolled up, they all wore the same foolish look of anticipation, thinking their little joke had prompted us to stop just to tell them to shut up. Confronted with the sight of a pair of Glock 7's pointing at them, they underwent a remarkable transformation through shock and surprise and finally fetching up on naked fear.

"I nearly shit myself," said Percy later.

The officers were both relieved and pissed off to know it had just been a hoax but they let us go with a warning.

Sometimes, the school dances we played introduced us to some of the most memorable characters, not least of whom were the teachers. There was always a few who'd been assigned to "chaperone" the proceedings, with varying levels of enthusiasm to bring to the duty.

At one afternoon sock-hop in a small northern town, we met a young man who told us he was the science teacher. He was very friendly and welcoming and took time to offer us a little tour of the school after we got set up.

His friendly banter began to change as we got away from the students and eventually found ourselves in the science lab with him. Little instances of what might have been construed to be sexual innuendo turned into an all out discussion on trans-gender experimentation, which cumulated with his proudly showing us the rabbits he'd been experimenting on by injecting them with hormones to change them from one sex to the other.

We managed to laugh it all off and got back to the gym without further incident, feeling distinctly weird about him but happy to let it slide.

About a year later, Percy noticed the guy's name in the Edmonton Journal. He'd been arrested for sexual interference with a minor. We were hardly surprised. I don't know how that ended up, or what has become of the man. I suppose, given the way that societies' attitudes towards trans-gender issues has changed, he's probably published his research and gone on to a stellar career in a new field of medicine.

Our most spectacular stage show was one that happened by accident. We had been trying for some time to penetrate the high school market, which had the potential of keeping us employed in town through the worst of the winter driving season. The thought of not having to hit the highway in -30 weather moved us to make a special effort to groom the band for the younger demographic, even to the point of learning new songs that were decidedly outside our usual lexicon.

We found ourselves mining the works of Kiss, Queen and BTO, searching for tunes that had some redeeming elements of musicality. The trick was to balance the popularity of the song among our new audience while finding tunes we could play without actually vomiting on stage.

We were rehearsing in the garage of the house that my girlfriend Janice shared with Doug's latest flame, Nelly. They'd met when both were working at a burger joint in Sherwood Park and hit it off immediately.

Nelly was a hoot. Nelly and Janice together were a trouble-makin' tag team. The two of them spent a lot of time laughing at us and at one another and they both got a great charge out of listening to us trying to play this drek as if we meant it.

That alone should have alerted us to the folly of pursuing that kind of material but hey-we needed work.

We resurrected a few timeless old chestnuts like "Smoke on the Water," in an effort to pad the set list with something the kids would like. It was horrible but anything was better than another winter spent driving out to god-knows-where in the teeth of a blizzard, so we persevered.

We found ourselves booked into one of the larger high schools in town for a mid-day "sock hop" dance. It felt odd, moving the equipment in broad daylight but once we started setting it up in the big gymnasium, enjoying all the room up on the stage, we really started looking forward to the gig.

The first set went over luke-warm. The acoustics were especially troublesome due to the total lack of sound-proofing in the gym. By the second set, we'd learned to compensate by cranking the monitor system up and the crowd seemed to be more receptive to our new repertoire.

The third set was to start off with-you guessed it-"Smoke On the Water," a sure-fire crowd pleaser (no pun intended).

What none of us had noticed up to this point was the nylon gym shirt that some track star had thrown up into the gantry above the stage, where it had been hanging until the vibrations shook it free, to drape itself over one of the big 2,000 watt Fresnel lights we were using. How long it had been lying there absorbing the tremendous heat from the spotlight, no one could say but, by the time Percy started into the opening riff, it was beginning to smoke. The convections above the stage wafted the thick, grey streams down across the front of the stage like a curtain. We couldn't have had a more theatrical beginning to the song, or a more appropriate one, if we'd designed it.

Then, just as Gary stepped up to the mike to start singing, the shirt burst into flames fell in a slow diagonal glide, to land just where he'd been standing seconds ago.

The crowd went wild. True professionals as we were, we just kept playing while Doug stamped out the embers, lest they burn through someone's cord.

We acquitted ourselves honorably that day and for several more high school engagements, but our hearts were never in it and we found ourselves more and more willing to put up with the discomforts of travel in order to play more adult venues.

By now we'd moved out of our tiny house in little Italy and taken up residence in a grand old Victorian four square off 124th street. The former parlour served as a great practice room, with the convenience of a sliding door between it and the living room for entertaining guests. Boy, did we entertain guests.

The parties we had there are talked about even today. It was an atmosphere of no rules, no holds barred and the devil take the hindmost. The only thing that kept the place from spinning off the planet altogether was the presence of our only female resident; long-suffering, ever patient, grounded and sensible Pat.

Pat was Doug's cousin and a bit older than most of us. She had some training in the nursing field which came in handy at times but her most valuable attribute was her ability to go with the flow until we began to get into areas of unsafe or harmful behavior and then to somehow steer things back to reason without confrontation or concern. She was our den mother, our chief cook and bottle washer, our neighborhood liaison and, when required, our medical officer.

I was smitten with desire for Pat, for a while. It was likely some kind of misplaced mother image thingy and never amounted to much but Pat was kind enough to respond to my advances and let it play out naturally.

It was Pat who organized the combination scavenger hunt/garden raiding parties by which we supplemented our larder when the band was in between gigs for too long.

It was a simple thing to enlist the dozen or so of us that were usually looking for some adventure 'round midnight and send us out with virtual shopping lists of veggies that could be found in the neighbor's garden beds.

It was amazing to see how much good food could be gleaned from them without arousing rancor from the gardeners. We saved a lot of money on groceries and ate a good deal better, as well. Of course, we always had money for beer and dope; such were the priorities in a band house. Besides, we had to save money for important things like getting our own vehicle.

We needed to secure our own transportation and we knew it. The only problem was that vehicles capable of carrying a couple of tons of equipment plus a half dozen musicians cost money. Catch twenty-two; as musicians, money was the one thing that we did not have a surfeit of.

Our first band vehicle was a used milk truck, purchased from the local dairy, who had made sure to get every bit of value out of it before sending it out to auction. It was of an uncertain vintage and in deplorable condition. The motor ran ok most days, but that was about all that worked reliably.

The headlights had an unnerving way of turning themselves off when it hit a bump and could only be turned on again by shutting the motor off and restarting it. Doug, who had made the purchase and did most of the driving, became adept at doing so without stopping.

The drivers' seat, which was designed to swivel as to allow quick exit and entry for the milkman on his route, was missing a cotter pin that secured it in the face- forward position, so it would swing around freely when cornering, which required a certain technique to the steering the thing. There were, of course, no seatbelts.

The drivers' door was a slider. Delivery vans like this one were all equipped with these horrible things to facilitate the rapid egress that a postman or milkman required to keep on schedule, with little regard to the fact that they were potential deathtraps.

There was a learning curve involved when you were simultaneously bringing the truck to a hard stop and sliding the door back to hop out. If you missed your timing, it was not uncommon for the momentum of the vehicle to throw the slider closed again just as you were getting out, with the most likely result being a dislocated or broken left shoulder.

The slider on Doug's milk truck was missing a latch to keep it closed, so it would open by itself on a sudden acceleration or an uphill grade. On rare occasions, when a tight right turn occurred going up a hill, the driver could find himself being flung out the open door by the swivel seat and hanging on to the steering wheel for dear life. It kept things interesting.

It was a wreck, but it was our wreck, so we were happy to load our stuff in the back and take off for the next engagement. Doug acquired the milk truck in the summer and for the first few months we had it, we would all pile in with the amps and gear and ride with him to the gigs.

We discovered, as the season wore on and the weather got colder, that one of the many things that did not function was the heater. After a particularly frigid late-night return from a one-nighter in the foothills, it was decided that we would start bringing another vehicle for the personnel.

We agreed that the car, being the more reliant of the two, would follow behind the truck in case of a break down along the way. From the rear, the milk truck presented a lopsided look, listing alarmingly to the passenger side. The thought of all the weight in amps and instruments stacked up inside was worrisome at first.

As we proceeded down the highway behind it, the milk truck seemed to be changing it's lean from one side to the other at each bump in the road. It began to take on a sort of comic appearance, like something out of an early cartoon, happily galumphing down the road in time to some cheery tune. We had started to speculate whether the body of the vehicle was still attached to the frame in any meaningful way, when the inevitable finally occurred.

We were coming into a town (I think it was Sangudo), which had a gravel approach up a hill. About half way up, the road took a sudden bend to the right and there was a good-sized bump just at the same spot. A lot of things happened at the same time.

The milk truck hit the bump as Doug was leaning into the corner, causing the seat to throw him towards the door, which chose that moment to slide open. The box and all its' weight lifted visibly off the frame and shifted a few inches to the left, before coming back down at a new angle, literally throwing Doug right out the door.

For a breathtaking instant, it looked as though the truck was going to over-balance and flop over on its' side on top of Doug, who was now actually outside the cab, still hanging on to the steering wheel and running along beside the truck. Then, miraculously, the road leveled out and the truck righted itself, just as Doug did a one-foot hop and managed to jump back into the drivers' seat. From the back, it looked like some invisible hook had reached out and jerked him bodily back inside.

We got to the top of the hill and stopped. Everyone got out of the car to see if Doug was all right, which he was, sitting there with a thoughtful expression on his face. It was some minutes before he moved from behind the wheel.

"We need to get a new truck," was all he had to say. Nobody argued with him.

Thus it was that Doug and I found ourselves on a trip to Little Italy, in answer to a notice in the classified section advertising a "window van." We found the address and saw the van parked in the driveway.

It was a nice looking '64 Econoline that had been white originally but now sported a bunch of copy in various colors advertising the "Italian Centre Shop." There was the company logo on one side and on the other was a map of Italy and a map of Alberta, with a big red arrow sweeping across the Atlantic to the west. The words "Espresso Coffee Pots" had been lettered over top the map and "Importers" appeared below it.

It looked clean and free of rust. There were no telltale puddles under it, nor had the weeds grown around the wheels, which would indicate it hadn't been moved for a while. We went to the door of the house and were about to knock when it flew open to exude an excited man of middle age.

He greeted us hugely in a mix of Italian and broken English, shaking our hands vigorously and grinning as if we were long lost cousins. Doug tried to ask a couple of questions about the maintenance records and such but couldn't manage to penetrate the language barrier. The man, who identified himself as Alfie, had only one thing to say on the subject.

"Is good! No worry!"

He produced the keys and unlocked the van, then handed them to Doug, inviting him to start it. The engine roared to life on the first try and then settled down to nice, even idle. It sounded good.

Alfie jumped in the back and insisted that I take the other front seat, leaving him to hunch down over the engine cowling, with a big arm around the backs of each seat. He hadn't stopped talking since he'd come out of the house but I couldn't understand more than one word in ten. It didn't matter. He was able to communicate using the force of his personality alone.

Doug put the van in gear and pulled out onto the street, driving slowly. We drove to the corner and turned, Doug checking to see if the indicator lights were functioning.

"Come on, lets a-go! Pedalli to the medal!" urged Alfie.

Doug obligingly stepped on it and we sped down the street.

"I'm going to test the brakes-hold on." Doug advised. He hit the brakes hard. Alfie apparently hadn't got the message and was thrown forward between us, head first into the dash, smacking his forehead sharply on the unpadded metal. He laughed it off, waving his hand dismissively.

"Is no thinga. Is good! No worry!"

Doug drove around the block back to Alfie's house, parking the van back in the driveway. Alfie, who had started to bleed from a small gash in his forehead, ushered us into the house. As we came up the stairs from the landing, a handsome woman of Alfie's age ran to him, speaking rapidly in Italian and casting suspicious glances a Doug and I. He spoke to her in their native tongue as she saw to his wound, then turned to us.

"Stupid woman, she thinka you beat me up! I tell her; no worry. Is good!"

Doug and I had managed to confer on the way in and decided to go ahead and buy the van. The ad in the paper had asked a thousand dollars and we'd come prepared with cash. We likely could have bargained him down a couple of hundred but the van looked so good and I think Doug felt so badly about the brake check incident that he offered the full amount.

Alfie was beside himself with joy. He wrote out the bill of sale and transfer of registration, then insisted that we stay and celebrate with a glass of his home-made wine. By the time we got out of there we had each drunk four or five glasses of the potent stuff with Alfie's wife looking on in obvious disapproval. She looked like she wanted to put an end to the proceedings but, with a thousand dollars cash sitting on the table, she held her tongue, perhaps banking on the booze putting her man in a more generous mood.

Neither of us was in any shape to be behind the wheel but then, these things were measured differently in 1971 and so, with Doug in the van and me following in his beat up old Volkswagon, we made our way home to the band house.

Next day, our buddy Joe came over to inspect our prize and after some tinkering around under the hood and a test drive of his own, pronounced it a good buy. We were happy to have his approval because we knew the guy had grown up in a house full of motor heads and knew more about automobiles than the rest of us put together.

"Gotta do something about that paint job, though," he said, "I'll get my grinder."

He came back an hour later with a grinding tool and began to remove the graphics from the sides of the van. He totally obliterated the "Italian Centre Shop logo off the one side and had started on the other when suddenly Bob yelled at him to stop.

"Wait! Look what it says!"

We looked. For whatever reason, Joe had started in the middle of the message and removed the word "Coffee" first. That left the message "Espresso Pot Machine."

"Take the "o" off, man."

Joe obliged. The result was, if you didn't look too hard; "Express Pot Machine," which, combined with the map and the remaining word "Importers" below, made it just too good to ruin.

Everybody loved it, although Joe had his doubts.

"You guys sure? You're gonna get stopped by every cop on the highway with that on the side."

We looked at each other. It wasn't even close. Joe touched up the spots he'd ground out with white rust inhibitor paint and left the rest as is. The Express Pot Machine was on the road.

One of the earliest trips in the ESPO took us northwest of the city on a highway made slick by a vicious storm. The rain and sleet had been followed by plummeting temperatures that froze the water on the road into patches of black ice. We were well acquainted with these kinds of conditions and were taking it slow.

Just outside of Mayerthorpe, on an infamous uphill grade in the highway that was exposed to the prevailing winds and famous for black ice, we came across a debris field. It looked like someone had dumped a load of trash in the ditch. Bits of wood and aluminum littered the side of the road, mixed with a variety of what appeared to be household items over a distance of several hundred feet. As we came round the curve we saw that the rubbish trail ended at the site of a wrecked truck.

It was a Ford pickup that was sitting on its' side in the ditch, looking like it had rolled several times. A man was standing beside it. He looked at us as we approached and made a flapping motion with his arms as if to say, 'well, I don't know what to do now.'

A woman was walking down the side of the highway away from the wreck, stopping every now and then to peer at the stuff that lay in the snow, looking for something. Between the two of them was a little girl, maybe five or six, sitting by the side of the road.

She had nothing on but a pair of pink play pants and a little cotton blouse. Her feet were bare and her hair was caked with blood.

We pulled the van over into the opposing ditch, well out of the road and got out to see if we could help. Doug approached the man and asked if he was OK.

"Well, hell, yeah; I'm Ok but look at my Goddamned truck! I don't know how to fix this. I'm not a body man, fer Chrissake! What the hell am I supposed to do with this?"

Percy and Gary had gone to see about the woman. She seemed to be in a similar state of shock.

"Ma'am, are you OK? Your daughter is hurt."

"I know. Don't you think I know? I'm trying to find her shoes. She shouldn't have been riding in the camper. She took her shoes off, and now I can't find them. Will you help me look? They're pink, like her slacks. Shiny pink shoes with silver buckles. I have to find them. She shouldn't be out in this weather without her shoes..."

Meanwhile, I had gone over to the little girl. She was sitting there, staring into space in her indoor clothes and she wasn't shivering. Her bottom lip was torn in a ragged line down to her chin. There was a gash on the side of her head that had bled a lot but now the blood was freezing in her hair.

I took off my jacket and wrapped her up in it, immediately feeling the sting of the cold even through my heavy sweater. As I pulled the coat closed, she stood up and put out her arms to me. I picked her up and held her to me as I returned to the warmth of the van, her head tucked under my chin.

Percy was trying to convince the mother to get into the van as well but she was fixated on finding the little girls' shoes.

"Where's the nearest hospital?" someone asked.

"Shit, they just built one in Mayerthorpe last year. It's only a mile or two up the road."

Doug was appealing to the man to talk to his wife, trying to get them both to get into the van and come with us to get some help but it was no good.

"Naw, I better stay here and try to get this here fixed up, somehow, I don't know. You go on and we'll stay here."

The little girl needed a doctor. There was no telling how long ago the accident had happened, how long she'd been out there in the cold. She was in shock, possibly hypothermic. We couldn't wait.

When we got to the hospital it looked deserted. The lights were on and the front door opened automatically as we came up the sidewalk but there didn't seem to be anybody inside the place.

"Hello?" Bob yelled down the hall, "Anybody here?"

His voice echoed down the hallway and finally there was some movement at the far end. A nurse appeared, an older woman who seemed reluctant to come closer to us, perhaps unsure of our intentions.

"We have and injured girl, here. There was an accident out on the highway. She's cut and probably in shock. There are two more people still out at the accident site."

The woman stood there looking at us, blinking her eyes as if she couldn't understand English.

"Look! Do you have a blanket? This little girl is in shock! She needs to get warm. Is there a doctor here?"

This was something she apparently understood, having orders barked at her. She shook herself and began to focus on the tasks at hand.

"Ah.. blanket, yes…Ok, there are blankets there, in the room. Doctor is at home, we call if he's needed…"

Percy ran and got a blanket from the room she'd indicated. I stood, holding the girl, still wrapped in my buckskin jacket, until he came back. We traded the coat for the blanket and I set her down in a chair.

The nurse had gone over to the phone.

"Call the RCMP as well. Those people on the road need help. They could have injuries, too." Bob told her.

The woman responded well to orders.

"The doctor will be right here; he only lives a block away. I'll get the police. Where did you say this accident was?"

"About a mile and a half east of town, right on the curve."

"All right, I'll tell them," she said, dialing.

We didn't wait for the cops to arrive, knowing they would want us all to go back to the detachment and fill out witness statements that couldn't possibly have any bearing on anything. We were already running an hour late for our gig. I watched the nurse bundle the little girl up and put her in a wheelchair to await the doctor's arrival.

It might have been him we passed coming into the hospital parking lot as we pulled out.

Joe's prediction didn't quite come true; driving the Express Pot Machine, we weren't stopped by every cop on the road-only the ones with no sense of humor. The RCMP pulled us over a few times and once, on the way home from a dance with some liquid refreshment foolishly displayed in the rear window, they made us pour eight beers out on the side of the road.

It was more a fun thing and became kind of a point of pride after a while but the fun went out of it the day we got stopped, ironically, just outside of Mayerthorpe again, and they found Gary's lid stoker in the glove compartment.

The two cops that pulled us over on suspicion told us all to line up along the side of the shoulder while they searched the van. It was thirty below with a vicious wind chill and none of us was dressed for extended periods outdoors. After going through our personal luggage, one of the officers opened the back and, looking in at the stacks of heavy equipment stated that, technically, they had the right to take every piece of equipment off the vehicle and open the backs of the amps.

He was informed that he was welcome to go ahead and do so, just don't expect us to help with the task. He looked at us, back at the thirty or so speaker enclosures and amps, and wisely closed the back door. It was about that time that his partner found the Lid Stoker.

The Lid Stoker was a pipe made out of an elk horn and capable of holding an entire ounce of pot. Once that baby was full, it was an all day party. It hadn't been used for months and Gary had no idea it was in the glovey. He had, in fact, thought he'd lost it somewhere.

It had, unfortunately, been well used and not cleaned afterwards and therefore reeked of the good stuff and had enough black residue caked inside to give the RC's all the evidence they needed for a bust. They asked us, standing shivering by the side of the road as we had been for twenty minutes, who owned the thing. Gary stepped up and took one for the team.

The officers then were good enough to release him on his own recognizance in time for us to get to the gig. The whole thing was conducted in a congenial atmosphere, their attitude almost sympathetic to our mild embarrassment at being caught with nothing but a neglected pipe. I think Gary was more pissed off that he wouldn't get the Lid Stoker back than anything else.

Gary told us later that he'd been more worried about them finding the ounce of pot he had in his boot, where he'd transferred it while sitting in the back seat of the squad car. Only then did our roadie Gene own up to having another lid in his shaving kit. We had all watched as the officer searched our personal luggage and, setting the shaving kit aside unopened, had gone through Gene's bag with a fine-toothed comb.

The cops instructed Gary to report to the local detachment for booking after the gig, which he did. Percy's dad was a lawyer at the time and did such a good job of representing Gary in court that he ended up with nothing more than a $60.00 fine and a couple of months probation.

Ah, the seventies; no more school, no more rules, no need for all those tedious old-world conventions about property ownership and law and shit. We were tuned in, turned on and had, effectively, dropped out. We were tuned to a higher conciosness and strove to free ourselves of the chains of materialism as we lived together communally in a spirit of sharing.

How else to explain how Gary, Bob and Gary's girl Lorrie decided one day to hop in the Express Pot Machine and, without bothering to tell anyone, drive to California for a little sight-seeing trip?

They weren't technically *stealing* the van. After all, being members of the collective that was Captain Nobody, Gary and Bob owned two fifths of it. I guess they felt that entitled them to the use of it for a few weeks, and how were they to know the engine was going to blow up on the way back from San Francisco?

Apparently, some passing hippies took them in and the next day they somehow managed to limp the van into a town. Only much later did it occur to Gary the risk they had taken by accepting free lodging with the local commune, especially in that part of the State. They could easily have found themselves at the mercy of one of the many cults that operated in the area. (Jim Jones had got his start just down the road in Ukiah.)

But the road gods smiled upon them, even enabling them to get the van to a friendly dealership in town. A new motor was $400.00, which was about $390.00 more than they had, so the only recourse was to sell it. The sympathetic dealer, out of the goodness of his heart, gave them $90.00 for it, which happened to be just about the price of a couple of greyhound tickets back to Canada. To hear them tell it, it was just an unfortunate turn of events.

It was a turn of events that, unfortunately, left us without a band vehicle.

I remember being pretty angry about it. There were words spoken. Looking back, though, I think I was mostly just pissed off that I hadn't gone along for the trip.

Along about this time, Gary and I, who had together been doing almost all of the lead singing in the band, decided we'd like to concentrate more on the ever-increasing demands of the instrumentals. We decided we needed a singer.

Ads were posted, auditions were held and we ended up hiring a guy named Charlie for the job. Charlie was a long drink of water from small-town Alberta who sported an impressive head of hair done up in an Afro and a set of pipes that far outdistanced me and Gary combined.

He had developed the patent rock and roll move of swinging the mike by its cord and catching it just in time to belt out the next line a la Led Zeppelin and by his stance and mannerisms it was plain he had a bad case of Robert Plant envy but, say what you might, the lad could sing.

When Charlie learned about our need for new transportation, he mentioned that his Dad had an old school bus he might want to sell.

"A SCHOOL BUS?!" we all cried out together. Well, OK, so maybe it wasn't quite that dramatic, but close.

After all, this was the dream that every rock band harbored deep in the hidden recesses of its' heart; to own one's own bus. Having your own bus elevated your band from hoi polloi and placed you in the pantheon of real, honest-to-goodness touring bands.

Who had their own bus? Bands who had recorded and released a record, that's who. A bus was part of the package that came with success in the music industry. Rolling up to the gig in a bus made a statement to everyone concerned; you weren't just there; you had *arrived*.

We lost no time getting the particulars; the bus was out at the farm where Charlie had grown up, near Camrose. It hadn't been used in a while, maybe a couple of years but the last time it was, it ran fine. Then came the really exciting news-Charlie's father had apparently converted the bus to a motor home for the family. According to Charlie, it already had a dining table that converted into a double bed, a sink and stove, bunks for four and storage closets halfway back. We would be travelling with *beds!*

No time was lost arranging to go out to Camrose and see it. Money was taken out of the bank and we went prepared to make an offer.

No group of five-year-olds on an outing to the zoo were ever more excited as we five (six, now counting Charlie, although I seem to remember him being a bit less enthusiastic than the rest of us) as we neared the farm and first spotted the big yellow vehicle parked by the barn.

It was a 1958 International Harvester 58-seater with big, bulbous front wheel wells and a funky grill. It had two big red warning lights mounted on top like comic ears, and three little amber warning lights in between them. The mirrors were thrust out three feet on either side on sturdy-looking arms with braces, screwed into the sides.

Inside, everything Charlie had said was true. His dad done a great job of turning the utilitarian space into a people-friendly environment, purpose-made for socializing.

The whole interior had been sheeted with wood grain paneling that went from the floor up to the bottom of the windows, like wainscoting. The first bench seat behind the driver had been reversed and, with the two intervening ones removed, faced the fourth seat across a hand-made wooden table that was designed to let down across the seats and form a double bed. Across the aisle, another seat had been turned and mounted with it's back against the side, providing couch-like seating for three or a spot for one rider to stretch out. A little kitchenette had been built into that side, complete with a pump-operated sink and a small propane range inserted into the Formica counter top. Underneath was a propane fridge just big enough for a couple of dozen beer cans.

A pair of closets faced each other across the aisle amidships and separated the "living" space from the sleeping area in the back. Two pairs of bunk beds were built into the sides, with a few feet of cargo space between them and the rear emergency door.

It was, in short, perfect.

Joe had promised to come out to the farm and check the bus out mechanically but by the time he showed up, we were so in love with the thing that I don't think it would have mattered if he'd found that it didn't have a motor; we still would have bought the bus if we'd had to push it home.

Joe walked around the vehicle, occasionally getting down to peer under it and mumbling to himself all the while. We stood around, waiting for his diagnosis. When he'd finished his exterior examination, Joe opened the hood and had a look under there and then he asked for the keys and started the bus up.

A cloud of acrid blue smoke belched from the exhaust and Joe made clucking sounds, but it seemed to run okay and when we went for a test drive down the gravel road, it showed no sign of anything wrong with the power train. Still, Joe was doubtful.

"It is an old bus, man. Real old. They do good maintenance on these while they run as school buses and it looks like it's been kept up since but it's still a very old bus. All this weight is hard on an engine, man, not to mention the transmission. No way that's the original mileage- it's probably gone around once for sure, maybe even twice. There is not a lot of life left in this power train but there's nothing wrong with it right now."

He was talking to himself as he usually did but when Joe looked up at us gathered around he must have realized he was wasting his breath. We had all agreed that we would go by his advice. None of us wanted to spend good money on a vehicle that was not mechanically sound but man, we wanted that bus.

It wasn't as if Joe had found anything specifically wrong with the bus, even if he did question the wisdom of taking a fifteen-year-old vehicle on the highway for long distances. As he looked around him at the our expectant faces, like a gaggle of five-year-olds waiting to know if we could have ice cream, Joe knew there was only one answer we wanted to hear.

"I don't see anything wrong with it, boys." he said.

What trip back to the city. We were over the moon. We had a bus to tour in. Our own band bus, outfitted for a rolling party.

That next week we got hired to play at the Spokane World's Fair, with two gigs in southern B.C. to do on the way. Captain Nobody was hitting the road. Ironically, Charlie decided to leave the band and would not accompany us on the buses' first big adventure.

Our bus would quickly prove to be somewhat less than the perfect transportation we dreamed that it should be.

Ever spent any time travelling by school bus? I don't mean a nice, comfy air-conditioned, heated modern Greyhound. I don't mean a twenty-minute ride to school. I'm talking about hours and hours – whole days on the highway in an old-style bus designed to provide cheap transport to lots of people for short drives.

The first thing you'll notice is the shocks are not very good. You tend to feel every little bump on the road and the big ones can put your dental work at risk.

After a while, you begin to be aware of another sensation; between the bumps. There is a constant vibration in a vehicle like that. It makes your voice sound odd and tires your eyes out from always compensating for it. It gets into your very being and, literally, rattles your bones. On really long trips it can drive you a bit nuts but you don't notice it until you get off the bus. Even a pee stop becomes a remarkable experience as you feel your body begin to relax and stress leaving your mind the instant you are away from the vibrations.

Then it's back on the bus and bzzzzzzz to the next stop. If the next stop is eight hundred miles away, you are in for a miserable time. There is only one way to combat the effects of being on the bus that long; you need to get zonked.

We hit Calgary at the afternoon rush, looking forward to the drive through the Rockies and still not too fucked over by the constant vibrations. Gary was behind the wheel and doing a fine job of navigating his way through the busy traffic when we came up on a red light. He eased the brakes down, then further down, then stomped the pedal to the floor-nothing.

"Holy fuck. I got no brakes."

"Use the emergency brake, man!" Doug wisely advised.

Gary grabbed the long brake lever and yanked up...and then handed it over to Doug.

"Here, man, you try it."

By this time, Gary had been forced to take an impromptu left turn in order to avoid running the red light. We found ourselves rumbling down a quiet residential street past nice sixties-style bungalows under a canopy of mature elms. I say *down* the street because it was on a hill. The bus was picking up speed despite Gary's efforts to use the gears to keep it under control.

"Somebody get the map out. I need to know where we are going," he yelled.

We jumped to comply. Doug ended up with the Calgary street map, trying frantically to find our location, by way of plotting a safe course either to some flat ground where we could roll to a stop, or at least to avoid the major traffic areas.

For the next ten minutes, the two of them worked together, Doug glued to the map, trying to guide Gary to the unpopulated routes through town, while the rest of us manned the windows, trying desperately to catch glimpses of the street signs as they flew by and relaying the updates to him.

"Fuck, if we could find a level place to let it roll to stop, but this town is all hills, man."

Gary declined to comment, absorbed by the task at hand. He was trying to anticipate the traffic, looking ahead four or five blocks to see where the lights were decayed or a car might be turning in our lane. We weren't going fast but we weren't able to stop, either, so he had to keep steering around the potential collisions and then Doug would re-route him back on track to get out of town.

We missed the Banff Trail and were forced to keep going south, ending up on highway #2, heading for Okotoks. As the city fell behind us the prairie flattened out a little and Gary finally found a place to pull out with a bit of an uphill incline. The bus coasted to a stop. Leaving it in gear, Gary choked the antique diesel off and we were safe.

"Didn't we bleed the brakes before we left?" Gary asked.

"Yeah, we did," said Doug, "there must have been a bubble in one of the cylinders, or something."

"Well, let's bleed 'em again. What are we going to collect the fluid in?"

It was over. We had survived driving our bus right through Calgary at rush hour with no brakes. The result was having to re-route south to the Crow's Nest highway, instead of our planned western route but, hey-we lived to tell the tale.

We'd scored some weed and stocked our tiny fridge with beer when we left and it was enough to see us through to the B.C. border but shortly before we hit our first engagement of the trip we ran out of everything.

It was on that leg of the trip that we developed, of necessity, the mobile piss technique. With six of us on the bus, and everyone on a diet of Labatt Blue, it soon became apparent that we would not make any time at all if we made a pee stop every time someone needed one.

I don't remember who it was that first became so desperate as to try peeing out the bus door while we were moving-it might have been Percy. When we hit a good-sized bump while he was standing on the bottom step with both hands occupied, it was just luck and Gary's remarkably quick reflexes that saved him from being thrown bodily from the bus in mid-stream. We needed to find a way to do this safely or risked losing a band member along the way. We soon hit on a two-man approach that involved a back-up person, seated on the top step and holding on to the back of the active participant's belt for the duration. It worked like a charm, providing there were no crosswinds. We were able to make more miles without stopping and without cutting beer consumption, which was the main thing.

We made such good time that we pulled into Fernie, our first stop on the tour, a full day before we were scheduled to play. We parked the bus beside the hall where the dance would be and hit the town. Fifteen minutes later, we were back at the bus, having seen everything that Fernie had to offer.

It was then that we remembered that B.C.'s legal drinking age was twenty-one, as opposed to "liberal" Alberta's eighteen. Nobody among us was yet twenty-one. We were screwed, unless we could find some friendly locals willing to help us out.

We decided we might as well see if we could get into the hall and set up the equipment, maybe run through a few tunes to check the sound. No sooner had this thought occurred than a couple of friendly young women showed up to see what the bus was about. One of them, an athletic looking blonde named Debby, turned out to be our reason for being there. She'd apparently seen the group in a bar when she was in Edmonton and made sure we were on the list of bands that the city hired to help them celebrate their festival.

She had the key to the hall and before long we were all set up and ready to play. A few of the local young people hung around with us that evening, someone prepared a nice simple meal in the hall kitchen and after partaking of some home-made hash brownies for dessert, we turned in early, our first night sleeping in the bus.

The next day was a beautiful summer day. The townies showed up and were mellow, with people stopping by to meet the band and just hang out. The hall became a sort of drop-in center for the town. Even the local cops stopped by to see what the deal was, giving the pot smokers some stress until they saw that we were just having a nice quiet time and left with a wink and a wave.

Someone found a box of decorations and it became an on-going pastime putting them up. Walks were made to the town center and groceries bought. Meals were prepared and eaten.

We managed to secure a couple of cases of beer through one of our new friends. Word got around that the band like to smoke, resulting in the appearance of several purveyors of magical substances who started off competing to see who could give the band the best price and ended up just smoking everybody up for free.

The warm summer day wore into a lovely, pine-scented evening and by the time the dance was due to start, a suitably festive mood prevailed. We mounted the stage as everyone who had been inside the hall dutifully went outside so they could come back in, paying at the door as they entered.

The dance went well. We were well rested and, having had plenty of time to set up and tune the sound system, the music went off without a hitch. It was, in short, just a really nice gig in a real nice place. We finished playing around midnight and joined some of the townsfolk around a fire pit they'd lit behind the hall.

Joints were passed around, wine was drunk and as people got sleepy they left for home until it was just us and a couple of the girls from the community.

We sat and stared into the flames for a while without speaking. It was perfect. All the nasty gigs in filthy old taverns and thankless sock-hops in high schools, all the hundreds of hours on the road in lethal conditions and inadequate transport seemed to fade away. There was just this lovely summer night, the tired, satisfied feeling of a gig well-played and the easy camaraderie that being in a band together brought. I remember thinking that, if I could spend my summer evenings like this for the next however-many years, I would consider my career a success.

The next night, being Saturday, we were booked to play the next town down the road, called Creston. It must have been a very similar experience to Fernie, because no one I've spoken to about it remembers the first thing about it.

I know we played there that night, because I still have the contract. I found it in a pile of papers and photos of the band. It says we were paid $425.00 for one (1) evening of live music, etc., etc., but I haven't any recollection of the engagement, nor do any of the other Nobodys. The contract says we'd been hired for the town dance in honor of the local Apple Blossom Festival. Indeed, the single memory of it we all can agree on is that, as we rolled into town the streets were lined with huge apple trees, all of which were in full bloom.

I can only assume that it was such an unremarkable evening that the details have just merged with the dozens of other unremarkable gigs we did in those years. Then, having put the preliminaries behind us, it was on to the main event-the World's Fair in Spokane, Idaho.

How we got booked to play there was a mystery. One look at the list of famous acts that shared the stage through the course of that celebration on the banks of the Spokane River tells me were out of our league. We were scheduled to warm up for up for Teen Angel and the Rockin' Rebels, one of the retro-rocker bands that had come out to take part in the popular "rock and roll revival" headed up by "Sha-Na-Na." Other acts to appear later on the same stage were Bachman

Turner Overdrive, Ray Charles, Chicago, The Pointer Sisters, Gordon Lightfoot, Ella Fitzgerald and Merle Haggard.

Of course, we had no notion of the stratospheric company we were keeping on the way down there, just an overall feeling prevailed that we were on our way to a date with destiny.

But first we had to get across the border.

There were several places we could have crossed the border into the states but, for some reason, we chose to cross on highway #95, at a place called Kingsgate. I don't know if it was chosen because it is a relatively tiny outpost as border crossings go but it wasn't a bad decision, given the lack of proper documentation we were carrying.

The school bus had not been registered after the sale, so all we had was the former owners' registration card, signed over to Doug on the back, to prove we owned it. No one had thought to get insurance on the bus, or perhaps the idea had been considered and put aside in fear of the expense it would have incurred. Instead, all we had to present at the international border was the old insurance from the Express Pot Machine, which listed the vehicle as a "Window Van."

The sole occupant of the little roadside kiosk that served as a Customs Port of Entry, a wizened, slightly perplexed looking elderly gent in a uniform two sizes too large, looked us over doubtfully. He was willing to let the registration pass but he balked at the insurance card.

"Says here, this is for a Window Van," he remarked.

"Well, plenty of windows on it, isn't there?" Gary replied.

It was hard to argue with that. Still, the man was reluctant to pass us through.

"You guys are aware," he said officiously, "that if I find reason to doubt your intentions going across the border, I can and will conduct a search of your vehicle and it's contents."

Now, where had we heard that before?

We said we understood that, wondering if he would really detain us for the length of time it would take to go through all our stuff. We needn't have worried.

He made his way to the rear of the bus and opened the emergency door. Looking up at the towering pile of amps, speaker enclosures and road cases that filled the rear compartment to bursting, he took his hat off and scratched his head. Then he somehow found it in his heart to forgive us our shortcomings.

"Well, I guess I can extend the benefit of the doubt, in the interest of good relations. You fellas go ahead and have a nice day."

So, off we went, into the United States of America, looking to find two things in that great land; pot and cold Coors beer. We found both at the first place we stopped-a lonely roadhouse at a place called Bonner's Ferry.

The roadhouse is a great American institution left over from the pioneer days, when travel by horse and wagon necessitated these stopping places every hundred miles or so along the major routes. Born of the travelers' need for food and shelter, a safe wayside shelter from a wild land, they have become taverns, restaurants, post offices, dance halls and general hangouts for new generations of Americans who now travel through a marginally less hostile landscape.

The one at Bonner's Ferry looked to have been there for a hundred years or more. The sagging roofline and tarpaper exterior told a story of makeshift repairs done where replacement was required. There were a couple of smaller outbuildings but the well-worn track to the door told us where the welcome might lie, if the neon beer signs in the window left any doubt.

As we stepped inside from the bright spring day, the interior was dark, cool and cluttered. Sports pennants festooned the ceiling beams and vied for space with a thousand signed dollar bills that marked the passing-through of celebrities real and imagined. The smell of draught beer and tobacco assaulted our noses along with cooking grease and a faint hint of something…else.

Several people were seated at the bar, cloaked in shadow as our eyes adjusted to the gloom. A middle-aged man with a shock of red hair and a handlebar moustache greeted us from behind the bar.

"Good afternoon, gentlemen. What can I do for you?"

"Coors all around, please."

"Coors it is."

The shadows resolved to reveal a couple of relaxed looking indi-viduals at the bar who slid down a couple of stools to make room for us all with friendly nods and 'Howdys'. The barman plied his trade and rapidly produced a squadron of foamy draught beers to order.

"That'll be five forty. Canadian money? Well, it's too early in the day for higher mathematics-we'll just take it on par."

He turned to an ancient nickel-plated cash register and produced change for the ten-dollar bill he'd been given.

"You boys on a road trip?"

"Yeah, going to Spokane for the World's Fair. We're playing there."

"I thought you might be a band. That's pretty cool-World's Fair, huh?"

"Yeah. We're pretty stoked. We're on the same bill with Teen Angel and the Rockin' Rebels."

"No kiddin'? Teen Angel is pretty big in these parts. Sounds like a good show. Maybe I oughtta head down there. Whattaya think, Frank? Think we should take off to the World's Fair? Catch Teen Angel and these guys, the...uh?"

"Captain Nobody and the Forgotten Joyband."

"No shit. Captain who and the what, now?"

"Captain Nobody and the Forgotten Joyband."

"Captain Nobody. Well, I'll be go to hell. Nice to meet you, Captain Nobody, my name's Reb. Now you got me interested. What kind of stuff you guys play?"

"Mixed bag. We do some Stones, some Fleetwood Mac, couple of Who numbers and mix it up with some Alex Harvey, early Trogs, Steely Dan and Beatles. We have a couple of originals we do."

"Wow, that sounds like an eclectic set, for sure. Maybe I will try to make it down."

We sipped our beers and relaxed, glad to be quit of the buses' constant vibrations and out of the dazzling sunlight and heat of the day. The bartender chatted amiably about the trip, asking about road conditions, etc. The appeal of the roadhouse began to make itself evident.

One of the other bar patrons addressed Gary in a confidential tone.

"Say, you fellas interested in buying some grass?"

"Oh, yeah. We are definitely interested. Is that something we might arrange to do here?"

"Not here, I don't carry it around with me but my place is just a half-mile up the road. I could go get it and be back in a few minutes, or why don't you come along for the ride; I'll show you my place."

Always up for a new adventure, Gary agreed. Bob decided to along for moral support. The band had a hurried conference and pooled our resources, sending him off with enough money to buy us an ounce of the good stuff. A new round of beer appeared, much to everyone's approval, and we settled into the cool, welcoming atmosphere of the place. Reb got the last of us served and then he turned to Doug.

"So, you guys are probably going to the rock concert, huh?"

We looked at each other.

"Rock Concert?" Doug queried, "Where's that?"

"Oh, you didn't know about that? Yeah, we're having our own little outdoor Rock Concert, right here in the valley. Should be starting up this evening, according to the poster. You didn't see the poster?"

He indicated the cork message board on the wall beside the door.

Doug and I got up to look. Right in the middle of a number of ads for vehicles for sale and babysitters needed was a vaguely psychedelic-looking poster advertising something called "Valleystock," which was billed to take place that very night and for three consecutive days in a place called the "Kooteney Bench." The headliner was a band called "It's a Beautiful Day," known to us as a California light-rock outfit who'd scored a medium hit with their single "White Bird," a couple of years ago. Not exactly rock royalty but respectable enough for an outdoor festival in the middle of nowhere, Idaho.

"Reb?" Doug called across the room, "where is the "Kooteney Bench?"

"Well, technically, you're standing on it. The benchland is just the flats that follow the river along this valley. What they are referring to is a point about two miles down the road, where it widens out to a nice big hayfield. That's where the stage is set up. Lots of room to party."

"So, it's on this road? On the way south?"

"Yep. Can't miss it. Just keep looking to your right as you drive down the valley and you'll see it below you. 'Bout two miles, like I said. There's a couple roads down to the flats. I guess they'll be using the one with the gate on it for admissions."

The poster said "ten dollars each, or fifty for a carful." We conferred briefly if we could afford it, having just sent most of our ready cash off with Gary. The obvious answer was no, but when music was involved, we weren't very good at taking no for an answer. It was decided that, as soon as Gary got back, we would check it out.

"Maybe if we offer to do a set, they'll let us in free." Percy speculated.

It was worth a try. We nursed our beers, not wanting to spend money on another round. We wanted to take some off-sale beer with us for the road. Reb must have sensed the slow down in consumption after ten or fifteen minutes.

"You guys want another draught while you wait?" and after we all declined, "those guys are probably going to have to test the product. Fred's real good about giving out the free samples. They might be a while. Tell you what-this one's on the house."

We expressed our gratitude.

"Well, hell, it ain't every day we get a real live rock band in the door. Here you go. Can't have you sitting around not drinking."

So we sat and chatted idly with him and his lone other customer, whose name was Bill. Bill knew a lot about the local history. According to him, Bonner's Ferry first saw Europeans in 1808, when David Thompson came through the area, surveying trading routes for the Northwest Trading Company.

"When gold got discovered up in BC, there was a rush through here on the old Wildhorse Trail. A fellow named Bonner put in the ferry where the trail crossed the Kooteney, pretty much just down the road, here. That was in the 1860's. By the 1880's, there was a steamship plying the river, servicing the gold fields up north. You wouldn't know it but this was a boomtown a hundred years or so ago."

We were just coming to end of our well-nursed free beers when Gary and Frank returned, looking a little high and smelling like home-grown ganja. The tantalizing background pong in the place was suddenly explained.

"You guys took your time." Doug remarked.

"What-someone in a rush?" Gary answered, and then turned to Frank. "You in a rush, Frank?"

That seemed to be about the funniest thing Frank had ever heard. He collapsed on the bar, laughing uproariously, while Gary beamed a big, silly stoned-out grin at him.

"Well, we're all here now. I guess we'd better hit the road," suggested Doug.

We did just that, thanking Reb for his generous hospitality and bidding Bill and Frank goodbye. We climbed back on the bus, blinking in the bright sunlight.

"Shit!" exclaimed Bob, "we forgot to get the off-sales."

While he and Doug went back in for supplies, the rest of us pumped Gary for information about his buying trip. Judging by the look of his eyes, it had been a trip, all right.

"You wouldn't believe it," he said, "fuckin' guy lives way up the side of this mountain, down this, like, goat track. Finally get to this farm that is so hidden in the jungle, I'd never be able to find it again. He had *tons* of pot, hanging from the rafters of his barn, drying."

Bob burst in to continue the story, carrying a case of beer.

"There was a fucking *hayloft* full of leaves, and all the buds were separated on this big bench, man."

"So, you scored, right?"

"Scored?" said Gary, reaching into his jacket pocket, "look at this. Frank is a very generous guy."

"Holy shit. What did you pay for that?"

That was a big economy sized baggy filled almost completely with dried flower buds of cannabis. There must have been close to a half a pound of the stuff.

"He charged us thirty bucks, for an ounce. Can you believe that? He even threw in a couple of books of rolling papers."

"Wow. That's what I call a score. We're set up for the whole trip."

"Let's just not get busted down here, all right? Roll a couple and then find a good place to stash it. Wow."

Doug came back with an additional "two-four" of frosty canned Coors, and our larder was stocked. We were ready. Rolling out onto the highway again, we told Gary and Bob about the outdoor concert.

"Sounds great, if we don't have to pay to get in, man. Fifty bucks is about all we got left for food."

"Yeah, we'll work something out. Just keep an eye out for this field."

A few hundred yards down the highway, we stopped to pick up a pair of hitch-hikers, a young guy and a girl.

They didn't look like your average hitchers at all. She was dressed demurely in brand-new levis' and a pretty floral top. She had on pink sneakers and carried a pristine backpack awkwardly. She was pretty and slim and had a lovely smile for everyone. Her companion was tall and athletic-looking, sporting a crew cut and dressed like he was going fishing, with a vest that must have had thirty pockets. His hiking boots looked so new, it hurt my feet just looking at them.

"Hi! Thanks for stopping."

"No problem. I don't know how far we can take you, though. We're just on our way to the concert."

"Concert?"

"Rock concert. It's supposed to be just down the road. We don't know if they'll let us in or not. We can't pay, so we thought we'd offer to play a set."

"You guys are a band? I wasn't sure what 'Captain Nobody and the Forgotten Joyband' meant."

"Yup, we're a band. Let me introduce you. This is Percy, Charley, Bob, Neil, Gary and I'm Doug."

"Nice to meet you all. I'm Larry. This is my wife, Minty. We're on our honeymoon."

"Really? You're hitching on your honeymoon?"

"Well, we thought about going to Hawaii, or Europe. Then we thought-'well, why not see America, first?' So we bought backpacks and some gear and here we are-'On the Road' like Kerouac."

"Like Kerouac!" Minty added, beaming.

"Well, that's pretty cool. So, you want to go to a Rock concert?"

They looked at each other for one second.

"Yah! That sounds great!"

"Great. Would you like a cold beer?"

They would.

We lit a doobie and rolled along the sunny road, looking to the right for signs of a gathering in a meadow, but the miles went by and there was nothing.

"He said it was just a couple of miles," said Doug, standing to see better through the screen of trees along the ditch.

"We must have gone three or four, by now, man."

"What the fuck? Did we miss it?"

"I hope not. How do you miss a whole concert?"

"You do that brown acid," said Bob, "I missed Jethro Tull that way. I was center front, man. Fucking 'Aqualung,' too. Missed the entire show."

"There," said Bob, pointing, "what's that?"

Sure enough, far off down the valley was something that at first looked like a little village. As we got closer, we could make out a big stage in the middle of a gaggle of tents, teepees and kiosks. People were milling about, concentrated in front of the stage. A parking lot was set apart from the crowd. There was no discernable road to or from the area.

"Well, that's it, but how do we get there?"

"He said there were two roads down."

"Wait-what's this? Is this a road?"

The bus slowed as we came abreast of a turn-off. It did not look promising, but by then we were getting the idea of just how rural a place we were in.

"Hell, man-give it a shot. We gotta get down the hill somehow."

We turned off the highway with a grinding of gears and proceeded to follow the side road as it took an increasingly steep route down towards the valley floor. Almost immediately, we were enveloped in a thick jungle of overgrown forest. All sense of our position relative to the objective was lost. Doug struggled to keep the speed moderate as the downhill grade continued to increase. The road took us deeper into the forest and then began to dissipate, becoming one with the unmarked forest floor. We found ourselves accelerating down a thickly wooded slope with no idea of direction and no hint of track or trail to follow.

Our speed started to get up to an unsafe rate notwithstanding Doug's efforts. We were crashing through the underbrush now, narrowly avoiding trees and stumps, bouncing insanely over unbroken ground. Branches smashed against the side of the bus and raked down the windows. People were thrown from their seats as amps and road cases were launched out of their births.

"Doug! Fuck's sake, man-slow down!"

"I can't! The fucking brakes are gone again!"

It was then that we all knew we were going to die. The situation had but one possible outcome. Flying unchecked down a forested mountainside with no way to stop, in a vehicle that was not equipped for such abuse, we knew what was about to occur.

Looks were exchanged. Stock was taken. Peace was arrived at. It had been a good run. We'd played a couple of good gigs, a few of us had loved well and we were sufficiently stoned to accept what was about to occur with calm minds. Smiles broke out. Nods were nodded, knowingly.

Then suddenly the forest belched us out onto a grassy sward that leveled out and brought us to a nice, rolling stop about a hundred feet behind the stage.

A big hairy guy with dreadlocks came walking over with a clipboard in his hand. After dutifully recording the band name from the side of the vehicle, he jumped on board and addressed us from the top step.

"Great entrance, guys. Okay, I don't have you on my list but that's OK, I don't have half the bands on this fuckin' thing, anyways. Where you guys from?"

"Uh...Edmonton."

"Edmonton? Edmonton, Alberta? Like, Canada? Wow, man-I didn't know we had any international acts booked! Cool! All right, you guys just relax. I'll see when we can fit you in. Are you hungry? There's BBQ over there, and East Indian shit on the other side. Gonna be a corn roast at twilight, all included in the price of admission. Bands eat for free."

He looked down at Larry and Minty.

"You kids with the band?"

We assured him they were our manager and bookkeeper, respectively.

"OK, that's fine, then. Better not wait too long on that BBQ, she's goin' fast. Best ribs in the state. Welcome to Valleystock, man!"

And with that, he took his leave.

We sat looking at each other, not quite believing we'd been spared. Somebody cracked a shaken up beer, blowing sudsy foam across the aisle. Somebody else lit a joint.

"Well, let's party," somebody said. So we did.

We spilled out of the bus in a mix of relief at not being killed and excitement at finding the concert so open and welcoming. Another curiously dressed man came striding over the field towards us. He was wearing what appeared to be homespun cotton pants, held up with rainbow suspenders. He was barefoot.

"Say, you folks interested in buyin' a little acid? I got some of the best Purple Owlsley you ever did."

He was carrying a gallon jug of wine, which he proffered generously. We accepted and the jug made the rounds. It was sweet and strong and tasted homemade, almost like lemonade.

"How much is the acid?" he was asked.

"How much you got to spend?"

We held a hurried conference.

"If we don't have to pay for food, I guess we have bout fifteen bucks," Gary reported, handing over the cash, "How much will that buy us?"

"Well, if you pass that jug around once more, that'll be about right."

"You mean, the acid's in the wine?"

"You know a better place for it? That's my wife's dandelion wine-had a real good crop this year. Like drinkin' a little bit of last May all over again."

Everybody took another good pull off the jug and we thanked him for his generosity.

"I was thinking we might hold off on the acid until after we play," Doug commented.

"Oh, well. Too late now."

"So, we just did LSD? Really?" Minty was smiling her lovely smile, enchanted at the notion.

"Wow, this is our first time," said Larry, perhaps a tad less enthusiastic. "I feel like we should have…well, prepared ourselves, somehow."

"You'll be all right. Just enjoy. Just go with the flow."

"Ok," Larry said, doubtfully.

There was a creek running through the flat land, down to the river. It was shallow and stony, with lots of little pools where people were relaxing and cooling off. Most of them were nude and completely at ease. Children swam in the river under the watchful eyes of their parents.

Some of us wandered over to the food tents and helped ourselves to some ribs and corn on the cob. There was real lemonade and iced tea, as well. Everyone was outgoing and friendly, strolling about the field getting to know one another. Bands of half-dressed farm kids terrorized each other with wild abandon.

Presently a bluegrass band got up on stage and tore into a spirited rendition of "Orange Blossom Special." Folks got up to dance. I caught a glimpse of Minty in the middle of the dancers, whirling about in joyous abandon. Larry was nowhere to be seen.

The acid started to kick in and I realized that this was no run of the mill street dope. The guy with the wine jug had said it was real 'Purple Owsley' and, as a whirlwind of magnified sensations began to rock my senses, I began to believe him. Even if it hadn't been made by the legendary grand wizard of psychedelics himself, this was potent stuff.

The afternoon grew hot. I found myself sitting in a shady bend in the creek, dabbling my toes in the cool water. Some kids ran by, splashing their way through the water and soaking me in the process.

The sensation of the chilly water suddenly hitting my chest made me draw my breath in so sharply my head spun. The children's laughter melded with the splashing water and the tingling of my skin. I heard the water, felt the laughter, watched the cold shock on my skin. The next thing I knew I was running with them, in and out of the stream, splash laughing sunlight shade warm cool. River-jump swim fish. Cool mud bank lay basking warm sun dry clay flakes falling crunch under red feet back up creek to bus Doug speak. Word speak play time.

Play time?

"It's time to play. We're using the house equipment. You can play the drums that are on stage. We need to be on in ten minutes. Are you all right?"

Doug should have known better than to ask someone on acid a question like that. 'Are you all right?' Why, the philosophical implications alone are stag-ag-ag-gering. Like me. Stum-bum-bumbling up the make-shift sta-sta-stairs to the sta-stage, standing, looking out at the expectant faces looking back, wondering what I was supposed to do.

Finding a set of drums there, sticks and all, some stage-hand guy asking if I wanted a vocal mike. Now, there's an interesting question, and one well worthy of consideration. Do I want a vocal mike? Well, I guess I should have one, in case I'm called upon to sing something but, if I say yes, does that mean I'm consenting to sing? Do I feel like singing? There's more to the question than you might think...

"Right...so, I'll just set this one up on the boom stand here and leave it off but if you want to use it, just switch it back on, OK?"

"OK," sez I. That settles that.

Now I just need to address the fact that these are not my drums and everything is in the wrong place. It's going to take a while to adjust things...

"One, two, three four!"

Fuck! Gary's counting in a tune. But what tune? I didn't hear anyone call out a song. Jesus Christ-the band has started playing...playing... "All You Need is Love," the Beatles anthem for the Peace generation. That's OK, the intro is so ambiguous that it didn't matter that I missed it. I can come in with the vocals.

The Vocals?! I'm supposed to sing the third part in the chorus, which is also the intro. Get the mike over to my mouth. Nothing! Stage hand guy gesturing from the wings, making flicking motions with his fingers.

Of course, I need to turn the mike on. There. Oww! Feedback screeches through my head, quickly snuffed out by stagehand guy with a pail of cold control he keeps in a jar by the door.

Bless John Lennon for writing simple songs, easy to play while you watch the misty colors of the harmonies drift into the crowd and settle, fog-like to the ground, where the grass picks up the overtones and turns it to a whiter shade of pale.

Whoever owns these drums has a taste for bizarre cymbals. There's one with rivets drilled through that reverberate atonally and another that's inverted and sounds like someone hitting a garbage can with a bat. Every time I hit it, it yells back at me. I can't do my normal, business-like set on these things. So, what's the advice?

"Just go with the flow."

By now, I'm not the only one realizing he's just too stoned to do a standard performance. We need an inspiration. It comes from Percy, who waits for the last chord of "All You Need..." to fade out before launching into the opening guitar riffs from "Rain-O."

Fucking "Rain-O," man. Chilliwack's bluesy, rambling jam-inducing, hippy-friendly lyrics are perfect for the situation. We once played an outdoor gig at Cooking Lake, set up right on the shore and ended up doing "Rain-O" for about a half an hour. It was Perfect then and it's Perfect now.

Grins all 'round as, one by one, we realize what a stroke of genius choosing this song at this time is. By the time we get through the preliminary two verses and start into the jam section, we're all lost in the tune, total subjectivity on the stage. I close my eyes and surrendered to the groove. It's beautiful. The crowd just loves it. We wring old "Rain-O' out for all she's worth, likely another 30-minute version but then, who's counting? I remember tears in my eyes about half way through.

When we finish, it's time to rock and roll. I start into our version of "Sympathy for the Devil," based on a kind of rocked-up samba rhythm that I'd come up with while trying to emulate the entire Rolling Stones on percussion instruments in the studio. Great dance tune and the tempo made a nice counter balance to last one.

I don't remember what else we played that day, only that we had a great time on stage and the people there really enjoyed the set. We were instant celebs for the evening, as other acts took the stage and we all wandered about, taking part in what had turned out to be about the best outdoor concert I remember ever being at.

At one point, Larry came up to me and told me he was "feeling strange." I replied that he should expect to feel that way for another hour or two and the only strange thing would be if he didn't feel strange after ingesting what I conservatively estimated to be about five hundred mics of bitchin' LSD.

"Go with the flow, huh?" he enquired.

"Exactly. If you are feeling strange, maybe it's because you're hungry. Did you get some ribs?"

"I don't eat pig," he said.

"Oh, okay, well, there's supposed to be some East Indian food over there-they'll have some vegetarian stuff, right? Why don't you go over and have a look, or a smell, and see if anything appeals."

"Yeah, okay, but…what if I eat something and I'm still feeling this way?"

"Right, well, you may want to act out your feelings. Try dancing to the music, whatever. Can you think of a better place to be seen acting strange? How many chances do you think you're going to have in life to act totally weird and have no one think the least thing about it?"

Larry considered this at some length, while a big, toothy grin slowly spread itself across his face. He laughed.

"You are right! Thanks!" he cried. He gave me a big hug and ran off to act strange somewhere. I watched him go, hoping he didn't get to acting *too* strange.

The evening was wearing into night as a bonfire was lit and bamboo torches appeared and were distributed about the grounds. I found myself gazing hypnotically into the flames with lovely halluci-nations playing themselves across my retinas.

"Hi there! Drummer!"

I turned to the voice, hailing me from a knot of people. It was Minty. She had a new scarf of some diaphanous material, which she was wearing as a headband. Her feet were bare and there were little blue cornflowers woven into her hair.

"Drummer!" she cried again, and flung herself into my arms, giving me a big, sloppy kiss and a hug. She stayed with her arms around my neck, mine resting uncertainly on her hips. Such nice, slim hips.

"Hi Minty. How are you?"

"How am I? That is so sweet of you to ask. I am so, so good. I have never felt this good in my entire life! I hope I will feel this way forever."

She was literally glowing in the firelight from a nearby bonfire, her face haloed by the light. She was looking unflinchingly into my eyes, her lips parted just oh, so little. I looked around nervously for Larry.

"What's the matter?" Minty asked.

"I was just wondering where Larry is." I replied.

"Larry?"

"Yeah-you know, your husband?"

"Oh! Larry! Hahahah...I had completely forgotten about him. Wait. Is that weird? That's weird, isn't it. I shouldn't forget about Larry, should I? He married me! Oh, I don't feel good about that."

"Hey, listen, you're stoned on acid. It will mess with your head. You don't want to be worrying about what your brain does when you're stoned. One time, I spent three hours examining a kumquat. Let it slide."

"Promise?"

"Promise. You want me to help you find Larry?"

"Would you do that for me?"

She still had me in her arms, hanging off me as she relaxed a bit.

"Sure. Come on, let's circulate."

We started walking, holding hands, around the edges of the firelight. I spotted Larry almost right away. He was twirling around in the dark, just outside the firelight like a whirling dervish with his arms flung out to his sides, head back, laughing and shouting.

"I feel Strange! Hahahah! I *Feel* strange!"

Minty ran to him and threw herself around his waist, knocking him over. They fell together in a heap on the grass.

"Minty! I feel strange!"

"You do?"

"Yes! It's Wonderful!"

"Oh, well then. That's good."

I left them and wandered back to the stage, where a bunch of young local kids had screwed up their courage and got up to do a set. They couldn't have been more than thirteen or fourteen, making up for their lack of experience or any real musicianship with youthful exuberance. A small crowd of their friends were standing around and dancing at the front of the stage, occasionally shouting encouragement.

I listened for a few minutes, smiling in understanding of just where they were at, then I went off, away from the lights and crowd, looking for the creek. When I got there I was alone under a blanket of stars in a clear night sky. It was warm, still from the hot day, warmer than our nights ever get at home.

The noise and lights of the party were just far enough away to provide a backdrop to the quiet of the evening.

I sat down on the bank, just listening to the babble of the water, feeling peaceful and drowsy, coming down nicely from the high. Something moved on the opposite bank, something white and brown in the grass. It moved again, a little hop-it was a rabbit; a floppy eared, brown and grey bunny, nibbling on the succulent grass at the edge of the creek.

Just when I thought that was about the cutest thing that could have happened, some fireflies came squadroning out of the bushes, hovering three feet off the ground, each glowing with its own tiny light. I was charmed completely. I lay down with my head resting on my arm and gazed at the magical scene before me, half expecting to see a leprechaun next, sprinkling pixie dust about.

The next thing I knew, the sun was up. A suspiciously familiar looking group of kids came splashing down the creek, whooping and hollering with abandon. I was *hungry*.

The stage was occupied by a duo, a man and a woman, singing folk songs and accompanying themselves on autoharp and some other manner of stringed instrument, a dobro, I think. They were good, adding to the ambience of the place.

Where the ribs had been yesterday there was a crew of cooks turning out pancakes as fast as they could brown them. I sidled into line and wound up beside Percy.

"Hey, Percy, man-how you doin'?"

"I am here, alive and all my limbs are functioning. More than this, I cannot ask."

"That was some good acid, eh?"

"No shit. First good trip I've had in years. I was ready to swear off the stuff but if you can get shit like that, wow."

"Right on. Man, I'm starving. Those pancakes are looking mighty good."

"You're in America, man. Those aren't pancakes-they're flapjacks."

"Right you are, when in Rome. Seen anybody else?"

"Gary's crashed out in the bus. I tried to wake him up but he's gone, man. Someone else is sleeping in the back. Two someones, I think. Couldn't make I.D.s. Bob went with some guys to get supplies. They left about ten minutes ago."

"Supplies meaning, of course, beer."

"Coors, to be exact. He was taking a collection. Must have had a hundred bucks when he left."

"Well, Reb will be glad to see him, I guess."

"As long as he doesn't get rolled for it and left on the highway."

"Hah!"

We looked at each other.

"Hey, man-you don't suppose..."

"Naw-no way. With this crowd? These people are hippies, man, and besides-they all know each other."

"You guys eating or talking?"

It was our turn. Big stacks of golden brown flapjacks and all the corn syrup you wanted. Just what the doctor ordered. We found ourselves some shade and squatted down to break fast.

Doug joined us presently and after a while Gary emerged from behind the stage, looking like death warmed over. After he'd secured his plate, he came over.

"Hey, there's coffee. They just put a big urn up."

"Coffee?"

We were galvanized into action. Presently, we were all settled back down, enjoying steaming cups of 'welcome back to the human race' brew. I told everyone about my magical visitation by the creek.

"I thought I'd found 'middle earth', or something."

"This whole scene is once removed, man. I mean-autoharp? Come on."

"Like I said, man. These people are hippies. We are in the summer of love, guys. It's 1962 all over again."

"I love it. There's this guy I was rapping with last night, moved here from New York. Took over an old farm that was abandoned. Just moved in and started fixing the place up, planted some corn and shit. Stayed three years before the county visited and sold him the place for a dollar, just to make it official."

"Back to the Earth, man. You can smell the musky pages of the Whole Earth Catalog on their clothes."

"Don't knock it, man. A lot of these people got shit on the ball. There's a couple keeping bees. The guy was telling me about the mead they are making. Started selling it locally, got so popular they are building a national brand, buying honey from other keepers to fill the quota. Guy's going to be rich, man. Making mead."

"Please don't talk about booze, you guys. I'm going to lose my flapjacks."

"What the fuck did you get into last night?"

"I met a man who makes moonshine. White lightning. Corn liquor. I told him I didn't have any cash and he laughed at me. Said he was happy to get my opinion on his product. Stuff was smooth, man. Went down like fine cognac. I think I drank about a jam jar full of it."

"Pint, or quart?"

"Pint, man. What, do you think I'm crazy? Still; 'way too much. Stuff creeps up on you, man. And on top of that acid, I didn't know what was going on."

"That much was obvious. Do you remember playing air guitar on stage?"

"No. Oh, God-did I?"

"No one could figure out why you didn't just pickup a guitar and join in. You were in your own place, man."

"Oh, well, if you have to make a fool of yourself, I guess this is good place for it."

"Oh, yeah."

It was then that Larry and Minty approached, holding hands like little kids, looking happy and rested.

"So, we just wanted to let you guys know that we won't be coming to Spokane, after all."

"Oh yeah? Why's that?"

"We met some people, here. Really nice people. They asked if we'd like to stay around here for a bit, help out on their place in return for bed and board. This lady is going to teach me quilting. Larry is going to be helping to harvest the early corn. They get two crops of corn, here-did you know that?"

Larry stood beside Minty, grinning happily. They were in a good place. Who could blame them for wanting to stay for a while?

"I, um, I wanted to thank you for helping me find Larry last night."

I could tell that what she meant was 'thanks for not taking advantage of my blissfully stoned horny state and boinking me senseless when you could so easily have done so.'

"I'm just thankful we found him as soon as we did." I told her, bringing a small blush to her cheeks and a tiny smile to her lips. Really nice lips. Oh, well.

Bob came striding across the field with a flat of beers in his arms.

"We had better start thinking about finding the highway, man. We need to be in Spokane to play tonight."

So, we gathered our belongings and loaded them and ourselves back on the bus, bid our new friends adieu and followed a small caravan up the mountain on a real road that intersected with the road we needed to be on.

Doug had taken the wheel, as Gary was in no condition. We settled in for long day of vibration and sight-seeing, rolling through the luscious hills and valleys of western Idaho.

The two-lane highway wound its way, this way and that, in series of gentle curves. The possibility was ever present of meeting oncoming traffic, unseen until the last second, so without a shoulder it well behooved a driver to keep to his own lane.

Even so, the curving road provided surprises. You never knew what might be around the next bend till you were virtually on top of it, as could be testified by the road crew we suddenly came upon and drove straight through before anyone had a chance to react.

Doug grew weary and Gary insisted on taking over, saying he needed to do something to take his mind off his hangover.

On we drove, through fields of corn on the winding road until suddenly, Gary inexplicitly geared down, braking and pulled over to the shoulder.

"What the fuck, man?"

"Check this out," he said.

We all looked out the windows and wondered if we were still stoned.

Standing by the side of the road, taking in the bus with a look of mild amusement, was a vision from a wet dream.

She was young-maybe twenty, blond and beautiful-*model* beautiful with a body to match, nicely displayed in a halter-top and a pair of cut-off shorts that came within a hair's breadth of being pornographic. She had on rugged looking hiking boots that, on her, somehow managed to look as sexy as the rest of her outfit. Giving definition where none was needed to her shapely hips was a wide black leather belt that sported a big silver buckle and on one hip a bone-handled Bowie knife about a foot long and on the other a holster containing what appeared to be a six-shooter.

Sitting beside her in the road was a big German Sheppard on a sturdy leash, which she held in her left hand, presumably in order to keep her right free for hitching, or possibly shooting people.

We came to stop in a cloud of dust with the door of the bus about ten feet away from her.

After she eyed the bus critically for a moment or two, she approached the door, which Gary threw open. They regarded each other as the dust settled.

"Hi," was all Gary could think of to say.

"Howdy," she replied, "how far you goin"?"

The rest of us were staring out the windows of the bus at her. She didn't seem real, this apparition of the cornfields, so closely matching our every drowsy daydream fantasy on this hot, lonely road in the middle of nowhere. We couldn't believe our eyes.

"We're going all the way to Spokane," Gary replied, "Hop in."

She hesitated for one more second and then, urging her dog to go first, took the three stairs up into the bus. The Sheppard took in the gaggle of faces all ogling his mistress and let out a low growl.

"Nixon," she said, and the dog was quiet.

"Your dog's name is Nixon?" I asked.

"Yep, old tricky Dicky."

The dog looked into her face for assurance, gave a little worried whine. She patted him on the neck.

"'Saright, Nix," then to us, "he gets nervous when there's more men than women in the room."

I instinctively reached out toward him to let him sniff my hand. Instantly, she pulled him back by the collar. The dog bared his teeth with another rumbling growl.

"That would not be a good idea. He's trained to not get friendly with people, especially males."

"Men, you mean."

"OK. So, what-you guys are a band, or something?"

"Yeah. Captain Nobody and the Forgotten Joyband. We're going to Spokane for the World's Fair. We got a gig, playing there."

"At the World's Fair? That sounds like fun."

"I hope you don't mind me asking but-is that a real gun?"

"Sure is. It's a Colt Peacemaker. What, you thought I'd be wandering around with a cap pistol on my belt?"

"Ha! No, I just...we don't see a lot of people wearing guns where we come from."

"Yah? Where's that?"

"Alberta. Canada. That's in Canada."

"You guys are from Canada? That's cool. You're a long ways from home."

The idle small talk went on in tacit oblivion to what was really happening in the confined quarters of the bus, which was the six of us all falling hopelessly, helplessly and irretrievably head over heels in love with her.

The combination of her extreme good looks and complete confidence in her unapproachable status, guaranteed by the dog and the weaponry made her the most desirable woman any of us had ever been this close to. It was not lost on me that she had six bullets in her pistol, one for each of us.

It was incredible, sitting there chatting about this and that, knowing that if any of us were to make an unwelcome advance or, for all we knew a racy comment, she could easily just shoot us all to death and then slice all our nuts off for dog food.

Then, as all good things must, it ended. She looked out the window and said that she was where she wanted to be. We stopped and let her off at an intersection in the middle of, as far as we knew, nowhere. The last we saw of her, she was standing by the side of the road exactly as she had first appeared, beautiful, dangerous, unapproachable and desirable in a way that can only be achieved with the threat of deadly force.

"Was that for real?" someone asked.

"No shit. What a babe."

"What a knife."

"What a gun."

"What a dog."

"I'm going to be dreaming about her for years."

Percy stood and began making his way to the back of the bus.

"Where are you going?"

"I'm going to go jack off while her memory is still fresh in my mind."

And so it was, as we continued on our way, each with his own private thoughts. The country began to take on a slightly more urban feel as the fields gave way to small industrial yards and the towns grew closer together. We rolled past market gardens and U-pick berry farms, feed lots packed with happy-looking cattle and endless fields of potatoes, the mature plants topping their hills with their white flowers announcing harvest time.

The southern stretch on Highway #95 ended at the interstate, where we turned west on the four-lane through Post Falls. By the time we got to Coeur d'Alene, the flap-jacks were a distant memory.

We drove around town a bit, looking for someplace cheap for lunch, finally spotting a drive-thru called the "Bag 'o'Burgers."

"That sounds about right," said Gary, "how much dough do we have left?"

"About eight bucks," Doug said, counting.

"I doubt we can get much for eight bucks," said Bob.

But he was wrong. The "Bag 'o' Burgers" franchise was one of the many new style diners that were popping up all over America at the time, based on the principle of applying mass-production techniques to the restaurant business.

It had been discovered that, by doing so, a limited menu could be produced at such savings that the price point on a lunch item like a hamburger could be brought down to where people couldn't afford *not* to eat there. There were a dozen such franchises in North America at that time, vying for market share. The only one to survive the eighties was Macdonald's.

The bus wouldn't fit through the drive-in, so we had to go in to get our meal. The menu offered two items-hamburgers and cheeseburgers. You could get a bag of six burgers for five dollars. They weren't anything to write home about, but they were identical and freshly made.

"I love America," I said, munching happily.

"America loves you, too," said Gary, "as long as you have money to spend, which we don't. We had better get paid tonight or we'll be harvesting corn for food on the way home."

The World's Fair was being held on an island, serendipitously called 'Canada Island' in the Spokane River. It was easy to see why they'd chosen the site-it was gorgeous. The river was fast and littered with boulders, split by the island and bridged picturesquely. The island was big and well forested, with a large park in the center.

There must have been three acres of parking, all organized by uniformed attendants. We were given a sign to put in the window that corresponded with a signed area, right next to the venue where we were to play. The place was enormous, some kind of field house with thirty foot ceilings and an area that would easily accommodate indoor soccer games.

The stage was set up in one corner and although it was a good size, it looked tiny and out of scale in the space. It did have all the features that one might expect in a major sports facility, including one that our bus sadly lacked-showers. Oh, the joy!

We had been on the road five days now and except for the occasional sponge bath in filling station washrooms, we'd gone pretty much unwashed. The feeling of getting naked under a bounteous supply of hot water and soap was indescribable.

We found some dollies to make the task of moving the equipment in easier, only to be admonished by the sound technician not to bother. They had a complete set up on stage already and were planning on having each of the several acts that would be performing that night just plug into their amps and go, which would greatly expedite the pace of the show and avoid lengthy delays between shows. I did, however, insist on setting up my own drums.

That task behind us, we wandered about the fair grounds a bit, looking for a cheap place to eat supper. It was early in the fairs' run and a lot of the exhibits were still under construction, so there wasn't a lot to see. The Mexican pavilion consisted of a large space filled with tables of cheap souvenirs for sale. Percy, who was the only one who'd actually been to Mexico, confirmed our suspicions.

"Yep," he said, "it's just like Mexico."

We asked around the people who were working there and found they all agreed that the cheapest place to eat was the Russian pavilion.

"Order the Borscht," one helpful broom pusher advised, "it comes with this amazing bread, all you eat for ninety five cents."

It turned out to be true. We sat down to big, steaming bowls of beet soup full of various veggies in a nice chicken broth. It was so good we didn't bother to question the pieces of North American style hot dog wieners floating about in it. The best part of the meal was the dark black Russian bread that came sliced about two inches thick in unlimited supply.

So fortified, we made our way back to the bus, to find that it had become the center of some attention from the other musicians at the gig. Most of them were hauling their stuff in U-hauls and vans, as we had been doing just a scant week ago, so they were all pretty impressed with our mobile party wagon.

We invited a few people over. Joints were lit and beers were popped and before too long, a festive atmosphere pervaded the area. I remember rapping with another drummer who was wondering if he should use his own setup, too and then I found myself looking into the smiling face of Nora; Doug's friend from Yellowknife. She was with a friend, named Gina, a tallish brunette with a big laugh and a calm disposition.

These two enterprising young women had hitchhiked their way from the Northwest Territories to San Francisco and were on their way back to Canada when they heard that we were playing the fair and decided to look us up.

This was typical of the times, as a generation of courageous, free-spirited young women took it upon themselves to re-write the females' role in western society. I was duly impressed.

We went on stage first that evening, warming up for a couple of other acts before the headliner "Teen Angel and the Rockin' Rebels" hit the stage. The sound was horrendous in that monstrous cavern, but nobody cared. It was the Worlds' Fair, man. Party time!

After the fun was over, having worked up a sweat playing and dancing to other acts, we decided to hit the showers. Nora and Gina decided to join us.

So, without having this narrative descend to the level of porno-graphic description that it so easily could do, suffice it to say; it was the seventies. We were young and there were drugs about and every-one was in a Mardi Gras mood. Sex was had.

It wasn't surprising when, in the morning, the girls announced that they would be coming back to Edmonton with us. This changed the dynamic inside the bus only slightly because of the way those two fit in with the group so well.

The trip home was relatively uneventful, discounting the amusing return across the border as the Americans seemed only too pleased to see us leave their country and the Canadians just shook their heads in bemused wonder.

As luck would have it, it was to be the only trip we ever made in the bus. Outside of Calgary it threw a rod and, with no alternative but to try to make it home anyways, we proceeded to do all kinds of damage to the power train by driving the remaining way home.

I remember the way I felt as we pulled up in front of Joe's place. It was more or less the way I always felt at the end of a road trip, kind of sad to see it end and reluctant to return to the drab day-to-day existence between gigs but, as I stepped down from the bus onto the sidewalk, there was something different this time. It felt like we had come to the end of not just this trip, but of an era in our lives. Somehow I knew, as I think we all did, that this one had been the best. There would be no topping our trip to the Worlds' Fair.

fin

YELLOWKNIFE

It is one thousand four hundred ninety six kilometers from Edmonton to Yellowknife.

That's three hundred kms longer than to Vancouver. Edmonton to Vancouver is a long drive, but you pass through some of the most beautiful country on the planet, so nobody minds.

Going the other way to, say; Winnipeg, it's a hundred ninety one kms less than to Yellowknife. People do complain about that drive because most of it is across the flat plains of Saskatchewan, with no real scenery until you get into Manitoba.

But that's the thing; you have something to look forward to; you know that at some point the tedious flat prairie will give way to lakes and forest again and there will be towns and cities and life. The hope of coming to the end of the desolation sustains you on the way.

Not so, on the way to Yellowknife. There's nothing at the end of that road except Yellowknife.

At 62 degrees 26 minutes North, it's not the northernmost settlement in Canada but, with a permanent population of over 19,000, it is arguably our northernmost *city*, with apologies to Pond Inlet.

You leave Edmonton driving west on highway #16 and pass through the little towns of Winterburn, Spruce Grove and Stony Plain and on through Wabamun, Fallis, Gainford and Seba Beach. Once you hit Entwistle it's time to make a choice. You can turn north just past Evansburg and take #22 up through Mayerthorpe, or continue on west through Wildwood, Nojack and Niton Junction until you hit Carrot Creek. If you go that way, just past Carrot Creek you must turn north onto highway #32 and after that, the towns start to get a bit fewer and farther between.

Not much to see in those towns now but in 1974 they each had at least one hotel with a tavern and every tavern had a stage. We played 'em all, sometimes several times each.

It was easy to believe that the crowds we played to in those bars came to see the band, but the truth is, nobody would ever have come if it wasn't for the beer.

In 1974, the price of an eight-ounce glass of draft beer in Alberta was twenty cents. You would put your hand up in a high-five and lay a dollar bill on the table. Your beers would arrive in the regulation slimly tapered glass with a fill line about an inch from the top. If any of them weren't filled to the line, you could send it back for one that was. That was also regulated.

At that time, everything in the taverns of Alberta was regulated.

There was a standard table, which was about 24 inches around and covered with a red terry-towel cloth edged in elastic. At the end of the night the waiters would just whip them off and replace them with a clean, or at least dry one. The chairs were regulated too-chromed steel frames with plastic armrests and black vinyl seats and backs.

There was nothing of the décor you see in pubs today, nothing to distract you from the serious business of drinking beer.

Mind you, any similarity between real lager and the insipid, watery yellow stuff they served in those tapered glasses was strictly incidental. It smelled and tasted like someone had forgotten to rinse the glass (which they frequently did) but it was the regulated 3.5% alcohol by volume and therefore technically, at least, beer. Drink enough of the stuff and you would get a buzz.

This regulation of things in the taverns had a curious effect when we were out of town, sometimes for a month at a time, playing one tavern after another for a week at a time.

The fact that every tavern in the province had the same tables and chairs gave the experience a weird, homogenized feeling. The view from the stage was virtually identical in almost all of the places we played. There were times when I had no idea what town I was in, which made it tough to pump up the crowd. (It's good to be back in… uh, where are we, anyways?)

Not that it mattered much. Nothing seemed to matter much in those times and those places, especially if you drank enough beer.

And believe me, we drank enough of it. In 1971, when the drinking age in Alberta went from 21 to 18, the high schools emptied and the taverns were immediately flooded with eager teenagers who lacked, among other things, any sense of proportion.

The older guys who worked in the taverns were set upon to deliver drinks at a rate they'd previously only seen on special holidays and playoff nights. These unfortunate individuals found themselves unwittingly enlisted to baby-sit as the baby boomers learned to drink.

Like everything else that generation did, they took it to extremes. The formerly reserved atmosphere in the tavern changed virtually overnight into something more closely resembling a scene from an Octoberfest, every night of the week.

Bars in town, like our regular haunt the "Klondiker," that had formerly catered to an older crowd, used to Country & Western music, turned into rock 'n' roll venues virtually overnight.

Interactions between the regulars and the younger newcomers were instructional.

Drinking contests were standard procedure, with the more experienced competitors enjoying whole evenings of drinking for free at the expense of the newbies. Every bar had its champ and the Klondikers' was Wayne-the Klondike Sewer Pipe. This guy could pick a glass of draft up off the table, down it and return the empty glass with a bang before most normal people even got their hands around their glass. He did it every night about fifteen times before retiring to the corner to nurse one.

When the drinking age first changed, there was still no dancing allowed in the bars. For us, this meant total freedom when it came to choosing our repertoire. With no consideration needed as to whether or not a piece of music could be danced to, we were free to play anything we wanted, and did.

Unfortunately, it also left the audience with no way to work off the beers they drank. They sat and they drank, often 'way too much.

It took a while for things to get out of control enough that the owners started to institute rules about how many beers could be ordered at a time. In the meanwhile, the norm was to fill one's table just before cut-off, which was generally at midnight. The law said you were allowed to drink what was on your table, which effectively extended the hours of operation by a half hour or more.

For the band, this meant an extra set at the end of the night, sort of a perforce encore. We always saved a couple of good tunes for the last set.

It also meant that at midnight, the place would be full of severely inebriated youngsters sitting at tables loaded to groaning with full beer glasses. At the Klondiker, as at a lot of these places, the tables were arranged to give us a view from the stage of a sea of draft glasses extending from the front of the stage all the way to the back of the room.

For the most part, the peace, love and rock 'n roll generation ended their evenings in a spirit of drunken goodwill but every now and again the mixture of over-indulged amateur drinkers and raging adolescent hormones would produce a return to less lofty behavior and a fight would break out. It was quite a sight when all those draft-laden tables started going over like so many dominos. Like witnessing the parting of the Red Sea, only with drunks instead of Jews.

In three years of playing in bars, the band had seen its share of minor fracases. It was far more common in the small towns.

There is a complex psychology involved in the social make-up of small towns. You could gauge the likelihood of a fight breaking out by the general feel of a town.

There's always a tough guy in every small prairie town, always some kind of pecking order that has been established as the local guys grow up together and each finds his place on the totem pole.

There's usually a guy who considers himself the toughest guy in town. Sometimes this is true and sometimes not. As often as not, the real toughest guy in town is too laid back to give a shit what the guy who thinks he's the toughest guy in town does. As long as he and his little entourage (and there *always* is an entourage) don't mess with him or his, the toughest guy in town keeps his own council and minds his own business. The guy who thinks he's the toughest guy in town knows this, as he knows that, as long as he doesn't cross the real toughest guy in town, he will be allowed to play out his fantasy and bully everybody else.

Sometimes the guy who thinks he's the toughest guy in town happens to love rock and roll. If so, the band does not get beat up.

It would be a good bet that, if the guy who thinks he is the toughest guy in town hates rock and roll, the toughest guy in town loves it. This meant the band would not get beat up.

Occasionally, the guy who thought he was the toughest guy in town was, in fact the toughest guy in town and hated rock and roll. This left the band beholden to the security staff in the tavern to protect them from the violence that would inevitably be focused on them as the night wore on and the beer consumption mounted.

In very rare cases, usually in a really backward, pissant little town with a history of extensive in-breeding and no civic pride whatsoever, hotels were allowed to operate without a security staff, leaving these sociopathic yobbos free to terrorize anyone they felt like, including the bands.

Like the Ranchman's Inn, in Ponoka.

Captain Nobodys' first and last gig in Ponoka started out pretty normal. The band was using the old milk truck to carry the gear, and it had definitely seen better days. The suspension was no longer functional, the steering was questionable and the ignition had given up the ghost entirely, so that it had to be hot wired to start and had a habit of shaking the wires loose and dying in traffic.

We had invited our buddy Ross to do the driving and help with general roadie chores. It was mid-winter, cold as hell with a lot of snow on the ground, so his labors were much appreciated and worth every penny he was paid.

Things started out pretty normally; we were greeted by the manager and shown the facilities. After taking our personal luggage to the assigned rooms, we set up on the modest but adequate stage, relaxed in the rooms for a couple of hours and went out to do the show.

The first few tunes went well and seemed to be accepted by the audience, who'd responded with a smattering of applause.

Then, just as Percy was going into his guitar solo on the fourth tune in the set, and turned away from his mike to make an adjustment on his amp, an ashtray flew out of the crowd and smashed on his mike. A split second sooner and it would have exploded right in his face, with an excellent possibility of Percy getting a shard of glass or five in his eyes.

Those old glass ashtrays didn't shatter easily. They were meant to be used in a bar and would stand up to being dropped over and over. It took a lot of force to have one disintegrate as this one had; it had to have been thrown with a clear intent to hurt somebody. The song ground to halt.

We all were shocked. Gary was incensed.

"All right; who threw that?" he demanded over the mike. There was no answer, besides some childish snickering coming from a table in the middle of the room.

Seated there were four or five of the most stereotypical small town losers I had ever seen. They were dressed alike in the uniform of the country jackass; worn baseball caps with some logo or another on the crest, filthy armless T-shirts and ill-fitting jeans to match, mud caked cowboy boots. On average, these guys looked to be about six foot and weighed somewhere about fifty pounds over. They all seemed to share the same razor, which had gone missing a couple of weeks ago and the two that wore glasses both had them held together with liberal applications of scotch tape. The tables nearest this troupe of circus performers were empty owing, presumably, to the collective body odor emanating from them.

"Did anybody see who threw that ashtray?" Gary asked. No reply.

"Any more of that and we'll be packing up. We're just here to play music but we're not going to do it with people chucking stuff at us. If you guys want some music tonight, you better tell whoever threw that to knock it off."

More snickering from the brain trust.

The band started the song over and finished it without incident. We continued on with the set, keeping a watchful eye on the suspects.

Sure enough, halfway through the next set, the biggest guy at the table suddenly flung back his arm and launched a half-full beer bottle at the stage. It sailed between Doug and Percy and hit one of my cymbals; a glancing strike that failed to break the glass. The bottle skipped off the cymbal and over my left shoulder to smack into the wall at the back of the stage. I was splashed with beer as it passed.

This time, there was no doubt. We stopped playing and Gary took off his guitar. Hopping down from the stage, he went straight over to the bar, where the manager was pouring draft, oblivious. The rest of the band got off the stage and milled about, waiting to see what might transpire.

Gary's conversation with the manager became animated. He pointed out the offending group, still seated, still snickering. The manager shrugged. Gary said something else. The man turned away and started polishing glasses.

The band waited as Gary returned to the stage.

"You would not believe what I just heard," he said, "this jerk-off manager does not have any security staff. He says, if we have a problem with someone throwing shit, we'll have to deal with it ourselves."

"Fuck that. I'm not sitting up on that stage, waiting for these morons to get their aim right. That beer was half full!" I said.

"I know. What the hell else can we do? We drove in here on fumes. The milk truck doesn't run on good intentions, man. If we had enough gas to get back to town, I'd be with you, but we don't."

"So, what? We go back to work and wait for the next beer bottle to hit someone in the face? Not me, man; I quit."

"What do you mean, "you quit"? You can't just up and quit while we are stranded in town. "

"You watch me. I am not going to sit up on that stage playing sitting duck for a bunch of homicidal miscreants. If anything changes, I'll be in my room."

I felt a lot of things about that. I was feeling guilty about bailing out on the rest of the band, although I suspected that any or all of them would have come to the same decision, given time. I was a bit apprehensive about the final impact of this decision; what if we got fired from the gig and ended up stranded in town without even a place to stay?

There wasn't a lot I could do about it. The one thing I knew for sure was that I wasn't going to allow myself to be victim of some ignorant track star's twisted sense of humor. I'd seen enough people get glassed in taverns to know what a beer bottle could do to a person's face. I retired to my room. The gig was over.

That night, the boys were invited to a party on the outskirts of town. It seemed like a bad idea to Doug and me, so we stayed in my room watching TV.

Percy, Gary and Ross decided they would go, and somehow the milk truck suddenly had just enough gas to get them out to the place and hopefully back again.

As they pulled into the yard of the farmhouse, they could hear heavy metal music being played at unnecessary volumes. There were a number of vehicles, mostly pickups, parked around the circle drive that led back out to the road. The party was in full swing.

There were some surly looks exchanged when the boys entered the house but the party went on uninterrupted. Beers were passed around, introductions made and conversations struck up with local girls, one of whom turned out to have arrived there with the head tough guy from the hotel tavern. She seemed to have decided that Percy was somehow deserving of her special attentions, much to the disgruntlement of her ride.

At some point, the offended party decided it was time to initiate the time tested little dance that would have inevitably led to his pounding the be-Jesus out of Percy. He hadn't gotten far into the ritual when the boys recognized where the evening was going and wisely made the collective decision to book it the hell out of there.

They left the house and, ignoring the head bully-boys' taunts and insults, got to the milk truck and started it up. The incensed belligerent, frustrated at being robbed of his rightful chance to beat the crap out of somebody, resorted to his other favourite hobby; chucking full beers at folks.

Four or five bottles hit the side of the milk truck as the band members, with Ross at the wheel, attempted to make good their escape. Before they had made it around the circle drive and got pointed out to the road, another half dozen fully loaded missiles exploded off the sides and roof of the old truck.

As the road came into view, so did the beer chucker. He was blocking the only exit, standing up to his knees in the freshly fallen snow, aiming another beer directly at the windshield of the approaching vehicle. Ross didn't hesitate. In his mind, it was self-defense. A full beer could easily smash right through the windscreen and hit someone inside. There was only one thing to do.

He stepped on the gas and ran the bastard down.

There was no way for Ross or the boys to know that the idiot had slipped an instant before the front bumper hit him and landed in deep enough snow that, when the milk truck passed over him with it's high clearance, he'd been untouched and unhurt.

They thought they'd killed the guy.

Racing down the country road, trying to make it to the highway back to town, it was with horror that the guys in the milk truck noticed headlights appearing in the rear view mirror. Several vehicles had left the farmyard behind them and were now in pursuit on the narrow, slippery back road.

Ross was doing his best, trying to coax some speed out of the ancient power train but it was clear the lights behind were gaining.

As they reached the highway and performed a perilous four wheel drift into the far lane, their lead had dwindled to a couple of hundred feet. The milk truck roared through the night, the engine complaining loudly about such treatment, until they crested a hill in the road and hit a bump on the other side.

The milk truck's motor died.

The lights went out along with everything else and for a heart stopping moment they were helpless as they coasted to the side of the highway, still half a mile from town, a howling mob of drunken assholes fast approaching with revenge in their hearts and murder on their booze and dope-addled minds.

Ross was struggling in the dark with the jury-rigged ignition when the first car full of goombas came over the hill behind them.

At first they missed the darkened milk truck in their haste and in the gloom, then the driver pounded on the brakes and came to a skewed stop in the middle of the highway, fifty feet ahead. The tail-lights flashed as the driver slammed it into reverse and punched the gas, just as the second crew from the farmhouse, in a big new pickup truck, came over the rise. No way they were going to stop in time.

The pickup plowed into the back of the car at speed, smashing the trunk and driving the front of the pickup up over the rear end. The truck's radiator blew, spewing steam and anti freeze as the two wrecked vehicles skidded to a halt in the center meridian.

Just then, Ross succeeded in getting the milk truck to start.

"We better see if anyone got hurt," he said. Putting it in gear, he drove slowly down the shoulder towards the wreck. Just before they got there, the doors flew open on the pickup and two people half fell out into the snow. Before a word was spoken, the both off them took off, running down the highway, one of them with a pronounced limp in his gait.

"What the fuck?" Percy mumbled.

"They must think we're going to kill them," Ross surmised.

As he spoke, the car emptied and another three or four people joined the exodus.

"I feel a bit silly," Percy said.

"I don't know what to do," Ross added, "If we go back to town, we're going to catch up with them. What'll we do then?"

"I don't think we have to worry about it," Gary interjected, looking in the rear view, "the RCMP are here."

It took a while to explain the whole thing to the officers but, after examining the evidence of a dozen beer-smelling dents in the body-work of the milk truck, they figured the boys were telling the truth.

"You guys want to press charges?" the one cop asked, a bit eagerly. It seemed they knew exactly whose pickup was piggy-backing whose car in the ditch and looked upon the incident as a chance to finally get some serious charges to stick in a long-standing history.

"We might have to talk about that, sir but, would it be OK if we parked our vehicle in front of the detachment for the rest of the night? No telling what these dummies might try, if you don't apprehend them, first."

So, that's what happened. We managed to shame the hotel manager into pro-rating us enough pay to get home, and the RC's gave us a police escort out of town the next day.

Ponoka was marked with a big black spot on the map on the band house wall. We never went back but we all knew there were more Ponokas that we had yet to find.

When an evening in the taver ended without any fights, there were usually a few overly ambitious groups that found they had ordered more beer than they could get down before being asked to leave. Sometimes there would be ten or twenty untouched glasses of beer left on the table.

We called them "snaffles." What a blessing were snaffles for broke musicians. We were happy to take advantage of these oversights but there was some tricky timing involved. We had to get there after the customers had left but before the waiters cleared the table.

Playing the bars was fun and we had enjoyed a couple of years of it but it was time for a something different.

The gig in Yellowknife promised to be a welcome change from what had become a bit of a rut for us, then. We were excited to be on the trip, eager to see some fresh country. We were going to have a long ways to go, though, before we ran out of highways we'd already travelled. We knew the roads north of Edmonton pretty well.

It's 72 kilometers from Carrot Creek up to Whitecourt. There you can turn left and take #43 on through Fox Creek and Little Smoky to Valleyview, a distance of 166 kms.

Up to now you've been travelling through the Central Aspen Parkland, with great swaths of grass broken by stands of Balsam Poplar and Aspen, with the occasional Jack or Lodgepole pine.

I used to wonder how any amount of hard work could possibly have cut down the trees and cleared that much land for planting in the scant few generations since the Europeans arrived in the west. It was years before I realized that it had always been like this.

The buffalo herds moved through this country following the grasslands North and South each year for tens of thousands of years and with them moved the hunters; the Blackfoot and the Plains Cree, the Nez-Perce, and the Dakota, Lakota and Nakota Sioux-the "buffalo nation." The great grasslands supported an ecology that changed little before the coming of the Europeans. The bison are gone but the country is still the same.

The highway cuts through a dense understory of dogwood, willow, snowberry and low-bush cranberry. Patches of saskatoon, chokecherry and pin cherry invite the pickers in summer but in the winter the tangled undergrowth is bare.

Gradually, as you continue north, the Balsams and Aspen thin and eventually give way to the conifers as you leave the parkland and enter the vast Boreal Forest. Spruce, Fir, Pines and Tamarack take over the land and without the shrubbery you can see further into the forest as you pass. The Swan Hills fall behind and the pine forest engulfs you, hiding the horizon with an evergreen wall thirty feet high along the road.

From Valleyview, a straight shot north on #49 takes you past New Fish Creek and Guy on the way through Donnelly where the road north changes to #2.

Soon you notice that the Poplars and Aspens have returned. You've entered that great, isolated island of parkland known as the Peace Country. After a journey of 63 kms you look down the hill at the mighty Peace River and the town that shares it's name. You've come 487 kms from Edmonton, about a six-hour drive, allowing for lunch and pee stops.

Have a look at the map. It surprises you how little of the total you've actually covered. It feels like more but you've barely made a start.

You have over a thousand kilometers to go, and the scenery is about to disappear. North of Peace River the Pines and Fir claim the country again and brook no interruption until the tree line north of Great Slave Lake marks the beginning of the Arctic Tundra.

Three hundred kilometers on, at the town of High Level, you might be surprised to see on the map that you haven't even left Alberta yet. Nine hours on the road. You've come a little under half way.

Why am I telling you all this? I don't know; I guess I'd just like to impart to you just what a monumental trip it was.

The roads are better now and vehicles more trustworthy but, in 1974, things were different. For the uninitiated, driving from Edmonton to Yellowknife could be a daunting, scary and exhausting journey. Even now, a trip like this is not a thing to be taken lightly, or embarked upon at a whim.

Your vehicle must be in good condition. The wise traveler makes sure he knows the route and that people know his schedule, should he go missing along the way.

One must go prepared for any contingency, as there are long stretches of untamed wilderness between human habitations. It's a good idea to check the weather forecast. In the winter, sustained readings of -40 are not uncommon. That far north the temperature can drop tens of degrees without warning in a few hours.

It is unwise to start a drive like this in less than top physical condition. A person should be well rested and fed, alert and ready for the long road ahead. It's a serious business, to be taken seriously.

So, naturally, we did acid.

We stayed up all night partying, drinking and generally wearing ourselves into a state of exhaustion. A few of us got a few hours sleep but it was a sorry looking troupe that made it out to the car about noon the next day.

With the exception of Joe, who took his driving responsibilities seriously, we were in no condition to start off on what was conservatively estimated to be a twenty- hour road trip. The last thing we needed at that point was to put a bunch of street quality pharmaceuticals into our dilapidated bodies, but that's what we did.

The girls, God bless 'em, had gotten up early and prepared a big bag of food for us to take; sandwiches and squares and such. We said our goodbyes and found our places in the old Pontiac. As we pulled away from the curb, the U-haul trailer rocking with the weight of all our gear, we had no idea the kind of traumatic, near death excursion we'd embarked upon.

The first few hours passed quickly. We made good time on the well-travelled highways we'd been on dozens of times before. With nothing new to see, most of us took the opportunity to catch up on our sleep. We knew it would be a while before the drugs kicked in.

Late afternoon found us north of Whitecourt, heading for Valleyview and stoned out of our fucking gourds.

Generally speaking, a road trip is not a bad way to spend your time if you're going to do acid. The feeling of being in motion, of *going somewhere* is conducive to a good trip. Provided the driver stays straight and sober for the duration, being in a vehicle on the way to somewhere can be one of the better ways to ride the dragon.

The altered perceptions that a person on acid experiences can easily lead to fixation and obsession if his senses are not offered a variety of stimulations, preferably changing ones. Thus the ever-fresh landscape outside the windows of a moving car can keep one's addled mind engaged and entertained without becoming overly preoccupied with any one thing.

So it was for us, as the miles slipped under the tires and the pretty Northern Alberta winter countryside sped by. We spent our time like children on holiday, spotting wildlife and points of interest, spinning fantasies about the things we saw and having, all in all, a pretty good time.

When the conversation waned, I found myself whiling away the time marveling at the delicate intricacy of the vinyl upholstery on the backs of the Pontiacs' seats and wondering what the growing feeling in my gut was. After two or three hours, it occurred to me that I might be getting hungry.

Our supplies of sandwiches had long since disappeared and it was getting on suppertime as we neared the Donnelly Corner, where highway #49 north inexplicably takes a sharp left, leaving the unwary driver to wonder why he's suddenly travelling highway #2 instead, when he hasn't made any turns.

Joe was making noises about the car using more oil than it should and wanted to stop and stock up, anyways, so we turned into the old service station/café there at the crossing.

Donnelly Corner was known to us. We'd been there a couple of times in the past, on the way to one of the small towns in the area to play at the legion hall or the high school. Donnelly was about the furthest north any of us had been before, so stopping there was a little like taking a final breath before plunging together into the enormity of unknown country ahead.

We pulled in and Joe stopped at the pumps to fill up, while the rest of us headed inside to order some food. It wasn't much of a restaurant. The oil-stained floor gave testimony to its origins as one of the garage bays. A half-dozen tables and some mismatched chairs were strewn about and a lunch counter that looked like it had been scavenged from some now defunct town bar occupied a corner.

The rest of the space was taken up by a number of shelves, containing a curiously disjointed selection of items for sale. It looked like the owner had at one time harbored ambitions of making the old station into a combination gas bar, restaurant, drug store and general store.

They'd probably bought up the old stock of local businesses as they failed and, load by load, ended up with almost anything you could imagine, gathering dust on the neglected shelves.

One of the tables was occupied. Three men sat watching us enter, coffee cups in hand. They were all dressed in working coveralls and baseball caps, with heavy work boots crossed casually into the aisle. Their table was situated so that we had to pass them to be seated ourselves. The one guy had to pull his legs in to let us by, which he did only after a significant moments' hesitation. We filed through the gap to an empty table beyond. They watched us with undisguised loathing as we did.

We must have looked a sight. After a full day of travel, we were in various stages of dishevelment but it was apparently our hair that had captured the attention of the trio. As I passed them, I foolishly made an attempt at bridging the gap.

"Hello," I said.

And that's when the trip started to go bad.

"Hello yourself, you long-eared sonofabitch," replied one of the three.

The threat of violence in that isolated place was more than I was capable of dealing with at the best of times, let alone while peaking on acid.

Instantly, paranoia set in. I started to hallucinate and at this point, I was joined on my trip by a familiar character I had come to know as 'Mr. Paranoid Guy.'

He existed only in my mind and came out to play when I was stoned on acid. Any time I ran across something that could be remotely construed by my drug altered brain as threatening, which ranged from real, potentially dangerous situations like this to the inane conjurings of an over stimulated imagination, I could count on Mr. Paranoid Guy to pop up and start speaking to me.

On his urging, I once spent an hour and a half cowering behind a garden shed under the misguided impression that evil vampire bunnies were searching for me in the back yard.

On another occasion, Mr. Paranoid Guy had me convinced the fir trees in the park were lunging towards me any time I got too close. I decided to share this intelligence with Percy, who had done two hits of the same potent acid. The result was the two of us running hysterically through the forest, pursued in our minds by every evergreen we passed. In my mind, our flight was accompanied by a soundtrack, which consisted of Mr. Paranoid Guy chanting;

"We'll all die! We'll all die!"

After that, I was careful to keep my conversations with Mr. P. G. to myself and I reminded myself of that policy as I continued past the table of hostile faces and sat down.

I tried not to look over at them but it was impossible. The farmers had begun to shape-shift. Their skin took on a greenish tinge and the dirt on their hands began to look more like fur. As I sat down, one of them looked over at his buddy and smiled, then looked sidelong at me. His eyes suddenly took on a reptilian cast and just for a second, when he licked his lips, his tongue looked forked.

I knew immediately that the three of them were conspiring to do us harm. They probably sat here, drinking their coffee and laying in wait for innocent travelers like us to come by so they could snatch them and cart them off to some hideous fate.

I was staring at the stains on the floor, wondering if it really *was* oil, when the owner/cook/waiter came out from behind the counter to take our order.

"What can I get you boys?" he asked.

My ears edited out all but "*get you boys...*"

I looked around at my band-mates with alarm. They seemed oblivious.

"Do you have any..." I meant to say steaks. It came out sounding like "safety."

The guy looked up from his pad.

"Steaks. I meant steaks." I stammered, afraid I'd given myself away. Was he in on the conspiracy?

I was trying to ignore the three belligerents across the floor from us as they continued to ogle us, exchanging murmured comments about us to each other. It was obvious to me that they were planning something diabolical.

They would wait for us to finish our meals and start to leave, then follow us outside and grab us.

No doubt they had some kind of farm vehicle outside that would hold us all. We'd be duct-taped and driven to some remote location and after being murdered in a variety of imaginative ways, slaughtered, perhaps to be served up in the restaurant the next day as hamburgers and...

"Steaks," said the waiter.

"What?!"

"I said, we ain't got no steaks. We got burgers and cutlets, no steaks."

"I'll just have a salad."

"*These guys knew we were coming,*" said Mr. Paranoid Guy inside my head. "*How do you think they knew? They probably belong to a vast secret network of redneck spies who keep track of bands and other nodes of non-redneck activity. They are alerted to our movements any time we leave the safety of the city and wander into their territory.*"

"Oh, come on-that's just silly," I argued silently, "they're just three guys. OK-admittedly rednecks-who were having coffee when we showed up. The one guy just wanted to get his two bits worth in about the hair, that's all."

This is how I typically spent the better part of every acid experience I've ever had; arguing with Mr. Paranoia Guy. I knew there was no point. I don't know why I bothered, other than to prevent myself being reduced to a gibbering wreck and carted off to the loony bin.

I don't know why I bothered even trying to get high at all anymore. Every trip ended in this ridiculous dance with my fantasies turning to fearful imaginings. It wasn't fun. But doing acid was like that; you get on the train full of great expectations and if the trip starts to go awry, well; too bad, 'cause you're still going to have to go to the end of the line. The important thing, I'd learned, was not to argue with Mr. Paranoia Guy out loud, for obvious reasons. So there I was again, doomed to listen to the voice in my head ranting and raving.

"*Don't be a fool!*" he whined, "*This could be the thing they've been waiting for all year; maybe the crops have been failing and they need a human sacrifice. Maybe they hate us because the oil patch is gobbling up all the available labor off the farms and they can't make living at it anymore. Who knows? You heard what he said; it's just the beginning! We're all going to die!*"

Joe came in from filling up the car and, to my horror, went right over to the three guys at their table.

"Any you guys got some spare oil a guy could buy?" he asked.

"Burnin' a little oil, are ya?"

"Naw, it ain't burning it, but it's going through some. I guess I got a leak somewhere, probably the head gasket. The guy at the service station says he's right out of 10/30. I just thought, if any of you guys had some extra, I'll pay you over market price."

This was awful. Poor Joe, he had no idea who he was dealing with. One of the lizard farmers pushed his chair back saying he reckoned he had a quart or two in the back of his truck. Joe turned to follow him back outside.

"They're gonna get Joe!" cried Mr. Paranoid Guy. *"Don't let them get him! Who's going to drive if they get Joe?"*

"Hey, Joe!" I shouted across the room. Curious eyes turned towards me. Joe waited.

"Um...can I come with you?"

Joe, well aware of the stoned state of his passengers, sighed a little sigh.

"Sure, man. If that's what you want to do," he said.

"These boys with you?" the farmer wanted to know.

"Yup. These are mine." Joe admitted.

"Okay," said the lizard/redneck/farmer doubtfully.

I followed them outside, wondering how to alert Joe of the danger. We walked over to a big black pickup truck at the side of the garage. The farmer rummaged around in the back.

"Weapons! He's getting his weapons!" cried the voice in my head.

I tugged at Joe's jacket. He turned and gave me look.

"Just a sec." he said.

The redneck pulled something from the tangled pile of stuff in the truck bed.

"Look out!" Mr. Paranoia Guy screamed. I braced myself, ready to run for it. Joe looked at me and shook his head a little.

"Well, you're in luck, buddy. Look here."

He produced a large black jug. He caught sight of me, poised to do the 100m, and paused.

"Your buddy alright, there, fella?"

I tried to relax and ignore the hysterical voice in my head.

"Oil! I told you it was about the oil! There's something in the oil; WE'LL ALL DIE!!"

"He's fine, just a bit simple. Thanks for asking."

"I got a whole gallon for you, if you want it. I can't testify to the age of it, but it's still got the seal on."

"That's great. What do want for it?"

"How's ten bucks sound?"

"Much obliged."

Joe paid the guy and they started back toward the restaurant.

"See that? He didn't do anything because we were here. They don't want any witnesses."

Back inside, the food had come. I sat down in front of plate of what might have euphemistically been referred to as 'salad', if one didn't study it too closely. The lettuce was wilted and brown along the edges, the tomato sadly past its prime. Some gelatinous substance had been drizzled over it. It appeared to be *moving*.

"Don't eat the food!" Mr. P. G. warned, *"they've put something in it to make us sleep!"*

I pushed the plate away. The rest of the band members were mid-way through their meals, blissfully unaware of the danger they were in. Joe had decided to sit with the rednecks. I sat there with my nerves on a hair trigger, waiting for something terrible to happen.

It didn't, of course. Everyone just finished eating, took turns visiting the washroom and got ready to get back on the road.

All the while, the voice in my head screamed alarm at every move made in the room as if *this one* was the thing that would spark the violent confrontation. All the way back outside, into the car and even as we pulled away without incident, Mr. Paranoid Guy kept it up.

Even then, safely back on our way, I had to listen to him.

"Watch out behind us! Obviously, the only reason they let us get away from there is so they can get us on the road, where there aren't any witnesses! Watch for headlights coming up from behind!"

There was no way I could do that with a U-haul trailer in the way, unless I was in the front seat where I could see the rear view mirror. I considered trying to convince Bob to exchange places, trying to think of an excuse for needing to be up front without letting on how fucked up I was.

"Hey, Doug," I began, "isn't it my turn to ride shotgun?"

Doug twisted around in his seat to look at me.

"Just how fucked up are you, man?"

"Wh-what do you mean?"

"It's just, ever since we stopped back there, you've been acting like Mr. Paranoid Guy. You all right?"

"He knows! They got to him! It must have happened while you were outside with Joe! They got him and now he's one of them! Maybe they all are!"

"Why do you say that? Why do say that in those particular words?"

"Jesus, you really are fucked up. Here-eat some vitamin C. It'll bring you down faster."

He handed me back a handful of tablets. I examined one. It said 'vit C 500' on it.

"You're not going to take that, are you!? Can't you see-that's probably how they got Doug!"

I pocketed the pills.

"Thanks, man," I said, in what I hoped was a sincere voice. Just then headlights lit up the interior of the car from behind. We were being passed by another vehicle.

"Oh, shit-here we go! It's them! They caught up with us! Now they'll run us off the road and get us!" screamed Mr. P. G.

A big pickup truck zoomed by and receded into the distance ahead.

"Fuck, now they're ahead of us, waiting up there somewhere to ambush us!"

"That looked like those guys from the restaurant," remarked Bob mildly.

"Yeah, that was their truck. Nice guys," Joe replied, "sold me a gallon of oil for ten bucks."

"That's right! The oil! We forgot about the oil! Joe put some in the car-it's probably going to wreck the engine! We'll be stranded at the side of the road and then they'll come and get us!"

"They were telling me to watch out for moose on the road, the next couple dozen miles. I guess somebody hit one just yesterday. Wrote off a ¾ ton," said Gary.

"Wow-imagine what one of those bastards would do to this thing," Percy speculated.

"No shit. I guess they stand so tall, what happens is you take the legs out with the front of the car and then the body comes through the windshield. Sometimes the impact doesn't even kill them. You can end up in the ditch, trapped in the wreck with a pissed off, wounded moose for company."

"Moose!? Aaaarggh! Now we have to watch out for fucking Moose!? We're all going to die!!!"

I hadn't eaten and couldn't sleep. The physical effects of the acid were coursing through me, causing muscle spasms and tension. My nerves were fried from long hours on the road and I was exhausted from the fear instilled by the stupid voice in my head. There was over a thousand kilometers to go-ten to fifteen hours, depending on the roads, and the roads were not about to get any better.

It looked like Mr. Paranoia Guy was along for the duration. Every dark clump of bush along the way harbored the lizard men, waiting in ambush. Every upturned root ball in the fields was the rack of a giant bull moose, poised to blunder out onto the road in front of us.

A raven flew across the road in front of us, visible for a second in the headlights before the blackness enveloped him again. My over-taxed mind turned him into a monster bat that turned to look into the car at *me* as he passed.

I looked around to see if anyone else had noticed. Gary looked at me in the rearview.

"Will you please try to get some sleep? You're starting to make *me* paranoid."

I tried. I snuggled down into my sleeping bag and kept my eyes off the windows. I focused on some song lyrics, something mild and harmless; Valdi, I think it was. I closed my eyes.

The reduction in sensory stimulation helped to calm my troubled mind and allowed me to focus on the roots of my unease. I remembered some conversation from before we'd left. I had been busy fucking around, as usual, when Doug and Gary sat down at the kitchen table to plan the trip.

They'd been talking about a bridge. The words "ice" and "breakup" resonated in my memory.

"Joe?"

"Yah, man?"

"Is there a bridge?"

"What do you mean, a bridge?" Joe asked. He and Doug exchanged a look. I thought I saw Doug shake his head just a little bit. Or was I just being paranoid?

"I thought I heard you guys talking about a bridge. Over some ice, or something."

"Oh, that. Yeah, don't worry about it. We'll be hitting Peace River soon. There's a hill down to the bridge that gets a bit icy sometimes, but we don't have to worry about it this time of year."

"Ya?"

"Ya. Don't worry about it, all right? Just try to get some sleep. It's still a long ways to go."

"All right."

Once again I made the attempt. This time I started singing a John Denver song in my head. That did it.

KRANG!!!

I jerked awake to the sound. Joe was wrestling the steering wheel, fighting to keep the car on the road, with the U-haul bucking and slewing around like a maddened bronco on its hitch.

"Fucking Hell!" he exclaimed, "What the fuck was *that!*"

"What happened?"

"Did we hit something?"

Everyone was awake, sitting up, looking around and wondering what had happened. Joe managed to guide the vehicle to the side of the road and bring it to a stop. He put the four-ways on and sat back with his eyes closed for a second.

"Fuck me," he said quietly and opened his door to get out.

"Joe! What the fuck just happened, man?"

"We hit a log."

"A LOG!?"

"A big, motherfucker of a log," Joe's voice said, as he walked away behind the car.

We began untangling ourselves from our sleeping bags and reaching for the door handles. Then we were all standing behind the U-haul, looking at a respectable sized log in the road. It was about twelve feet long and perhaps a foot in diameter.

"Fuckin' thing was right in middle of the goddamned road," Gary remarked.

"Jesus."

"Think it did any damage?"

"Oh, yeah, it did something," Joe said, "I could feel shit tearing off down there."

He started walking back to the front of the car, then stopped and went over to the side of the road about midway between the car and the log.

"Oh, shit," he said. I looked where he was looking and saw what appeared in the dark to be another, smaller log lying in the snow. Then I realized it what it was; the muffler, tailpipe and exhaust pipe off the Pontiac.

Joe sighed a big sigh. He retrieved the keys from the ignition. The headlights went out. It was suddenly very, very dark.

Joe went back and opened the trunk. He took out a big nine-volt flashlight and turned it on, shining it into the trunk so he could find another one, which he handed to me.

I automatically turned that one on, blinding Bob and Doug, who reached out to push the beam away from their eyes.

"Watch where you're pointing that thing, man."

"Sorry."

Joe handed me a nylon bag.

"Take this and walk seventy-five paces back the way we came. Open the bag and set up the triangle in the road. Then activate the flare. Be careful. Put the flare down beside the triangle and come back here. Got it?"

"Sure, Joe, I got it."

Joe hesitated for a second. He moved the flashlight so it illuminated my face a bit."

"Go with him, Percy."

"Sure. C'mon, man."

"I'm coming."

We walked, Percy counting our steps out loud, until he hit seventy-five. I rummaged around in the bag and found a plastic framework in the shape of a triangle. When I placed it in the road, it fell over.

"Here," said Percy.

He did something with the base of the thing and put it back down. This time it stayed up.

Meanwhile I had found the road flare inside the bag. It was a red cylinder a foot long and about an inch in diameter. Percy held the light while I read the instructions.

It was a simple thing to crack the top off and use it to strike the broken end of the tube, thus igniting the magnesium mixture within. The light was blindingly intense.

"Put it down, man-let's get back to the car."

He didn't have to tell me twice. With the flare lit, the flickering light of it had instantly thrown the surrounding bush into stark patterns of light and shadow, suggesting shapes and movement that were not really there.

Mr. Paranoia Guy had begun to stir.

We left the glare of the road flare and walked back to the car, following the beam of the flashlight. About halfway back, I stopped and turned the flashlight off. I'm not sure why. I think I just wanted to take stock, for a moment, of where I was.

I was, in fact, about thirty yards from the car. The car was about ten feet from the middle of the road. The road was...where was the road? Where, in fact was I, in relation to the rest of the world that I knew? I had no idea. And for the first time, that knowledge alone frightened the hell out of me.

I hurried to join the knot of shivering people at the car. Everyone was standing around the front of the car, where a pair of legs was sticking out from under it. The other flashlights beam caste around from down there.

"So, where are we, man?" I asked.

"We are screwed," Gary answered, misunderstanding the question, "but it could be worse."

"No, I mean-where are we?"

Joe pulled himself out from under the car and stood up.

"That is the question, all right," he said.

"Right. I'm glad we agree on that. So, what's the answer?"

"I don't fuckin' know. We passed through some shithole called Steen River about fifteen minutes ago. Didn't look like any services there."

Joe got the map out of the front seat and smoothed it out over the hood. He placed the flashlight so the beam illuminated it.

"The next place is 'Indian Cabins', about forty miles up the road. Boy, that sounds promising."

"Can we get there?" Doug asked.

"Well, the good news is, the log didn't take out the oil pan. If the oil pan was gone, we'd be walking. The bad news is, it did take out the exhaust system."

"The muffler? So what; it's going to be a little bit noisy?"

"No, no; I didn't say it took out the muffler. I said it took out the *exhaust system.* Right up to the manifold."

"Okay, but is it drivable?"

"Theoretically, yes. We're gonna lose a lot of compression, so we won't be able to make highway speeds and, yes-it is going to be noisy. The real problem is gonna be the fumes."

"The...fumes?"

"The exhaust fumes. Instead of going down the tail pipe and through the muffler and coming out back there, the fumes are coming out up here, in front. That means they're gonna come up through the firewall and the floor. We're gonna be breathing raw exhaust, carbon monoxide."

Joe was thinking out loud, working his way through the situation by talking about it.

"Shit. We're going to have to open all the windows."

"Open all the windows? Shit, it's like, twenty below, man."

"More like twenty-five, according to the last weather report on the radio. And it's getting colder."

"We've got no choice. I haven't seen another vehicle on this road in three hours. We've gotta try to get somewhere on our own. Hopefully this Indian Cabins place will have a telephone, or a CB radio or something and we can call for a tow. But we gotta get there first."

"Okay, but with the windows open? Jesus."

"If we drove this thing with the windows closed, we'd all be dead in half an hour."

"Man. Well, all right, you heard the man; let's get in and roll 'em down. Get under your sleeping bags, but keep your faces outside 'em."

"Hey, Gary?"

"What?"

"So, where are we?"

"We are between a rock and a hard place, man. Just try to stay awake, OK?"

He started the engine with a roar and put the car in gear. We moved off into the sub-arctic night with the sound of the un-baffled engine bellowing into the darkness.

It was *cold.*

Just standing around in air that cold is one thing, but moving through it at fifty miles an hour with nothing between you and it; that's *cold.* People who ride ski-doo's at those kinds of temperatures wear helmets, special insulated suits and gauntlets.

Fifty was all Joe could coax out of the damaged Pontiac without causing further damage to the wounded power train. It felt like we were crawling and according to the map, we were. At this rate our next safe haven at Indian cabins was almost an hour away.

I had a window seat because I'd been in the middle up to the accident. There was no way to get away from the blast of frozen air. I tried to bank my sleeping bag up and hide behind it but it didn't help. My face was numb in the first ten minutes. My breath froze in my beard, building icicles from my nose down to my chin.

It was so tempting to put my face down under the bag and get warm but I knew the fumes were coming up from the floor. There was death under the blankets. Above the blankets there was only hypothermia and frostbite.

After twenty minutes, we stopped to rotate the seating arrangement. Clearly, the people in the window seats needed a break. I moved up front and Doug went in to the back seat, looking drawn and pale.

The minute we started off again, I noticed the strong smell of exhaust coming from the dashboard.

"Fuck, man! The heater vents are open! That stuff is blasting into my face!"

We turned off the heaters and closed all the vents. I turned to look at Doug, to ask if he was all right. His face had turned an unlikely shade of green.

Great, so now we couldn't use the heater, either. We'd forgotten that it worked by moving air from the engine compartment into the cab through the vents. Just now that air was loaded with carbon monoxide fumes.

I looked around at the boys in the back seat.

Bob was in the middle, wrapped in his sleeping bag with his insulated lumberjack hat on. It was probably the first time he'd untied the ear-flaps and let them down. He had wrapped a thick woolen scarf around his neck and chin to keep them down in the icy breeze, leaving just his nose and eyes uncovered.

Gary had on a serious cold weather parka that reached to his knees. The hood extended forward almost a foot to form a little tunnel and the lip was trimmed with wolverine fur, the only fur that your breath won't ice up in extreme cold. I'd seen him put on a pair of fur lined gauntlets over his regular gloves and his feet were snug inside a pair of authentic northern muk-luks. Gary was fine.

Like me and Percy, Charlie was wearing a thinly insulated winter jacket made of some completely useless nylon fabric. The hoods on these things closed with a drawstring that, even if you did it up tightly under your nose felt exactly the same as when it wasn't on at all. Likewise, our ten-dollar gloves were no match for the temperatures we were being subjected to. If it hadn't been for the sleeping bags we had wrapped around us, we'd have been suffering hypothermia by now.

Mr. Paranoia man was huddled in the dark corner of my mind, whimpering like a little girl.

"*We're all gonna die,*" was all he said, over and over.

We crawled along, making the best speed we could, stopping every twenty minutes or so to rotate seating. People began getting silly about not wanting to move from their spot.

"Come on, man-we have to change seats," I said to Gary at one point.

"You don't want to get under these blankets," he replied, "there's farts under here."

I insisted, and he finally gave in but it was just indicative of how punchy we all were getting.

At one point, we came upon another log in the road, this one bigger than the one that had crippled us. We stopped, despite our sorry condition, and took the time to roll the damned thing into the ditch. I guess the thought that some other poor soul might suffer our fate was just not bearable.

"We should be coming into Indian Cabins soon," said Gary.

And we did. We came around a sweeping curve in the road and there were lights ahead. No one whooped for joy. No one expressed relief at arriving at this small oasis in the wilderness. We'd all seen the map.

I had looked hopefully over Doug's shoulder as he reckoned the mileage here from our last stop. I'd noticed the relative distances behind our estimated position and ahead of it and I knew; we had another five hundred kilometers to go. For all we'd been through, after almost sixteen hours on the road, we were only about two thirds of the way there. At the rate we were going now we'd need another sixteen hours to get there, if we ever did.

Indian Cabins was just exactly what the name suggested. All you could see from the road was a run-down garage by the side of the highway and a few similarly dilapidated structures off through the trees.

The chance that there was someone here who possessed the skills and the tools to do the work we needed done on the Pontiac was non-existent. All we could hope to get at Indian Cabins was a tank of gas to continue on as we had been, freezing our ears off in the breeze. That and a bathroom break.

Doug was the first to discover the outhouse by the side of the building. The extra monoxide exposure he'd gotten from the vents had really made him ill.

Joe went inside to confirm the inevitable, returning all too soon with the news.

"No mechanic on duty," he informed us, filling the tank, "Best this guy can do is to radio ahead to Hay River for a tow truck to come meet us halfway there. He says there's a heavy duty machine guy in Hay River."

The four of us remained where we were, waiting for our turn in the outhouse, reluctant to move from our inadequate cocoons.

Then Joe said; "There's hot coffee inside."

It took a few seconds to sink in. My mind skipped right over the word "hot." The words "coffee" and "inside" were too far removed from our miserable reality to have any meaning right away but as our dulled minds grasped what he meant, we started to move.

I found the door handle and pulled but nothing happened until I put my shoulder to it. All the car doors were frozen shut. We were weak as kittens but one by one we managed to exit the vehicle and extricate ourselves from our sleeping bags.

My legs had gone numb. My first tentative steps nearly pitched me on my face in the snow but I leaned on a fender and made my way towards the door of the place.

Coffee. Inside. Hot.

It had been so long since I had experienced anything other than freezing cold that entering the building was a shock. The place was warm. There was a wood-burning stove in one corner, pumping heat into the room. On top stood a blue and white- enameled percolator, burbling quietly in the small space.

Almost half of the tiny room was taken up by a wooden counter with an antique cash register on it.

"Come on in, you guys. Quick, fellas, let's get that door shut. Coffee all 'round?" the owner asked.

He put four Styrofoam cups on the table and filled each one with the contents of the pot. The smell of fresh-made coffee permeated the room. There was sugar in a Tupperware container and powdered whitener of some generic brand in an economy sized plastic bottle. We helped ourselves.

We stood, stirring our coffee with little wooden stir sticks, trying not to jostle each other in the confined space. We graduated from stirring to blowing and then, one by one we took our first sips of hot coffee.

"Mmmm," said Percy.

"Ahhh," replied Bob.

"Oh, that's good," Charlie commented.

All I could manage was a grunt of satisfaction. I don't know how to describe the effect of the hot coffee on my body. To say it *tasted* good would be to understate the sensation.

It certainly did taste good but then, as I swallowed the first sip, my entire body became involved as feelings of warmth radiated out to all my limbs in a slow, languid embrace. After the abuse my body had suffered over the past hours, it felt like sliding into a bath of delightfully re-affirming warmth.

And then the caffeine got into my blood and was carried up into my numbed brain, stimulating and massaging synapses back to life which had been unused for hours, as my body had begun emergency shut down of all system not required for survival.

It felt like coming back to life.

"*We're all still gonna die,*" said Mr. Paranoia Man.

"Oh, shut up," I mumbled to myself, luxuriating in my java-inspired resurrection.

Doug finally finished throwing up and came in from the outhouse, looking marginally better. We proceeded to take turns using the facilities, such as they were. Doug got the last cup of coffee from the pot and the owner started another.

"You guys are welcome to wait here for the tow truck," he said.

We looked at one another. The idea had a certain amount of merit, even if it meant spending a few hours standing there in the crowded office.

"That'd be nice," said Joe, in from the cold, "and thanks for the offer. But that tow truck is charging us by the mile and that includes every mile he has to come to us. If we don't at least meet him halfway, we'll end up losing money on this trip. Maybe we will, anyways-I don't know what they're going to charge to fix this motor."

The look on Joe's face told us he knew what he was asking of us.

"We should get going," he said, "the more miles we can make the more money we save."

As we started to file back out into the cold, the garage man spoke up.

"So, who's taking care of the tab, then?"

"Tab?" Joe asked, "I paid you for the gas."

"No, I meant for the coffee. Coffee's five bucks a cup."

"Five bucks a cup!? You gotta be shittin' me."

"Five cups at five bucks a pop; you owe me twenty-five dollars."

"Jesus. Here's ten. That's double what they charge at Donnelly Corner."

"This ain't Donnelly Corner, mister."

"Well, this ain't twenty-five bucks. If you're going to screw people, at least put up a sign."

We got back in the Pontiac and took our places, wrapping up in our sleeping bags once more. The warmth we'd felt inside the cosy refuge of the garage left us before we even started moving. If we had taken any comfort by stopping there, it took about three minutes before it felt like we never had.

As predicted, the day had gotten colder and the frigid air that assaulted our exposed faces had a new, lethal feel to it. We started rotating seats every fifteen minutes, then every ten as it became evident that the window seats were just not safe. Somebody was going to develop frostbite before we got halfway to anywhere.

About the fourth time we stopped there was some confusion as we changed seats. The numbers weren't right.

"Where the fuck is Charlie?" Percy asked.

"Oh, no. Don't tell me we left him back at the garage."

"No way, man. I saw him get in."

"I thought he was sitting beside me, in the window seat..."

"Here he is! Charlie? Fuck, man; he's been sleeping under the blankets! Charlie, wake up, man!"

Charlie had succumbed to the siren call of the warmth below the sleeping bags and curled up on the floor of the car where he'd been breathing pure CO_2 for the last ten minutes. He was not looking good.

His eyelids fluttered and he made shooing motions with his hands as we tried to revive him.

He started making incoherent vocalizations and drooling on himself, then, suddenly he came to and started throwing punches. He landed a pretty solid shot on Percy's nose.

"Ow! Fuck, that hurt. Charlie! Snap out of it, man."

Charlie looked around at us. He was clearly not himself.

"I ba, ibeh, In n n n…"

"It's all right, man, don't try to talk. Just walk him, will you? Get him away from the car and get some fresh air into his lungs."

I took Charlie's arm and ducked under it. Standing up with him, I started walking up the shoulder of the road with him doing the best he could to shuffle along with me. We went about thirty feet before we turned around and headed back to the car.

"How you doin', Charlie?"

"Ang. Anda ang uhnnn."

"Can't keep this up. Somebody's going to die."

"Maybe we better just wait here for the guy."

"I guess so. At least we can wind the windows up if the engine's not runnin'."

"Amen to that."

So there we sat by the side of the highway with the engine off and the windows up, taking turns walking Charlie up and down the shoulder. We knew the tow truck had left about the same time we had and that he'd been making way better speed than us. It was a pretty good bet that they'd arrive before we all froze to death, but it wasn't a sure thing.

Mr. Paranoia Guy wrung his hands and whined from the back of my head.

We waited for what seemed like a very long time indeed before a set of blue and white flashing lights appeared down the highway. A big blue truck pulled up and stopped on the other side of the road.

It wasn't the tow truck. It was the RCMP. A hearty voice greeted us from the interior of cab.

"How you guys makin' out?" it asked.

"We got one guy might need to see a doctor. He was breathing carbon monoxide for a while. The rest of us are OK, just freezing our balls off."

"I bet. Where's the patient? Oh, here he comes now."

"I ba. I bunh. In n n ..." Charlie said, by way of greeting.

"He's getting better, I think," I offered, "at least he's walking better now."

"Ok, well, I think he'd better come back to town with us. You can come with him if you want. We can take two more. Your tow truck is right behind us, should be here anytime."

As he spoke, a second set of flashing lights, these ones amber, came around the curve and slowed. It was a big flatbed with a huge cherry-picker mounted on the deck. The driver hopped out and approached us, shrugging into his parka on the way.

"I hear you boys need a lift," he grinned.

"We sure need something," said Joe, "how much do you figure for a tow into town?"

"Well, we'd have to talk about that but I'll tell you one thing; you're gonna have to pay up front. The way I hear it, you guys got a habit of walkin' out without paying the tab."

"Is that what you heard? No doubt from the guy at Indian Cabins. You pay five bucks a cup for his coffee?"

"Now, look here, Al," the Mountie butted in, "these guys are in a fix, here. We need to make sure everybody gets to town safe."

"So, the RCMP gonna pay me if these guys don't?"

"Come on, Al. You know what Bill's like. He probably tried to take these guys for a ride and they weren't going for it. Don't you think? You know what he's like."

"Yeah, I guess you're right."

"All right, then. I'm going to get these two fellas into town, and whatever two others want to come along. You take care of this vehicle and driver. Okay?"

"Okay, fine."

"Good man. Come on, guys, lets get you in the truck. Who else is coming?"

It was decided that Doug should come with Charlie and me, owing to his infirmity. Percy and Bob flipped a coin. Percy won and climbed in the truck. As we executed a three-point turn and headed back the way they'd come I could see Joe and the tow truck guy talking seriously by the front of the Pontiac.

"First time north of sixty?" the Mountie who wasn't driving asked.

"First time," Doug replied.

"Figured. Anybody who'd been on these roads before would have known a vehicle like that just doesn't cut the mustard. You're lucky nobody was hurt."

"I guess so."

We drove on in silence for a time. Inside the police vehicle it was warm and comfortable. I was almost nodding off when I noticed one of the cops sniffing the air.

"Smell that?" he asked his partner.

Mr. Paranoid Guy awoke and sat up in the back of my mind.

"You guys indulging in a little pot on the way?"

There was an uncomfortable quiet in the cab. Of course we had been smoking joints along the way. We must have stunk to high heaven of the stuff. I realized I had the better part of an ounce in the pocket of my jeans.

"Oh, Fuck. Now we're screwed! We're going to be busted!"

"It's all right. We're not going to hassle you about a little recreational use. Most folks up here take a little ganja now and then, especially in the winter, just to relieve the boredom."

He paused. Then he twisted in his seat to look back at us, crowded together in the back of the crew cab.

"As long as that's all it is."

He looked each one of us in the eye before he went on.

"Let me give you a piece of friendly advice, fellows; a lot of the people that live up here come from the south. Most of those that come up here, go back after their first winter. Life is just too tough in the North for most. Those that stay usually have a pretty good reason. For some, there's family down south that they want to stay away from. Others just find that the North suites them. Quite a few are up here because they can't be anywhere else. And of those, a lot of folks stay up here because down south they can't find a way to stay off dope."

Again he paused, looking at each of us in turn, letting his words sink in.

Mr. Paranoia Man cringed and whined with fear. The officer went on.

"There isn't any hard stuff in Hay River, and that's the way we like it. When I say we, I don't mean the police, although I'd be lying to you if I said that we don't appreciate the situation. The fact is, there are a number of people in town that do not take it kindly when somebody comes up here with the intent of selling hard drugs to them and their friends. They tend to take matters into their own hands."

He looked over at the driver, who was checking us out in the rear-view.

"The last guy that arrived in Hay River with a bunch of shit to sell found himself on the wrong end of a welcoming party, his second night in town. We got an anonymous tip that night. We found the guy ten miles south of town in his long johns, hoofing it down the road in minus eighteen weather."

The driver chuckled a little and chimed in. "They'd hung a pretty good beating on him, too."

"We took him down to Indian Cabins and put him on a Greyhound. He didn't quite need to go to the hospital."

Another pause.

"If you boys had a notion of increasing the profitability of your trip up here by peddling a bit of dope on the side, I would strongly advise you to forget about it. No one minds a little pot up here, so long as we're not setting up supply lines, but you sell hard drugs in this community at your own risk. OK?"

"Yes, sir."

"Got it."

"Thanks."

"*We're all gonna die!*"

I was just so relieved to realize that I was not going to be searched and arrested I didn't pay any attention to the voice in my head. The rest of the ride into town was quiet, if a little tense.

Once they had made sure that Charlie was coming around and didn't need medical care, the cops suggested they drop us off at the "Youth Center." This turned out to be a building right across the street from the RCMP detachment, on the main street. There was a café and some pool tables, one of which was empty.

We doffed our outer gear and got coffees at the counter, then proceeded to play a game of hopelessly inept billiards, much to the amusement of the local youngsters there. The whole thing had an aura of unreality after the last few hours. It didn't seem possible to be there, inside the warm room, drinking weak coffee and, little by little, relaxing.

One of the RC's came over from across the road to tell us the news from the radio.

"It's seems your vehicle is coming in on it's own steam. Looks like your driver wasn't able to come to terms with Al. You guys got moxy, I'll say that for you."

A few minutes later the roar of an un-muffled V8 announced Joe and Bob's arrival in a cloud of smoke.

We'd made it. We were ready to rock Hay River, NWT.

As it turned out, Hay River was ready to be rocked. They hadn't had any decent music in town for a long time and no one I talked to could remember the last rock and roll band to play there.

It had been decided that, because the repairs to the Pontiac were going to take a few days, we would play that week in a local lounge. The owner had heard of our arrival (as had everybody else in town) via something referred to as the "moccasin telegraph."

I still don't know exactly how the moccasin telegraph worked, back then in the days before cell phones, only that it did work, and amazingly well at that.

The news that there was a bona-fide rock band in town had run through the community like wildfire, sparking all kinds of activity. The lounge owner, whose name was Bill, was a native "Hay River Rat" who possessed the innate northerners' instinct for taking advantage of opportunities as they arose.

This was something we would witness in the people we met up there time and again; it was a survival skill.

Within an hour of our arrival, the decision had been taken to have us play in the lounge. A labor force had materialized and converted one of the booths at the back of the room into a tiny stage. Our trailer had been transferred to another vehicle and driven to the venue where it had been unloaded and all our gear deposited in a polite stack against the wall. We didn't have to lift a finger and a couple of burly lads hung about as we set up, eager to assist us with the heavy lifting, while the kitchen staff prepared a generous dinner for us, on the house.

This was more like it. By the time we had finished eating and doing a sound check, arrangements had been made for accommodations in town. We were driven there and shown to the door by another helpful guy, named Zack.

Zack thought the whole thing was just hilarious. He had a big, booming laugh that seemed to emanate from his whole body at once. After a few minutes in Zack's company you found yourself laughing along with him, heedless to the fact that there wasn't anything in particular to laugh at.

He wheeled us merrily across town and came to a halt in front of the four-story building. I say *the* four-story building because it was the only one in town. The only building taller was the six floor communications building three blocks away. Everything else in town was one or two story. The town seemed to hunker down in the cold, as if it didn't want to expose any more of itself to the chilly arctic wind coming off the lake than it had to.

It was slightly amazing to me how rapidly all these arrangements had been made but I was to learn that the people who lived up north were adept at moving swiftly to take advantage of anything good that came their way. We were the first thing even resembling entertainment that most of them had seen in six or seven months and they were ready and able to make the most of us.

Zack somehow carried all of our luggage upstairs to the two apartments that had been vacated for us in one trip and left us, laughing.

Showers were taken and plans were made to go out and check out the town. Then somebody found the whiskey.

The original idea had been to buy a case of Canadian Club at Alberta prices, which averaged about 25% lower than those in the NWT, and trade the club manager to pay off our bar tab at the end of the gig. So much for the plan.

The whiskey made the rounds and as the stress of the voyage ebbed and the mood mellowed, the prospect of leaving the warmth of our new-found home to go out into the sub-zero temperatures lost it's cachet. One by one we succumbed to a post-trauma snooze.

Captain Nobody spent their first ten hours in Hay River asleep. We'd have been ready for a nap after that long a drive even without all the drama. The stress of being stranded in the middle of nowhere combined with the cold and the fumes we'd breathed had done us in. We were, as some wit observed just before oblivion took us all, exhausted.

Next day, a rested and restless Captain Nobody finished breakfast and started looking for something to do. Without a vehicle we were on shanks' ponies to get around town but then, there really wasn't very far to go in any direction to the edge of Hay River. We got going around noon and, once outside, were delighted to find the temperature had moderated to a balmy -15.

We had an idea we might save some money by doing our own cooking in the apartment, so the first order of business was an expedition to the local grocery store. Notwithstanding the milder weather, we were still pretty cold by the time we had walked the three or four blocks to the store.

When we got there, I was amused to see, along the side of the building, a row of-not bicycles, but cross-country skis leaning against the bricks. There were several pairs of snowshoes there, as well. I didn't waste any time pondering what the instance of snowshoe theft might be in town but the thought intrigued me just the same.

We loaded up on sundries, including lots of carbohydrates to help us fight the cold, and splurged on some very pricey mix for the CC.

Back we went to our warm little apartment, feeling that we had accomplished something.

Only six more hours to gig time. There was no TV service in Hay River at the time; cable had yet to be invented and the latitude made satellite service impractical. Someone had a deck of cards. We talked about making a trip to the local library for some reading material, but we never did. And there was lots of whiskey to help while away the time.

We managed to get to the venue sober enough to play our first night. The stage was horribly cramped and the room was so small that we must have been blasting peoples' eardrums but they loved every minute of it. The joint was jumping all night, filled to capacity with young folks who hadn't heard live music in months. We played OK, for musicians who had previously been deep frozen and didn't have room to move. Charlie was feeling especially cramped when he realized he would have to curtail his usual microphone flailing in the interest of not braining anyone.

All in all, we managed to acquit ourselves reasonably and the best part was we couldn't buy a drink all night; the townsfolk were so overwhelmed with gratitude at having something to listen to other than the river ice cracking that they kept an endless variety of beverages flowing up to the stage.

It was then that we began to get the first inklings of the kind of creativity that characterizes the people who live north of the sixtieth parallel.

Lacking any other medium by which to put a personal stamp on their messages of thanks, they resorted to testing the bartenders' skill with orders for the most outlandish drinks ever invented. At one point the speaker enclosure that I was using for an end table was adorned with a Mai Tai, a Pink Lady, two Singapore Slings and a Pina Colada complete with a tiny umbrella.

The only evidence I had that I made it back to the apartment that night was that I awoke there in the morning with a hangover of truly epic proportions. The thought of breakfast was an affront to my delicate sensibilities, so I decided that what I needed was some fresh air. Donning my flimsy parka, I made my way down the two flights of stairs to the street.

I must have been in such a state that the cold didn't register until I'd made my way two or three blocks. By the time I realized how cold it was, I was as far from the apartment as I was from the store. I'd never felt cold quite like it; my skin actually hurt from it. My eyelashes were freezing together from the tears that had started in my eyes from the pain. My feet had begun to go numb.

There was no point in turning back, so I went on until I came to the first open door, which turned out to be a sort of combination gift store, crafters' co-op and art gallery, simply called "the Ptarmigan".

I hurried through the door, as folks do when they are coming in from extreme cold. The shopkeeper, a middle-aged woman of pleasant countenance, looked up in surprise from the back of the room, where she was opening boxes.

"C'mon in! You weren't walkin' around in that, were youz?"

"I was. Pretty cold out."

"Pretty cold? You got that right. You always in the habit of walkin' around dressed like that in minus forty weather?"

"Minus forty? Is that how cold it is? No wonder."

"No wonder what?" she inquired, turning back to her task.

"Uh, well...no wonder I'm freezing my butt off, I guess."

She stopped cutting boxes open again and looked at me.

"There's hot coffee over there," she said, gesturing toward the back of the room.

"You're with that band, aren't you?" she asked.

"Yep. How did you guess?"

"Only a newbie would be out wandering around, dressed like that, in this weather. Only newbies I know of in town is you guys. I'm Terry. Didn't you think it might be an idea to check the temperature before you went out?"

"Neil. Nice to meet you. No, I didn't. When did it get so cold?" I helped myself to cup of strong, hot coffee. It tasted like heaven.

"It was fifteen below last night. This morning it was minus eighteen at 6:00am. This stuff came in over the last four-five hours. Right now it is..." she leaned across the counter in front of her to peer at the thermometer outside the window, "exactly forty one degrees below zero. There's such a thing as frostbite, you know."

Terry then busied herself again, taking things out of the boxes and putting them out on the counter. They were soapstone carvings, about a dozen in the first box. Most of them were about fist-sized, but one or two were twice that.

"I've heard. So, local people don't go out when it gets this cold?"

"Not unless they have to. Nothing works at this temperature. Vehicles freeze up-anything that runs on fuel. Gas turns to jelly-propane too. Hoses freeze up and crack, soft metal gets brittle and snaps. Can't count on machinery at forty below. Gets this cold, the sensible thing to do is hole up somewhere warm and wait it out."

She opened the second box.

"I guess I blew it, then, eh?" I tore myself away from the sculptures she was unloading and started looking around the rest of the shop. The place wasn't large but there was an enormous amount of stock. There were beaded muk-luks and gorgeous parkas trimmed with fur. One wall display sported a variety of rawhide gauntlets, like Gary's, another held moose hide skirts and shirts as soft and pliable as chamois.

"Funny you should put it that way. Blowing is the problem; it never stays this cold for long, this time of year. It'll probably last overnight and by morning it'll start warmin' up again, but in the meantime, it's going to get windy."

A table in the far corner caught my eye. It was empty except for what appeared to be a little gong, brass or copper, hanging in a frame made of driftwood.

"It was starting to on my way here."

"Yup, well; forty below and still is one thing and nothing to be foolin' with. Forty below and windy-that's a whole other ball of wax, there. When air that cold starts moving across exposed skin, it ain't funny. Your walk over here was nothing compared to the walk you'll have back."

I made my way over to the gong. It was no more that eight inches across, the surface dimpled with a thousand tiny bumps. I ran my fingers over them.

"Hand-hammered copper," Terry said, "Made out of a frying pan, if you can believe that, by an Inuit hunter. Probably got the pan in trade for some fur, took it home and spent his off hours hammering it out. Took him all winter. Want to try it?"

"Yes, please."

Terry reached under her counter and produced a short mallet. The handle was whittled from some supple wood and looked to be about nine inches long, with a loop of rawhide on one end. On the other was a mallet head, the like of which I'd never seen before, made of some thick, white fur.

"Polar bear. Feel it."

I did.

"Soft, eh?"

"No kidding."

I was wondering how a striker that soft could produce sound from anything. I took it over to the corner.

"Just a sec."

She'd gone over to turn off the stereo that had been playing soft new age music in the background. When the room was completely silent, she nodded at me.

"Go ahead."

I turned to the gong and, taking the beater by the end to get maximum leverage, delivered as solid a stroke as I could in the center of it. The result was a total surprise.

"Bwaaaaaaaaaaaaaaaaaah…"

The little gong produced as clear and pure a tone as I had ever heard any musical instrument produce. The timbre was a rich, round alto that opened up and sustained undiminished for an astounding length of time before fading gently to oblivion. I couldn't believe my ears.

Turning back to Terry, I found her looking at me with an expectant grin on her face.

"Pretty cool, huh? Nobody can believe the sound of that little thing. It's like he got it perfect, somehow."

"I'll say. Wow. I've never heard such a pure tone from any percussion instrument, except maybe a glockenspiel."

"Well, I don't know what that is, but I know a good sound when I hear it and that thing gives me goose bumps. I keep thinking about this hunter, holed up in his tent, or igloo for weeks on end, out there on the ice, hammering away at that copper. Working on it until he got it right."

"It's pretty amazing. But then, the best cymbals were always hand hammered. The Turks have been making them for centuries. You can still get them, if you can afford one. Too rich for my blood. Is this for sale?"

"It is, if you have a spare fifteen hundred bucks. I'll never see another one."

"I guess not. Maybe you should buy some copper cooking pots and leave them out on the shore."

"Ha! You think so? That's not a bad idea. So you're the drummer, I take it?"

"That's right. I do some singing, too."

"Is that right? You sing? Are you any good?"

It was the kind of bold, in-your-face question I was to hear time and again in the north where, I was soon to learn, people had nothing to hide from one another and expected you to have the same honest self knowledge as they all seemed to possess.

I faltered.

"Well, I don't know, I mean I think so..."

"You mean you don't know if you're any good or not but you get up and do it in front of people every night? That must be fun."

"No, I mean, I think I'm good. Lots of the people we play for think so, I mean, they request the songs I sing and stuff..."

"Wow. For somebody who makes a living performing in front of crowds, you sure don't exude a lot of self-confidence, friend."

"I just don't want to come off sounding conceited, you know?"

"Well, no worries there. Where did you guys come from, anyways?"

"Edmonton. We drove up on the weekend."

"I heard. Everybody heard about that-everybody from here to Yellowknife and back. You guys are part of the lore, now."

"Yeah? What's that-the lore?"

"The lore of the North. Up here there is not a lot to do so folks spend a lot of time tellin' stories. 'Strange things done in the midnight sun' and like that. People up here love a good story. Any time someone does something interesting, like driving a hundred miles in minus thirty weather with the windows open, for example, it gets turned into a story. The story gets told and re-told and a little bit added on each time until the people that actually took part in the original event wouldn't recognize their own story. That's when it becomes part of the Lore."

"Wow. So that's what they mean by the 'Moccasin Telegraph" I guess."

"Ahh, not really, although the two things are related. The M. T. is how things get around. Lots of people don't have telephones up here, you know? Some folks have CB's or satellite radio, lots don't have anything but word of mouth. So the M.T.'s is all of that and more-if you deliver water to people, you also deliver the news. If you come into town once a month for groceries, you stop in for a chat and find out what the buzz is. Then, on your way home, you might be dropping off a few things at your neighbors' and they get the news from you. One way or another, things get around up here. Folks make sure of it."

"Are there newspapers at all?"

"Oh, yeah-we got the Hub here in Hay River. It ain't bad for details, editorial views and reviews of things but nobody relies on the Hub for the news, 'cause by the time it comes out, the M.T. has already taken care of that."

"Huh. That's pretty cool. It's like a kind of... I don't know, a community consciousness kind of thing."

"If you say so. I don't go in for a lot of that psycho-babble stuff, myself. Are you planning to do any more strolling about today?"

"Strolling? Oh, no-I was going to have a walk about, but now that I know the temperature, I'll probably just head back to the apartment."

"Very wise. Still, you've got a ways to go and you are not dressed for these kinds of temperatures. If it was any colder, I'd offer you a ride but you should be OK if you dress up a bit."

So saying, Terry had gone over to a rack of clothing in the middle of the room. She selected a few items and brought them back to the counter. There was a handsome parka of cream-colored moose hide with a hood that covered the wearers' entire face and enveloped it in soft fur, with a telescopic front that allowed no wind unless you faced directly to it. She'd thoughtfully included a pair of the ubiquitous Inuit gauntlets that went on over your standard gloves and went up to your elbows.

"You'll be alright with these, just don't dilly-dally in those boots."

I looked down at my inadequate city boots, good for ten minutes at ten below and not much else.

"I won't. Listen, Terry-there's no way I can afford this stuff..." I had glanced at the price tags.

"You think I'm trying to sell you this stuff? Ha!" she threw her head back and let go a great guffaw, then, shaking her head in disbelief, said, "You really are fresh out of the pond, aren't you? I'm just loaning you this stuff to get home in. You make sure you take it all to the lounge tonight, I'll come pick it up. OK?"

"Really?"

"Well, the first live band in town since I-don't-know-how-long; I guess I better catch at least one night."

"OK, great! Thanks a lot. I'll see you tonight, then."

"See you."

And with that, I went back out into the cold, and immediately got what Terry had meant about the wind. I could feel it the second I stepped out-the kind of bone-chilling wind that can do serious damage if you're not dressed for it. I was fine, though, in my borrowed parka. The gauntlets kept my hands completely comfy as well. The wind was blowing at an angle to my route and with the design of the hood, I didn't have to worry about it. The only chinks in my thermal armor were my boots, which proved themselves completely inadequate for the task of keeping my feet from freezing in short order. By the time I had walked the short distance home, my toes were numb and turning blue. I resolved to buy myself some proper cold weather footwear at the earliest opportunity.

That evening, I wore the borrowed clothing to the lounge, although the weather had moderated a bit by then. It was only minus 34 on the thermometer by the door as we went through the outer coatroom and entered the lounge to find it once again packed to the ceiling.

I kept an eye out for Terry as I made my way up to the stage, taking the expensive parka and gloves with me but, if she was there I couldn't see her in the crowd. Percy and Doug were tuning up their guitars when I finally made it through the press. Gary and Bob were over at the bar getting a start on the liquid intake for the evening. Charlie was sitting on the front of the stage with his legs crossed, holding his mike in his hand.

"Hey guys. Hey, Charlie; what's up, man? You look like you're ready to run a race. We won't be starting for another twenty minutes, you know."

"Hi Neil. Yeah, I know I just-there isn't a lot of other places to sit, you know?"

"True enough. 'Scuse me, man, I need to get behind the kit for a second. Yeah, just; watch your foot there…Ok, made it, thank you."

"Hey, Neil?"

"Yeah, man."

"Do you think they like us, all these people? Do they come to hear us, or is it just…I don't know-would the place be this packed every night if another band was playing? Any band?"

"I don't know, Charlie. I guess it might be. Apparently we are the first live entertainment they've had in town for months, so I guess they are pretty cranked up just about that."

"So, if some other band had gotten here first, like last week, do you think they would still be coming? This many people, every night?"

"I don't know, man. Does it matter? I mean, here we are; here they are, why don't we just, you know; go with it? You know? Let the good times roll."

Gary came through the crowd to take his turn with the guitar tuner. He must have overheard a part of the exchange.

"Gentlemen, listen and take my advice; pull down your pants and slide on the ice."

I got a laugh out of that but Charlie looked up at Gary with a blank face.

"What does that mean, man?"

"Old Inuit proverb," he said, "you know how inscrutable they are, man."

"Yeah, but what does it mean?"

Gary and I exchanged looks.

"Don't worry about it, Charlie. In fact, don't worry about anything. We are young, we are free, we have a date to play and the house is ready to rock, so let's just enjoy, Ok?"

Charlie considered this at some length, just sitting there, holding his mike, before he replied.

"All right."

Worries about Charlie's state of mind were quickly drowned out in the music and the din of the crowd. Whatever it was that was bothering Charlie didn't prevent him from turning in a stellar performance. I continued to keep an eye out for Terry but, as the evening wore on and closing time loomed, she still hadn't appeared.

As predicted, the weather had continued to improve and by the time we left the lounge at the end of he night, it was a balmy ten below. I was nevertheless thankful for the borrowed cold weather gear after spending four or five hours inside the hot, crowded room.

The following day I made my way to Terry's shop on foot to return the parka and gloves, only to find the place closed. The sign in the door said "Back Soon." Nothing to do but wander around town for a while, hoping she might return soon.

I took a stroll down to the old part of town, admiring the weathered old buildings and making plans to return with my sketch book. A tanker truck passed by, looking like it had seen better days. When it stopped beside a rickety-looking residence and the driver got out to hook up hoses to barrels, I realized that he must be delivering water.

Of course, I thought. Here in the sub-arctic, unlike further south, the permafrost made it impossible to bury water pipes to keep them from freezing. Unless you wanted to dig trenches twenty feet deep, you were better off keeping your water in heated barrels or cisterns than to try to rely on a piped supply.

There was no sign of Terry that night at the lounge either and I began to wonder if I had inherited a mighty nice moosehide parka.

The next day was a Friday and made special by the appearance of my girlfriend, Janice and Gary's partner, Lorrie in town, having driven up from Edmonton in Janice's Volkswagon Beetle. Let me just, at the risk of being repetitive, reiterate that; The two of them drove up to Hay River from Edmonton in a Volkswagon Beetle just to see us. They had decided that they couldn't be without us any longer and braved the elements to be with us and to bring us a small supply of dope to help beat the tedium.

I honestly don't know which was more welcome at the time, the girls or the drugs. Certainly the fact that she had driven all that way to see me gave me cause to reflect on just how serious my relationship with Janice was getting.

The girls took rooms in the local motel and we lost no time renewing the physical side of our union, with a brief intermission to go play the gig.

Unbelievably, the two of them had only come up for the weekend and had to work on Monday. To allow time enough for both the drive back and recuperation, they had to leave on Saturday. We parted company most reluctantly, vowing to be true and looking forward to seeing each other again asap. It was with a certain sadness that I watched the tail lights of the VW fade in the distance.

But, hey; they'd brought dope.

Saturday night Gary, Percy and I dropped acid the minute we finished the last set at the lounge. The weather had taken another radical turn and warmed to no more than ten degrees below zero which, after the rigors of the week felt positively balmy. After having been cooped up in the apartments for five days and nights and going out only to scurry to the lounge and back, we craved diversion, preferably outdoors.

We were intent on an exploration of the town of Hay River and environs. The tour began with a trip to Old town, where we stopped in at the home of Doug's new friend, a tall, lanky blonde tomboy named Nora.

Nora had a big, booming laugh and no use for manners. She lived in a one-room cabin that was at least a hundred years old, heated with a wood burning potbelly stove. In one corner of the single room was the water barrel.

Joe was there when we arrived. He took one look at our stoned out faces and asked;

"What's on the menu tonight, guys?"

We told him we'd taken acid. Joe was not impressed.

"We're going to be up here another month. You guys need to pace yourselves."

"Don't worry, man," I said, showing the bottle of rye I had brought with me, "we are tempering the effects of the dope with this."

"Very wise," offered Joe dryly, "well, play safe. I'm headed back to the apartment. Anybody want a ride?"

We declined, intent on a midnight ramble through old town. The weather had stayed moderate and the forecast was for more of the same, so we felt confident walking about. We wandered around the streets of old town marveling at the rustic, not to say impoverished, look of the place.

The acid kicked in hard after a while and gave the most mundane of things an added mystique. We tripped out on a huge moose trophy mounted on someone's cabin, looking for all the world like some dinosaur death's head. The wind sculpted snow banks along the river provided us with entertainment as we followed the shore and somehow ended up at the banks of the lake.

The sight of a dozen big fishing boats pulled up on the shore and covered with snow was bizarre. Masts and spars festooned with icicles, windows glazed over with frost, they stood starkly outlined against the night sky like some maritime graveyard from a fairy tale. It was irresistible.

How we managed to scale the ice-laden ladders up the sides of the boats, I do not know. We wandered around on the decks, just tripping on the oddness of the place and not even trying to open doors or get into the boat.

At one point I noticed the mast had a crows' nest; a lookout platform built around the mast. This one was about sixty feet up, accessible by a little steel ladder, which, like everything else on board, was covered in ice.

We were getting down to the bottom of the bottle of whiskey at that point and peaking on the LSD to boot. I had no recollection of what occurred after that until Percy reminded me the next day.

"You scared the shit out of me," he said, "that ladder was coated with ice about an inch thick. I don't how you made it to the top without slipping right off that thing."

"The top?" I felt a bit sick to my stomach at the thought, "you mean I went all the way up to the top?"

"Yup. Then you were hanging off of the rail with one hand, yelling your ass off."

"Really? I don't remember a thing. What was I yelling?"

"I don't know, the usual shit about being the king of the world and stuff."

"The king of the world."

"Among other things. You're lucky you didn't wake someone up, like the owner. The only thing that brought you back down was when you dropped the bottle."

"The bottle."

"Yup. You carried the bottle all the way up there and then you dropped it. Almost killed Gary-missed him by inches. At least it made you come back down. That was about as much fun to watch as when you went up. Do remember slipping?"

"Slipping?"

"You were coming down, hand over hand, and then you slipped. About twenty feet up. You slid the rest of the way down. You don't recall this?"

"Not a thing. I must have been really stoned."

"Well, you drank most of that rye. Nobody else wanted any so you just kept swigging it back. That's a shit load of booze on top of acid, man. You better slow down. You are going to do yourself a damage."

"I guess you're right." And he was. I was pushing my luck in an unfriendly environment. I resolved to temper the booze consumption. There was no more dope, so that was that and probably for the best.

Strange thing about doing acid before drinking too much-no hangover. I felt fine, if a bit stiff, no doubt from the aerial gymnastics. I took myself for a walk and ended up at Terry's store.

It was open, so I let myself in. There she was, just like the first time I saw her, opening boxes.

"Hey! How you doin'?"

"Howdy, stranger. Long time, no see."

"Yah, I had some business to take care of out of town."

"Business?"

"A buddy of mine had some trouble with his propane system. Hose froze up and snapped while he was changing tanks. Idiot didn't have a spare, so I had to take him one."

"Out of town, you said? How far?"

"'Bout a hundred and fifty miles, I guess. Bad roads. Took me five hours to get out there, by then his water and sceptic was all froze, too. Had to hang around and help him get things workin' again. Ended up staying overnight. Next day my truck wouldn't start. Block heater had packed it in. Had to heat her up the old way, with a torch. That took all afternoon. Driving home in the dark, I hit a goddamn moose. Lucky I was going slow, hardly any damage to the truck. Moose had a couple broken legs, though-had to put it down. So then I had to dress it out and get the meat packed up. That took god-knows-long. Didn't get back to town 'till midday and I was so tired I just hit the sack for the afternoon. You guys want some moose meat?"

"Wow. You mean, you took three days and drove three hundred miles in minus 30 weather for a frozen hose?"

"No, I took three days and drove three hundred miles in minus 30 weather for a friend."

"Right. I guess there's a fine distinction, there."

"Nothin' fine about it. It's just the way we do things up here. A person doesn't have the option of bein' a loner in the North-you help people when they need it, and they help you back."

"I guess it makes you into a community."

Again, at the mention of a lofty ideal behind her actions,Terry stopped and looked at me like the idea had never occurred to her before. This, I was to learn, was typical of the people in the Territories. They didn't have a lot of time for "philosophizing," as one resident put it. They possessed a huge wealth of communal spirit but did not take the time to dwell on it, or even to celebrate it in any way, other than in the other thing they shared-the dry, self-deprecating northern sense of humor that I grew to love and admire.

Nothing ever illustrated this better than the campaign to name the residual Northwest Territories Bob.

In 1999, it was decided that the Northwest Territory would be divided into two distinct new territories.

The new Eastern Territory had been given a name-it would be called "Nunavut." Many assumed that the rest of the original territory in the west would just retain the old name but a controversy sprang up about this. Lots of northerners felt-had always felt that "Northwest Territories" was just too long.

As a result, there was a contest held to solicit suggestions for a new name and to choose among the suggestions by plebiscite. A smattering of ideas came in but for a while it looked like most northerners just considered the whole thing silly and pretentious, until NWT cabinet member Stephen Kakfwi appealed to his constituents to step up and take advantage of the opportunity to give their home a name that was less indicative of it's relationship with Ottawa.

This seems to have struck nerve with people and served to elicit an upsurge in ideas for the new name. Soon folks were rallying their support behind the one suggestion that seemed to reflect how they felt about their land and about the whole issue. No one remembers who first came up with it but the suggestion that came to be the people's choice was; "Bob."

Someone put out a circular to promote the idea and son there had been a committee formed to rally more support behind it. A list of reasons why "Bob" would be the best choice was published in all the northern papers;

10) Government would no longer be 'big brother' because 'Bob's your Uncle!'

9) Millions of Parents-both aboriginal and non-aboriginal-can't be wrong. Bob has been chosen by many.

8)"Bob says..." has a much better sound than "The Government of the Northwest Territories says..."

7) Politicians could take junkets to the twinned jurisdiction of ZimBOBwe.

6) 'Kurzewski-stan' is too long...(referring to a local big-wig)

5) Lots of neat official stuff would be immediately available to the government-the official sport could be "bobsledding. The official hairdo could be the "Bob. The RCMP could be called "Bobbies," etc.

4) Bob is dyslexic friendly.

3) Allows parents to show pride in their territory by naming their kids 'Jim-Bob, "Bily-Bob, etc.

2) Bob sounds the same in all the official languages of the territory-Chiewyan, Cree, Dogrib, English, Gwich'in, Inuvialuktan, North Slavey and South Slavey.

1) The Bob and Doug MacKenzie River runs through it.

Although this all occurred long after I'd returned to the south, it was typical of the way the people I met up there viewed themselves and their land.

Terry had no opinion about the question of community, she was simply too busy taking part in it to think about it.

"I guess," she said, "So, you think you wanna take some moose off my hands? My freezer is full."

"Sure, I guess. What kind of meat?"

"Moose. It was a younger bull, three or four years old, so it won't be too tough."

"So, like just ground meat, or…" I had no idea what wild meat looked like.

"Yeah, I can give you some hamburger. I'm having forty pounds ground up over at the Co-op. I could let you have some steaks, if you like, or ribs. You don't have to take just burger."

"No, that's fine-just, whatever you have. I'm keen to try it."

"Keen, are ya? You mean you never had moose meat before?"

"Nope. Never had any wild meat before. I'm looking forward to it. Are there special instructions for cooking it?"

"Special instruc…no, no-you just fry it up, or roast it. Just a little dryer than your beef, is all. You can stew it, if you want."

"Sure, well thanks."

"I'll be going for lunch in ten minutes, you like to join me? Nothin' fancy; just a burger at the Caribou."

So we went for lunch. Terry had to pick up some boxes at a freight yard on the way, so we took her truck.

"Wow, that's quite the cow catcher you're sportin'," I commented, referring to the grid of welded metal that was mounted on the front of her vehicle. There were bits of hide and meat still clinging to the metal after her recent encounter.

"Yup, had it made up special. First truck I had up here, I wrote off under a 1600 lb. Bull moose. Just about got killed, too. I can't afford to buy a new truck every year."

"I guess."

I helped her load up at the trucking depot and we made our way the few blocks to the restaurant. There was a small crowd of early lunch customers already seated in the booths, all of whom greeted Terry by name. I was introduced to enough strangers that I was confident I wouldn't remember any of their names.

The Caribou was a modest little diner on the main street, offering the standard menu with a few Northern twists. Right under the hamburger was listed the "Moose burger", along with something called "Guess what Stew."

"He just throws in whatever he has on hand that morning and leaves it to you guess what's in it," Terry explained.

"He" turned out to be a guy named Dave, who was the owner of the place. He came out of the kitchen to personally say hi to Terry and we were introduced. He was a big guy with a disarming smile and huge hands that he kept wiping on a cloth.

"Folks call him 'Crazy Dave,' but I don't. He's no crazier than a lot of 'em."

"Why do they call him that?"

"Well, I guess it started when he arrived here from Edmonton, that was back in '64-'65, I guess. Arrived in town with nothing but the clothes on his back, hair down to his waist. Asked around town and found no work. He hitchhiked up to Yellowknife and when he got there he went straight out to the Giant Mine to apply for a job. The foreman there looked him up and down and said he might have work for a guy if he was to get about half that hair cut off."

Dave came back to our booth to take our order. I ordered the stew, curious to see what I got. Terry ordered a hamburger. She waited until Dave went back into the kitchen before resuming her story.

"So, Dave goes back into town and he has the barber shave him completely bald on the right side of his head. Then he puts the other half in braids. Or, a braid, I guess. Anyways, he goes back to the mine the next day and the foreman thinks that's so funny, he gives Dave a job anyways."

"So they started calling him Crazy Dave because of that?"

"That and some other things. Mostly just harmless pranks and stunts."

"Mostly?"

"Here's the food."

The stew turned out to be elk that day with big chunks of spuds and carrot and turnip floating in it with the onions and something I didn't recognize.

"Daikon," said Dave when I asked him, and then, when he notice the look on my face, "Japanese radish. Adds a little spice."

I agreed. The strange vegetable added an exotic flavor to what would have been a good stew anyways. It was delicious.

We lingered over coffee and as the lunch crowd thinned, Dave came over and joined us.

"So, you're with the band, eh?" he asked, stirring his tea.

"Yup."

"I caught you the other night. You guys are pretty good. I like the material."

"Yeah? Thanks. Anything in particular?"

"No, I guess it's all good stuff. Maybe what I like best is that you do it all together, Beatles and Stones and then Nilsson and right into Alex Harvey. It's a cool mix. It's like the only reason for doing a song is that you like it."

"That's pretty much the way it is. We like a lot of different stuff, the weirder the better. Humor is a big thing. We all like funny lyrics, off beat topics."

"It shows. I like it. Ever hear of "Wilderness Road?""

"Wilderness Road. No, I can't ay I have."

"California band. Funny as hell. I got a copy of their LP at my place. You outta come over and give a listen. Bring your buddies. Bring the whole band, if you want. My place is big enough."

"That sounds like fun. How do we find you?"

"Tell you what-I'll find you guys. It's my day off tomorrow, why don't I come down , see you guys and after you're finished we'll convoy up. I'm just a couple miles out of town."

"Sounds like a plan. How about you, Terry, you comin' to the gig tonight?"

"Not me. I told Uncle Bill I'd come over and help shovel the snow off his roof. That has to get done before I open the shop, so...thanks, anyways."

Dave finished his tea and went back to work. Terry turned to me.

"If you are going over to Dave's place to party, you need to keep your wits about you."

"What do you mean?"

"Well, I told you about Dave's reputation for playing jokes on people. He likes to target people who stick out."

"Stick out?"

"Yeah, you know; noticeable people. It's almost like he thinks of it as a contest. Dave is well-known because of is jokes, so anybody who becomes well-known for something like that becomes his competition."

"I see. So, because we're in the band...?"

"Well, that and the other stuff."

"Other stuff?"

"You know-like those shenanigans down at the shore the other night."

"Did you just say 'shenanigans?'"

"Ok, be a smart ass. But take my advice; if you're going out to Dave's place, you watch your back. And don't fall asleep, whatever you do."

"Why, what happens if you fall asleep?"

"See that guy two booths over?"

"The one with the tattoos all over his head?"

"They're not tattoos. Dave decorated his head while he slept on the couch after Dave's last party. He used permanent markers. That was five weeks ago-they've faded a lot. Another month or two, you'll hardly notice."

"I see. Thanks for the heads-up."

"You're welcome. Time to go. I gotta get back to work. Can I drop you off?"

"Yeah, sure. Don't you need help off-loading that stuff in the truck?"

"Nope. That was Dave's stuff. He's already unloaded it."

"Just doing more favors for friends?"

"Did you see a bill for lunch?"

"Oh."

Terry dropped me off at the apartment building, making sure I remembered to take the green garbage bag of moose meat with me.

As I made my way down the hall, I could hear voices coming from the room I shared with Gary and Percy. One of them belonged to neither.

"I'm a tella you guys, you listen to me. I take-a you to Roma, do a concert in-a the

Colosseum!"

"The Colosseum? Do they even allow concerts there?" That was Percy's voice. "Yeah, the vibrations would shake the place apart, man." This from Gary.

As I came into the room, the two of them were sitting at the kitchen table opposite a guy I hadn't seen before. He was a swarthy individual clad in a muscle shirt and jeans, with curly black hair worn in a mullet. He was addressing my band-mates with obvious enthusiasm.

"No, no–I'm-a from there, man! All-a the big bands do a-concerts in the Colosseum. Make-a more money than you can-a burn!"

"Hi Neil."

"Hey, man, this is Mario. Mario, this is Neil."

The guy jumped to his feet and offered me his hand.

"Neil-a. I'm honored to meet you," he said earnestly, while he pumped my arm with gusto, "You are a genius on-a the drums, my friend. What a drummer! Ginger Baker? Keith Moon? Pshah!"

He spat on the floor, much to everyone's surprise, and went on.

"I'm-a watch you play, I'm-a think; this man is-a the drummer for the world, my friend. For the world!"

I noticed Percy grinning. Gary was laughing out-right, giving the impression that they'd each been the recipient of such praise.

"Well, thanks very much, Mario. It's nice to be appreciated."

"That's a –what I'm a tell-a Percy and Gary. It's a sin you guys working 'ere, in this-a shithole! You should be in-a Europe, playing to people who are-a capable of a-seein' 'ow good you are, not these peegs."

"Ah."

"You, Neil-you are a man of a-vision. I can see it in a-your eyes. 'elp me to make-a them see. You don't a-belong-a here, Neil. Let me take a-you to Europe! To stardom!"

Percy had broken out into laughter. Gary was sitting there with a look of disbelief mixed with disdain on his face. He looked like he was trying to decide whether or not to throw the guy out.

"Well, it sounds good but I have to ask; how are we going to get there?"

"Is a-no problem. We take a boat."

"A boat."

"Si, si. I got a lot of friends in the Italian Navy."

"The navy? You want us to take an Italian Navy ship to Italy?"

"Si, we do it all a-the time. I been 'ome to visit my familia three, four times. I just wait for the Navy to come to Vancouver, go to a the boat, give a guy a leetle money, walk up-a the gangplank."

By now it was obvious the guy was out to lunch. I looked over at Percy, who was still shaking with mirth.

"I love this guy!" he said, "he's a riot!"

I helped myself to some coffee. Mario continued his rantings, insisting that he could arrange a tour of Europe for us without any need for money or backing. It very soon got very old. I went for a shower.

When I came out of the bathroom the apartment was empty. It was mid afternoon. The weak sub-arctic sun was already on the decline, casting long shadows across the snow.

I was tired. The past week had taken a toll both physically and mentally on all of us. The long days with minimal sunlight, followed by night after night of hard playing and harder partying were beginning to add up.

I decided to take a nap before dinner, and woke to the sounds of my roommates getting ready to go to work. I realized that I hadn't had any supper. With the prospect of Dave's party after a full night of playing, I felt it would be ill-advised to go to the gig without eating.

I looked in the fridge and found nothing, except the garbage bag of moose meat from Terry. Unwrapping it, I saw that she'd taken the time to wrap the meat in butchers' paper and label it. There were five one-pound packages labeled; "Hamburger" and three others that said "steaks".

Selecting a steak pack, I rewrapped the rest and put it back in the fridge. The package I'd selected yielded three good-sized steaks, looking like a beef sirloin cut but a different shade of red.

Lacking time and knowledge, I grabbed a cast iron fry pan and put it on high heat. By the time I found the salt and pepper in the cupboard and seasoned the meat, it was smoking. There was no cooking oil or butter in the place but, looking through the cupboards I found a spray can of 'Pan' and used that. The steak hit the pan sizzling and sent up a great plume of smoke.

I gave it four minutes on a side and turned it out onto a plate. Then I paused. Looking at the remaining two steaks, I thought; 'why wrap them up and put them back raw, in the fridge? Here's this nice hot fry pan, which will have to be washed anyways-why not cook them all and put them away like that, ready to be warmed up fast in morning with eggs, or, more likely in the small hours when we get home from the party, famished?'

So, back on the heat went the pan and into the pan went the steaks as I headed off to the dining room to eat. The meat was tough and stringy but tasted good. I was chewing my way through the last of it when Gary came out of the bedroom, buttoning up his shirt.

"Fuck, man-did you have to fill the place with smoke?" he asked. He went into the kitchen .

"Hey, your steaks are burning."

"Oh, shit!" I cried as I rushed in to rescue them. They weren't quit burned on the one side, just needing turning. I returned to my meal, intending to finish cooking the two spares and put the steaks in the fridge before I left.

"Hey, guys-how long does it take to get to the gig from here?" Percy asked, entering the apartment.

"About ten minutes, walking," Gary replied, "Why?"

"Well, because it's already ten after nine."

"What?! No way! The clock says eight twenty five!"

"I got 9:10," Percy said, looking at his watch.

I looked under the table, where the cheap plastic wall clock was supposed to be plugged in. It wasn't. I held up the cord.

Just then, the phone rang.

"Illinois Central," said Gary, answering, "yes, we just figured that out. We're on our way. Tell him we'll play an extra set...Okay, see you in ten."

"Boys, we are late for the gig. Doug says there's a riot starting up at the restaurant."

We rushed to get out the door, pulling on coats and boots as we went. A hurried walk to the gig got us there in time to start forty minutes late. The usual crowd was exceptionally rowdy because of the delay.

"What were you guys doing?" asked Charlie.

"The clock stopped. It's OK, we'll play late."

"I don't know why I should be expected to play late. I was here on time."

"You got a lot to do after midnight in this town, do you Charlie?"

"That's isn't the point. I just don't see why I should have to play a late set when it was you guys that screwed up."

"Fine. You know what? Don't. You go on back to the apartment after the third set and we'll play the last set without you."

"Oh, sure. That'll look good."

"Well, what do you want to do, Charlie? The clock stopped and we're late. Nothing we can do about it now."

"What do you mean-'the clock stopped'?

The look on Charlie's face was out of sync with the conversation. He suddenly looked like he'd seen a ghost.

"Just that. The fucking clock in the apartment stopped working because somebody kicked the cord out of the wall socket. That's why we were late."

Charlie visibly relaxed at this. The color, which had drained from his face, began to return.

"You all right, Charlie?"

"Yah. No, I'm OK. I just…I thought you meant something…"

At that moment, Bob started the intro to the first song; "Let Me Be Your Swampsnake 'till the Real One Comes Along" by the Sensational Alex Harvey Band.

Later, I remembered the look on Charlie's face. I brought it up with Doug.

"Yeah, he's been putting out a curiously disturbing vibe ever since the exhaust incident. I guess there are some residual effects, or something."

"Well, as long as it doesn't stop him singing, I guess there's not a lot we can do."

"I guess not. Maybe I'll have a chat with him later."

I never did find out what bizarre paranoid musings were taking place in Charlie's brain. He stuck around and played the late set with us, with no trace of how he felt about it apparent in his performance.

After the set, Crazy Dave came over and made arrangements for us to follow him back to his place. It was a couple of miles out of town, just off the road and down a plowed drive. In the middle of a clearing stood his house-or rather, his structure. To refer to it as a house would not do justice to the eccentric nature of the place.

It seemed to have started out as a mobile home, what they called a "double-wide"- a pre-fabricated trailer that had been plopped down on some poured concrete pilings. Another structure, which looked like it might have started life as grainery, had been spliced onto the back of the trailer with a sort of sagging walkway between them. On the roof of the mobile home there was a hump, which on closer examination was actually the body of a Winnibago. It gave the whole structure a silhouette like some kind of a submarine.

Stepping inside, there was a foyer/mudroom that Dave called his "airlock," about four feet by six. The walls were insulated with multiple layers of egg flats, stapled together four or five thick to keep the outside air from blowing freely through the interior every time the door was opened.

Through the airlock door was a rather nicely, if sparsely furnished living room. Dave's taste in décor ran decidedly to the sixties with things like bean bag chairs and lava lamps, UV tubes installed over black light posters and a big hookah pipe in the middle of the coffee table. There was a large aquarium between the living room and the kitchen, with several large tropical species evident.

Crazy Dave insisted on giving the band the tour of his place, which included the "Studio" which he accessed by way of the unsound passageway to the auxiliary building. It turned out to be Dave's combination music room and crafts space.

There were several guitars in various states of repair hanging on the wall and one that looked only half built sitting on his workbench. Keeping it company was a mandolin and a pair of banjos, all of which had seen better days.

Another bench held a set of leather working tools and a rack of belts that were decorated with a combination of beadwork and branding. A selection of silver buckles graced the adjacent wall.

"Gotta do somethin' to keep from going completely looney up here in the winter," said Dave.

He then took us back through the living room to a set of stairs that led up through a hole in the ceiling to his bedroom. He had adapted the Winnebago into a cosy suite with windows looking out on the frozen landscape and a collection of books that covered three walls.

"This is where all the mysteries of the universe unfold."

I wasn't sure if he was referring to the library, or the king-sized four-poster at the back of the room. It was certainly the warmest part of house, anyways.

Then people started arriving by the truckload and the foyer door got held open. Pounding the stairs, Dave yelled;

"Close the door! You're gonna kill the fish!"

The stereo was blasting out Johnny Rivers' "Memphis Tennessee" when we arrived but as the evening progressed Dave's record collection proved to be an eclectic one.

He had LPs by the Beatles, and the Stones, the Band and The Who, all standards of the day, but he owned an equal number of country and country swing records by the likes of Bob Wills and the Texas Playboys, the Light Crust Doughboys and Milton Brown and his Musical Brownies. In addition, there was one recording that he was particularly proud of by Asleep at the Wheel, a new band from the south that was carrying on the Texas Swing tradition.

"My buddy Jake found 'em out and sent me this copy. It's their first but it ain't gonna be their last. Texas swing is back! Yee-haw!"

We sat about on the floor, taking gentle hits of hash from the hookah and sipping beers. We listened to music and rapped until we all started to get drowsy. Even Charlie relaxed and seemed to lose the edge he'd been on.

"Stay the night if you want. There's plenty of blankets," Dave offered. I declined, mindful of Terry's warning. We all decided to go back to town.

"Hey! You can't go until I play you that album I was tellin' you about! Wilderness Road! Just got this one from my buddy Vern, in California. You're gonna love these guys."

And we did. The album was a sort of country/rock satire, poking fun at the southern gospel radio stations in the southern U.S. We listened through the whole thing and then we had to go. We were knackered.

"C'mon back any time! You guys are great! See you tomorrow night. Close the fuckin' door before you kill my fish!"

When we got back to the apartments, the building manager was waiting for us. It seems the steaks that I had left on the stove in my rush to get to the gig had burned to a crisp, filling the building with smoke and causing someone to call the fire department.

After the false emergency was dealt with, the question came up as to who was living in the apartment. It seemed that the whole place was owned by the telephone company and was intended for the use of their employees.

Only.

So, the next day, we were evicted. There was a rumor that reports of Percy having been seen riding somebody's bicycle up and down the halls in the buff might have contributed to the manager's decision.

No way we could afford to pay motel room rates. Luckily, the car was fixed and ready to continue on to Yellowknife. We packed up the equipment a little sadly and bid goodbye to our hosts.

And we left Hay River, headed North.

THE ICE BRIDGE

Did I say there was nothing at the end of the road to Yellowknife except Yellowknife? You must forgive me; I was overlooking a little detail called Great Slave Lake.

How could a person neglect to mention something like that? It's the reason for Yellowknife being there, after all, along with the local gold deposits. And it's not, of course, little at all.

It's big.

It's really, really big. There are probably not enough adjectives in my vocabulary to describe how very big it is. So I'll resort to the numbers.

Great Slave Lake is 480 km long. At it's widest point it's just over 108 km wide. With a surface area of 27,200 square kms, it's over four times the size of Lake Ontario. Of all the Great Lakes, only Lake Superior surpasses Great Slave Lake, but only in surface area.

Her average depth is 41 meters but there are places where the bottom is 614 meters down. That's 2,014 feet, making Great Slave the deepest lake in North America. Although she takes most of her water from the Hay, the Taltson and Slave rivers, the thousands of smaller tributaries combine to drain a catchment area 971,000 kilometers square. It's the tenth largest lake in the world, keeping company with the likes of Baikal, Victoria and the Caspian Sea, which is technically a lake.

In terms of sheer volume, Great Slave Lake holds an estimated 1,580 *cubic kilometers* of water on average, but that can range up to 2,088 in the spring flood.

All things considered, this is one big fucking lake.

So, how could anyone forget to mention a thing with the immensity of Great Slave Lake? I don't know. But that's what I did. In fact, I spent three weeks there; right on the shore of it and *I never noticed it.*

It's embarrassing.

I caste my mind back to the time I was there and, to my surprise, I find absolutely no memory of the lake. What's more, I've spoken to several of the people who were there with me and they admit the same thing. Doug says that, once he got down to the shore to watch them dynamite the ice jam on the river, it did come home to him just how big a lake it must be but he would only have seen a small part of it.

We remember being aware of the huge, empty expanse of white covered nothingness stretching off beyond the horizon, commencing just a few hundred feet away but none of the rest of us can remember looking out there and saying to ourselves; 'Ah, that's the lake.'

How can this be? We weren't *that* stoned, at least not all the time. How could we have spent almost a month beside one of the most impressive geographic features of the Canadian North which, let's face it, doesn't lack for impressive geography-and not be consciously aware of it's existence?

I have a theory.

I think that, for a bunch of prairie raised southerners (which we were, to anyone who lived above the 60th parallel) who thought of the little sloughs and puddles that dot the landscape in central Alberta as lakes, the very size of Great Slave Lake rendered it incomprehensible to our minds. We were not capable of conceiving that vastness as belonging to the category in our brains where the concept of "lake' resided. It just did not compute, so our minds refused to let us recognize it for what it was.

It wasn't until we got to Yellowknife and I climbed to the top of the "Rock" outside Old Town, where the monument to the bush pilots sits, that I realized what I was looking at.

I'm getting ahead of myself, though. Before we got there, we were going to have to cross the river.

On the ice bridge.

Great Slave Lake is drained at the western end by the mighty Mackenzie River, the largest and longest river in Canada. It averages between one and three kilometers across, although in some places there are narrows where the river runs fast and deep.

The road from Hay River to Yellowknife backtracks twenty-five km to the junction with highway #35, (or highway #1 as it's known in the NWT), then follows the south bank of the Mackenzie for some sixty-five km until it turns north to Fort Providence.

Back then you had to have a very good reason to go to Fort Providence or Yellowknife in April or May because, in order to get there, you'd have to cross the ice bridge.

I can remember the first time I heard those words-'ice bridge.' It took me a moment to realize that the person who said them hadn't made a mistake; that they'd meant to say just what the phrase implies-a bridge across water, made of ice. My first reaction was; 'what a stupid idea.'

When I then realized that the person speaking intended *me* to cross it, my horror was tempered only with the hope that, surely they must be joking. But no, it became quite clear that I had somehow fallen in with lunatics who not only intended to go ahead with this mad scheme, but expected me to take part.

I imagine most sane people who are first presented with the proposal to drive across the frozen surface of a major lake or river would share my reluctance. I am at a loss to explain how so many of them are convinced to abandon their common sense and do it anyways, but they do. As difficult as it is to comprehend, every spring, thousands of northerners annually use the ice bridges on the Mackenzie and the Lesser Slave as a matter of course. What could possibly be so important about getting to the other side?

If you could wait a few weeks, you could take the Hardy Ferry across the river once the ice was clear.

If you were travelling in the winter, the Mackenzie River crossing was as safe an ice road as you'd find in the North; hardly distinguishable from the rest of the road.

Depending on the weather and its effect on the ice, the ice road stayed viable some years clear through to the end of May. The government sent men out on the road to collect core samples from mid-March on, in an attempt to gauge the bridges' strength and for the most part this gave them a pretty accurate idea of what was going on under the four or five feet of ice that made up the ice bridge.

Ice *that* thick will carry a lot of weight. The signs on either end of the crossing said it was given a load ceiling of 64,000 kgs which was very conservative but that was in the winter, when the temperature rarely if ever went up over -10 or -15. Once ice is frozen to a thickness like four feet, it takes an extended period of above zero to weaken it. But weaken it does.

Spring in the North comes in fits and starts, with two or three warm days followed by sudden cold snaps that yield to the warmth only to return with a vengeance, as if the ice is reluctant to relinquish its hold on the land even after the long, sunless winter was done.

These uneven conditions wreak their havoc on the ice, creating weak spots and air bubbles down below where they can't be seen. The ice bridges (there are more than one, although the main crossing is now replaced by a nice sensible bridge) become unreliable but there is no way to know where the worst spots are, except for the red flags the government survey guys post on the road.

Once the ice on the Mackenzie started to break up and travel across the ice bridge was over for that year, it was a three to four week wait before the ferry could operate safely.

The communities north of the river relied on the ice bridge to bring things to them all winter. As the inevitable break up time approached, people made contingency plans to stockpile perishable goods and have more flown in by helicopter should the need arise. Helicopter flights did not come cheap. The price of perishable goods went through the roof every spring.

In the end it became a matter of economics; just how much could you charge people for a dozen eggs or a steak before the market dried up completely? The answer was a hell of a lot, until the ferry started up and cheaper goods once again became available.

So, for the truckers that dared the ice bridge during those uncertain weeks in May, it turned into a lethal game of chance.

If you arrived at the crossing with a 'refer' full of garden fresh veggies or butchers' goods and found that the ice bridge wasn't looking good, there would usually be a half dozen of your peers parked at either end of the kilometer-long track, waiting to see who would go first and prove the bridge was safe, or not. Sometimes bets were made.

Some years an unofficial levy was collected from all who drove the highway, with the pot going to salvage the unlucky soul who braved the odds and lost. Often it wasn't a question of who felt lucky that day but rather who couldn't afford to turn back.

If some unlikely combination of extreme bad luck and economic pressure dictated that you were going to be the one to see if the bridge was going to hold that day, there were accepted procedures.

You didn't go fast. Too much speed going across the bridge, even when it was in good condition, meant trouble as a heavy vehicle would push down on the ice and displace the water below, setting up a bow wave that preceded one's progress across the river, hit the other side and then rebounded back to meet the vehicle still progressing towards the bank. The result of the old wave meeting the new was often an upheaval of the ice directly under the vehicle which, if strong enough, could crack the ice and send the speeder to the bottom, some eighteen meters below.

For similar reasons, it was considered unwise to stop on the bridge. As long as you kept moving, the weight of your rig couldn't put concentrated stress on any one area of the ice. Once you let it come to a stop, it was only a matter of time before the weight overcame the structural integrity of the crumbling crust.

Many drivers who crossed when it wasn't safe did so standing on the running board, steering through the open window and ready to jump for it at the sound of the ice letting go.

The day we arrived at the crossing, nobody was feeling lucky. It had been unseasonably warm for a few days. The bright sunshine reflected from various spots out on the river road. The ice was looking so iffy that there wasn't a trucker there, out of the seven or eight rigs parked on the shore, who was hard up enough to chance it. They all just sat, some of them since the early morning, waiting for someone else to take the plunge, so to speak.

When we arrived, the whole game changed.

With our unlikely combination of the old Pontiac and the over-loaded U-haul on the back, we looked strangely like the perfect test vehicle for seeing if the ice bridge would carry a load.

Joe got out to talk with the drivers and assess the situation and was treated to the biggest load of pure hogwash ever heard on the shores of the Mackenzie. They convinced him that, while they couldn't risk the ice with their big eighteen wheelers, we could cross safely with our load, no problem. He returned to the car brimming with confidence.

"No problem, man. We're way below the safe weight for these conditions. We'll be in Yellowknife in time for supper."

"Are you sure, man? That looks like patches of open water out there."

"Sure, there's some puddles on the surface. The ice is melting, man. But underneath it's like, six feet thick. It'll take our weight five times over."

"I don't know, man. I am freaked out. I mean; what if it doesn't go well, and we go through the fucking ice. We're fucked, man! The equipment would be gone."

"Listen, it's not like we have any choice, here man. What would you like to do, turn around and go back to Hay River? Do you have any idea what it would cost us to stay in the motel while we wait for the ice to go out? How much we'd have to fork out for food? And for how long? Nobody knows when the ice is going to go out; it could be a week, it could be a month. We'd be in the hole so deep, I'm tellin' you guys-we gotta go.

Look, the truckers gave me some tips. We gotta go slow across here, real slow. If you're nervous about this, roll down your window and sit on the door with one leg outside. That way, if anything happens, you can get clear fast."

"Oh, great, so the four guys with door seats get out. What about the rest of us; what do we do, push?"

"The trailer has those wide running boards. Two guys can stand on 'em and ride across that way."

And so it was. We must have looked as silly as most of us felt, starting across with two of us riding on the skirts of the trailer. Doug and I'd lost the draw and had to go in the Pontiac. I wasn't keen on sitting inside, waiting for the sound of the ice cracking. I wound the window the window all the way down and sat on the door with only one leg inside the car, ready to bail. The others decided to do the same.

We eased out onto the bridge at idling speed. Heedful of the truckers' advice, we proceeded at a moderate ten or fifteen mph. We hit the first puddle a few hundred feet out and I, for one, felt better knowing that it was, in fact, just that; a puddle of melt water sitting in a depression on the surface of the otherwise sound ice.

Then I saw the first crack. It was hundreds of feet long and a good foot wide where it crossed the road. Of course, it was full of water and therefore impossible to gauge for depth. The wheels dipped slightly as we went over it, making the vehicles rock unnervingly. On we went, for lack of selection.

The puddles on the surface of the ice became ponds, then joined into one big shallow lake that seemed to cover the rest of the crossing ahead. It had only been a few inches deep closer to the bank but as we neared the middle it started to get deeper until it was half way up the tires and threatening to come over the bottom of the Pontiacs' doors. We made a visible wake as we proceeded through.

The next crack came on us suddenly, hidden as it was under the water. Doug saw it first and yelled out to Joe, who instinctively hit the brakes.

"Don't stop!" someone shouted.

Remembering the truckers' instructions, Joe hit the gas again, perhaps a trifle hard. The big car surged ahead, yanking the trailer along. We hit the submerged crack and were horrified to hear a sound like muffled thunder from directly under us.

"Fuck! Keep going, man!" someone whined. It might have been myself.

The trailer hit the crack a second later, producing more submerged rumblings. Far across the ice, in the direction the crack went, came a loud bang, answered by an unearthly groaning sound. As we left the crack behind, water boiled up along the length of the fissure as if from a geyser.

Forced to stay at a crawl, we proceeded on our way. Behind me, I heard someone on the trailer begin to mumble under his breath. It sounded suspiciously like a prayer.

There were three more cracks to cross but none of them was any worse than that one. At some point I looked up and saw that we were noticeably closer to the far side, where I could make out the shapes of more big rigs, the drivers watching our progress with interest. Before long we made the shore and stopped to collect ourselves and retake our seats. As we did, I saw one of the local drivers take out his wallet and pass some bills over to the man standing beside him.

"These guys had bets going on whether we'd make it or not." I said.

"Just as long as we never have to do that again," said Percy, "I only packed so much clean underwear."

The ice bridge had been crossed. Yellowknife beckoned.

The End.

BILLY

Billy Sanderson was the weirdest kid I've ever known, and hopefully ever will know.

He didn't look weird. At first glance you might dismiss him as just another typical pre-teen, a stocky boy with a shock of reddish-blonde hair and freckles dressed in Levis and a turtleneck. It was only on closer inspection that the little things might tip one as to the volcanic personality lurking within.

Billy was always smiling. It may well be that this is the thing that fooled most people when they first met him. When he got excited he tended to drool a bit. He wasn't a bit shy and easily joined any group or conversation he encountered but at times he would push limits, cross lines. It wasn't unusual for other kids to find themselves a bit uncomfortable in Bill's company.

He had a good sense of humor and wasn't above laughing at himself, although there were times when he was the only one who seemed to get the joke. We would stand around, pretending to get it, fake-laughing, nervously waiting for an explanation that never came, most days.

That was the thing, though; most days Billy seemed absolutely normal but for a few idiosyncrasies.

The problem was that he also had days when, for no apparent reason, he went completely, uncontrollably and irretrievably off the deep end.

And the thing is, you never knew when it would happen.

I remember going over to Billy's place after school one day. We hung out downstairs, playing records and looking at his comic book collection. Billy's dad was doing something in the other room and at one point Billy addressed him.

"Dad, can we get a color TV?" he asked.

"No. We can't. Billy, you know we can't afford it."

"Dad..." Billy's voice had taken on a threatening, menacing tone.

"Billy..." came a similarly warning timbre.

"CRASH!" The next thing I knew, Billy had hauled off and put his foot right through the screen of the television. A flash of sparks was followed by an implosive whoosh as the picture tube ruptured.

Mr. Sanderson appeared at the door to the family room.

"Billy!" he yelled, and launched himself at his son, tackling him and pinning his arms to his sides. Billy fought back with surprising strength and the two of them crashed together around the room. At one point the father's face turned to me, wild with anger and exertion, and he yelled;

"Get out! Go on, get out of here!"

I wasted no time in complying. On my way home I had time to replay the scene in my mind. I realized with a bit of a chill that at no time during the whole thing had the smile left Billy's lips.

The next day at school Billy came up to me and my friend, Myles. He had a blue and purple bruise on his forehead and walked with a limp. He was smiling still.

"So how come you took off so fast yesterday, Ward?" he asked, somehow managing to smile and sneer at the same time. His tone was accusatory, as if I'd shown a lack of fibre by not sticking around.

"Are you kidding? Your old man was screaming at me to get out, man."

"So what? You scared of the old fart?"

"Well, he is your dad, Billy."

Billy didn't answer. We were standing on the second floor of the school hallway, beside the stairs. Without another word, Billy turned and, taking one step, vaulted over the railing into the stairwell and fell a full story to the hard tiled steps below.

"Jesus Christ," Myles said, as we ran to see if he was OK, "what did he do that for?"

Billy lay across the bottom two or three stairs in obvious pain. As we looked down, he struggled to his feet, emitting a groan, and went off down the hall. His limp was noticeably more pronounced. I found out later that he'd actually fractured his ankle in the fall.

"That is one weird guy, man." Myles said, and I agreed but I knew Myles felt the same way I did about Billy. Weird and unpredictable as he was, we couldn't help but admire him in an odd sort of way. I think all the kids wished they could be as wild and dangerous as Billy at some point.

I didn't see too much of Billy for a while. Truth be told, I guess I was avoiding him and for good reason.

The following winter, I was hanging around the local outdoor skating rink, at the bottom of the hill by the school, when I saw Billy again.

The kids had been packing the snow down on the hill with their toboggans until an unseasonal warm spell, followed by a deep freeze had turned it into glare ice. The more daring kids were trying to take the hill where it met the rink at the bottom, where the snow blowing machines had piled up drifts to the top of the boards, making a ski jump into the rink. One guy did it with his sled, starting half way down the hill, barely making it over the jump and landing on the ice rink with a thump. Another daredevil tried it standing up and lost his balance before he got to the boards.

Suddenly, everyone was pointing to the top of the hill, where a lone figure appeared to be climbing into a red wagon, maneuvering it to the lip of the slide.

It was Billy, grinning his grin, looking ridiculously small with his knees up around his ears, crammed into the tiny vehicle.

Those of us with a minimal grasp of physics quickly did the math and realized that what he was proposing to do was suicidal. The totally frictionless surface of the run, combined with the non-resistant wheels of the wagon, would give a vehicle with his mass in it a velocity that would surely propel him over the near boards and into the far side with deadly results.

We started shouting at him, pleading with him not to do it, which had the easily predictable result of egging Billy on.

Off he went, flying down the hill at incredible speed, zipping over the near boards and taking flight with a clearly lethal trajectory. Those who were in a position to see it said he never even came down before he hit the boards on the other side. People ran to the wreckage, expecting to find an ambulance case and were surprised to see Billy extricating himself from the broken wagon and standing up, grinning.

A ragged cheer went up. Billy was seen to give a wave to the crowd.

Then the rink maintenance guy showed up, angry with Billy for taking such a chance on his shift. He yelled at him, telling him if he wanted to commit suicide, he could do it at some other rink.

He told Billy he was crazy. Some of us who knew Billy better winced and took a step back.

Throwing his snow shovel down in frustration, the man turned his back on Billy and walked away.

Billy went over and picked up the shovel, a special tool that had been sharpened along the edge for shaving the rough ice, and hefted it like a spear.

"No, Billy! Don't do it!" we yelled.

But he did.

At the very last second, possibly alerted by our shouts, the rink guy turned to see what was up. He cringed away from the oncoming missile and by doing so was not decapitated by it. The shovel caught the side of his parka hood, instead, and sliced it clean through.

The poor guy called the cops, who arrived in minutes and were surprised to find that, instead of running away, Billy was just standing around like nothing had happened. Oddly, Billy gave no resistance as he was singled out and arrested. Word went around that he had gone before a judge and been remanded to his parents' custody pending trial on charges of assault with a deadly weapon.

A few weeks later, at the school's Christmas dance, Billy got into a fight with Keith Andulak, one of the school's more arrogant tough guys, at the school entrance.

These affairs generally didn't last very long. Most school fights were comprised of nothing more than a half-dozen exchanged blows, followed by a brief wrestling match before one of the belligerents cried uncle.

This one was different. They went at it for longer than the usual two or three minutes, with both guys on their feet, using fists and boots in an earnest attempt to do real bodily harm. Billy's opponent was the better fighter and landed several blows to Billy's face. It looked like his nose was broken and the blood was flowing freely down his face but Billy seemed completely oblivious as he fought on.

Slowly growing more desperate to bring the thing to an end, Keith lashed out with a solid kick that landed squarely in Billy's crotch. When even this had no visible effect on his rival, the tough guys' face suddenly showed the fear he must have been feeling.

A few seconds later, Billy landed a solid uppercut that snapped his opponent's jaw closed with an audible crack of broken teeth. It was enough for the tough guy, who slumped to the ground, unable to continue. The fight was over.

But not for Billy.

As the defeated boy lay there helplessly, Billy wound up and kicked him in the side so hard that he bounced several inches, with a groan of pain. A couple of us took a step forward, as if to intervene. We all considered Keith an asshole but even he didn't deserve this kind of treatment.

"You want some?" cried Billy. We did not.

When nobody pressed further forward, Billy kicked the boy again, as if to stress the point. He stayed there, standing over the inert body, occasionally delivering another blow, like a lion defending his kill from the jackals.

The police arrived, summoned by the school, and three burly officers tackled Billy and managed to get his hands cuffed behind his back-just. They picked him up and carried him bodily over to the squad car where he was placed non-too-gently into the back seat.

An ambulance arrived and Billy's victim was taken aboard on a gurney. Just as the ambulance was pulling away form the curb, there was another commotion near the police car.

Suddenly Billy was running down the street away from the school, hands still locked behind his back. The arresting officer had neglected to check the opposite door after putting Billy in the back seat. He'd just slid over and kicked the door handle to make his escape.

It was an easy thing to do, but the having the balls to do it was the kind of thing that set Billy apart.

The last we saw of him he was booking it up between two houses with two cops in hot pursuit, with the third peeling down the street in the squad car to cut him off on the other side of the block.

Nobody heard from Billy for a while after that. The rumors had it he'd been sent out to the medium security prison to await his trial date. After a while we just stopped thinking about him.

Then;

"Ward?"

The voice on the phone didn't sound familiar to me but somehow I knew it meant trouble.

"It's me. Billy."

"Billy. Hey, man. How's it goin?"

"It stinks, man. The pigs are lookin' for me. I broke out last night. I need you to help me."

"Oh, jeez, man, I don't know..."

"Hey, I thought you were my friend, Ward. Are you my friend, or not?"

"Yeah, sure, Billy. What is it you need?"

"I need some stuff from the drug store. You got a pen?"

An hour later, I was meeting Billy in the park by my folks' place with a bag of stuff from the Rexall. He looked rough, like he hadn't slept for a while.

"Did you get the hair dye?"

"I got it, but they didn't have the blond one. I had to get Auburn."

"Whatever, it'll be fine. Thanks, man."

"It was about twenty bucks, with the other shit."

"OK, I owe you twenty bucks. Just remember; you never saw me, right?"

"Sure Billy. I won't breathe a word."

It was maybe six weeks later that we heard Billy had been arrested, trying to get through the border into Montana. It was in the papers and everything. He had hitched a ride with a family from Lethbridge and asked them if they would mind pretending he was their son. The border guard apparently got suspicious because the families' brown hair contrasted with Billy's bright carrot orange.

After that, Billy was just gone. He disappeared into the system, and that was that.

It must have been three years later my band got booked to play the "Diagnostic and Treatment Center," which everybody knew was a polite name for the juvenile prison. We didn't know what to expect, but a gig was a gig and the government tended to rehire you if you did a good job.

It was mid-winter, in the middle of a cold snap. The temperature had been hovering below minus twenty-five all week and that night it was supposed to take a nose dive. I froze my fingers helping to load up.

We drove our equipment to the outskirts of town in a rented U-haul trailer. We waited to get through the automatic gate in the chain-link fence and pulled up to the low concrete building just around six. We were directed to a loading bay and a couple of guys in uniforms helped us unload the stuff, even finding a big freight dolly to move the amps and speakers through a short maze of grey painted hallways to the smallish auditorium stage.

"You guys get set up by 6:30, there's steak dinner in the cafeteria. You're welcome to join us. Just let someone know before you come."

Steak dinner? No two words went together more poetically for a bunch of eighteen-year-olds who had been subsisting on Kraft dinner and garden raiding. We set a new record getting the stage set up. We found one of the guards standing at the door to the gym and asked where the cafeteria was. He had a short conversation on his walkie-talkie with someone and told us to follow him.

Down the hall and around a corner and through some metal doors, we found ourselves on the set of a prison movie, only this was no movie.

The metal chairs, bolted to the floor, the bullet-proof sneeze guard between the inmates and the kitchen staff, the aluminum trays were all very real. We lined up behind the last few orange coveralled inmates and moved through the pass, collecting our meals as we went. Our guard/guide ushered us to the extreme end of a long table and seated us near the door.

We lost no time tucking into the meal, which made up for what it lacked in flavor by the generous portions. As we ate, one of the orange-garbed inmates at the other end of the table seemed to be trying to get our attention. The guards noticed him waving at us and stepped over to have a word with him but he persisted.

Suddenly Percy recognized him.

"Holy shit, man; that's Billy Sanderson!'

Four of us squinted at the animated figure. Sure enough. He looked a lot older and worse for wear but it was Billy, all right. His head was shaved completely and he'd packed on a lot of weight, but the thing that gave him away was the big, unmistakable shit-eating grin on his face. I'd have known that grin anywhere.

"You're right, man. That's him."

"Wow, I wonder what he's in for."

"I don't."

Just then the guards started telling everyone to eat up. Mealtime was over and they wanted to get everything cleared away so the "dance" could start on time. The guy who'd shown us the way came over to us.

"You guys just stay seated until we get the room cleared, OK? Everybody's going back to their rooms for a few minutes and then we'll get you back to the gym. We want you boys on stage before we bring 'em in, and we'd like you stay up on the stage all night, all right?"

At this, the guards started herding our audience out of the cafeteria, starting at the far ends of the table. It was all done in strict control, everybody in line and moving ahead only when told to do so.

Billy's line came right past where we remained seated. As he drew near he approached us.

"Hey, you guys! Are you the band? This is so cool. Man, I haven't seen you guys for a long time. How you doing?"

"Hey, Billy, good to see you."

"It's been a while."

"How's it hangin', Billy?"

And then he was gone, ushered out the door with his line, presumably back to his "room". The guard came over to us.

"Listen, guys, I don't think it's a good idea you makin' too friendly with any of these people, OK? There ain't a lot of good can come of it."

"Oh, no, sir; we know that guy."

"You know Billy? From where?"

"We all grew up together. We went to school with him."

The guard was suddenly looking very concerned.

"You *all* went to school with Billy Sanderson? Fuck." He thumbed the button on his radio.

"Bill? Listen; we may have a situation here. Turns out the guys in the band know Billy Sanderson. Grew up with him...yeah, he recognized them-came over to say hello. Right. That's what I'm thinking. OK, I'll handle this end. You check his room."

We looked at each other, wondering what all the fuss was about.

"I think we'll just have you guys stay here with me, for now, guys. You want a cup of coffee, or something? More jello?"

Just then the little light on his radio went on. He spoke into the mike, listened to his ear plug.

"Yeah, Bill. Right. You got it."

Then he spoke to the other two guards there in the room.

"Danny, Mike, we got a situation. Billy's not in his room. Mike; you want to go help Bill find him? Thank you. Danny, let's count the silverware."

Danny went around behind the Plexiglas and began doing just that. Our man stayed with us, keeping his eyes on the doorway. We sat wondering if we should laugh or not for maybe two minutes, then Danny came back out of the kitchen.

"One fork missing," he said. He joined us as the other guard spoke once more to his mike. Somewhere a buzzer started ringing.

"We are going to lock-down. Danny, if you want to lead the way, I'll take the rear and we'll get these gentlemen back to the gym. You ready? OK, lets go."

The two of them marched us back to the stage and took up station at the doors to the auditorium. The incessant ring of the buzzer was the only sound for several more minutes. Then the guard called "Mike" came back to us and told our man something we didn't hear over the alarm.

Leaving Mike to guard the door, our guide came over to the stage.

"Well, it looks like the dance is not going to happen, guys. Billy has gone missing and one of the other boys has been attacked. Stabbed in his room. He'll require hospitalization. Given the circumstances, our guidelines are quite clear; the dance is cancelled and we need to get you boys packed up and out of here, now. Don't worry; you'll still get paid; this wasn't you guys' fault. I'm sorry you had to come all the way out here just to load up again but that's the way it is."

So, we broke all the equipment down and piled it all back onto the dolly and into the U-haul. We had mixed feelings about the gig being cancelled. It was going to be weird night anyways, with no females in the room, but a gig is a gig and when you get ready to play, well, that's what you want to do, regardless of the circumstances.

Still, we were up one steak dinner and had the rest of the night off with pay. Plus, we'd gotten to see Billy again, no matter how briefly.

There was a somber silence in the car as we pulled away from the loading bay. Joe negotiated the parking lot, mindful of the trailer behind us and we made for the automated gate. Joe stopped ten feet from the gate and after a second it began to open for us. The thing was slow with the cold weather and screeched like a banshee as it rolled open on its wheeled track.

Then, suddenly, the gate stopped. There was a sound of switches engaging and it started to close again.

"What the hell?" mumbled Jeff. No sooner were the words out of his mouth than there was a clattering sound and a series of thumps from behind us. Looking in the big trailer-towing rear-view mirror, I saw a figure in orange, clambering down from the roof of the U-haul.

"What the hell?" I echoed.

It was Billy. He had somehow made it into the loading bay while the guards were searching for him inside and climbed up on the top of the U-haul. He must have been there all the time while we were loading the equipment into it, only the six-foot height of the trailer had kept anyone from seeing him.

I guess he'd planned on staying there until he was safely on the other side of the fence and then making his presence known. Instead, one of the guys at the center must have spotted him, maybe from a second floor window, orange coveralls stark against the white trailer roof. The alarm had been sounded, the gate closed, but not quite in time.

Billy jumped down from the wheel hub and ran past the car to squeeze, just in time, through the disappearing gap in the gate. Off he went, sprinting down the lonely road out to the main highway, hoping to make it there before the staff could organize a chase.

The gate clanged shut in front of us then almost immediately began to open again. Lights came on in the loading bay and the sound of motors starting reached us across the parking lot. Two pickup trucks, painted in Correction Service grey, came barreling towards us at high speed. The window rolled down on the lead truck.

"Hey, you guys! Get out of the way!"

We were blocking the road. The gate was all the way open by now, so Jeff drove us through and down the road far enough to angle the car and trailer as far over to the shoulder as he dared. The side of the road was ill-defined with snow banks and we were risking a trip into the ditch. The vehicles tilted alarmingly and the trailer swayed a bit as we came to a halt.

The first truck pulled out around us, the driver spinning his tires to catch up with Billy. He hit a bare patch of black ice just before he got clear, fishtailed and went nose first into the ditch on the other side of the narrow road, blocking it completely. He spun his tires frantically but with no success.

The driver of the second truck pulled up behind us and stopped. He jumped out of the cab and ran to the driver's side window.

"You're going to have to pull ahead, far enough for me to get by," he instructed, "Try to stay over as far as you can."

With that, he ran back to his truck while we started off again. Jeff sidled along carefully about a hundred feet. The prison truck drove through the emptied space and carefully steered around us. As soon as he'd cleared the car, the driver put the lights and siren on and gunned it down the road.

We followed at a slower pace, unsure if we wanted to get too close. There was no sign of Billy for a quarter mile.

"Look," said Percy, pointing.

A pair of bright orange coveralls hung from a tree, flapping gently in the breeze like some macabre Halloween decoration. There was no sign of Billy.

"Jesus Christ. That Sanderson is a crazy bastard." Doug said.

"Crazy like a fox," Gary replied, "He probably had this planned from the start, man. He took the fork at dinner, made a fuss with us at the table to get the guards excited and made it out to the loading bay before they started looking for him. Think about it. He knew they'd lock the place down, but he needed them to cancel the dance and send us home, or he was going to spend the evening freezing his nuts off on top of the U-haul, with no way over the fence."

"You mean he stabbed that guy..." I started. I was horrified at the thought that had just occurred to me.

"As a means to an end, man; all part of the plan. Like I said-crazy like a fox."

We drove on for another half a mile or so. We could see the flashing lights of the prison truck ahead of us. Rounding a curve we saw headlights moving along the highway. The truck ahead of us made a u-turn at the intersection and came back toward us, driving real slow and playing a spotlight into the ditch and the adjacent field. As we came abreast the driver rolled down his window. Jeff did likewise.

"Did you guys see anything?"

We told him about the coveralls.

"Yup, I saw that, too. Crazy bastard's runnin' around out here in his skivvies. Well, no use you guys hanging around..."

The other guard in the pickup said something to the driver.

"Just hold on a second, guys."

The passenger got out and went around to the rear of the truck. He climbed up on the bed and aimed the beam of a flashlight across the roof of the trailer. Apparently satisfied, he jumped down and got back in the cab.

"You really think he would have tried that again?" his partner asked.

"Hey, this is Billy we're talkin' about. Nothing that guy does surprises me anymore."

"Think he had time to get out to the highway? Catch a ride?"

"Who's gonna stop for some nut case in his underwear, in the middle of the night outside a correctional facility? Naw, he's out here, somewhere. I hope he freezes his ass off."

We said goodnight and drove out to the main road and home. There was no sign of Billy Sanderson, then or ever again. The last I ever saw of him, he was running past our car, making for the gate, still grinning like the Cheshire cat.

GHOST STORY

One of the things you need to get used to if you spend time in the North is the light. The higher latitudes are affected by the seasons in ways that can be disorienting to the tenderfoot, to say the least.

Yellowknife is on the 62nd parallel, a mere 512km from the Arctic Circle and therefore is subject to extremes of both daylight and darkness. On June 21, the winter solstice, the sun doesn't rise until 10:08am and goes down again at 3:05 in the afternoon.

During the summer the sun hardly goes down at all. It's the land of the midnight sun.

It's kind of novel, at first. You tend to stay awake all night and sleep only when you are too tired to stay up. The people who live there get a lot done in a day that's twenty plus hours long and they do get used to it but for the first time visitor there is a period of adjustment. It's kind of like jet lag-your interior clock is at odds with your reality. It can play tricks with your perceptions.

Of course, the cold temperatures are another force to be reckoned with. Even in springtime the winter chill can linger and keep you indoors for days at a time.

We had a week of mild weather when we first arrived, lulling us into a false sense of indifference to the weather and then it plummeted to thirty-five below for ten days solid. We were pretty tired of staying in the hotel by the time it let up a bit.

Gary and I decided to take advantage of the break in the weather and take a walk over to the part of town known as "old town." We were told that there was a peninsula of sorts, a group of little islets in the lake.

There was a little hill there, a rocky outcrop known locally as "The Rock" in the middle of all the old wooden buildings, crowned by a monument to the bush pilots who'd opened up this country. Not much to look at by all accounts but still, it was something to do.

We followed the road past a puzzling variety of properties, from steel Quonset huts and tarpaper shacks to log cabins, some of which looked to be a hundred years old. It would be hard to say what category the neighborhood would fall into if it were situated down south. Back home, there were zoning laws and regulations to separate the light industrial use of land from the residential but up here it seemed like everything was mixed.

It was another example of the harsh pragmatism that was forced on people who chose to live this far North. There was no room for polite concerns in a place like this. If you needed to do some welding on your floatplane in your driveway, there was no one to complain about it. None of your neighbors knew when they might need to do something similar.

We went past one yard that was home to about fifty dogs. Big, sturdy-looking huskys, they were obviously sled dogs. They did their obligatory barking, chains rattling as they leapt and strained against them, all except one big male that was caged apart from the others. He just stood still, watching us with a steady gaze until Gary remarked on it.

"Man, I'm glad that guy's in a cage."

"No shit. Look at size of him."

"I think he's a wolf."

"You're kidding."

"I heard they like to catch them as pups and raise them to breed with the huskys. A guy in the bar last night was talking about it. Said you're allowed to have a quarter wolf in your sled dogs."

We continued on past the dog yard, not wishing to tease them any more than we already had.

"You know, that makes sense, now that I think about it. There was somebody talking about how they shoot strays here. No questions asked, just blammo, doggone. He said it's because they can't take a chance it might be a wolf or a wolf cross."

"Well, I hope everybody has good fences."

"I bet they do. These dogs are really valuable up here. They run races in the winter, like a thousand fuckin' miles or something across the tundra-prizes are huge."

"Yeah, I heard."

"That'd be a trip, eh? Mushing across the empty wasteland at forty below, with only your trusty dogs for company."

"Yeah, I think you can go ahead. I'll just wait here and keep the beer cold."

"You have no romance in your soul, man."

"Romance I got. Also common sense and a deeply entrenched survival instinct."

We were coming to the hill where the monument stood stark against the ice blue sky. There was an old log structure on the side of the road with a sign over the door that read "Wild Cat Café".

It didn't look like it was open for business but it was hard to tell in the half-lit gloom. Gary tried the door. It was locked but as we turned back down the sidewalk, a voice came through the window.

"Come back at six!"

"uh.. OK!" I shouted back, "see you then!"

There was no answer. We continued on towards the "Rock." A set of wooden steps had been built into the bare rock of the hill, winding up to the top, perhaps a twenty foot vertical ascent made longer and easier by the meandering stairs.

We proceeded to the top and spent a moment reading the brass plaque that was bolted to the stone spire. The view was amazing. From up here, right on the little rocky outcrop and elevated above the treetops it was suddenly plain that Great Slave Lake was something to see.

The lake was still frozen over and appeared like a vast, empty white plain. It covered the horizon for half our view and stretched as far as the eye could see, which was pretty far. In the all-night twilight of a northern day in May, the whole scene looked unworldly.

I remember thinking that this might be what it looks like on Mars, with the endless desert stretching away for thousands of miles in all directions. It was easy to imagine oneself on another planet in that light. Then I remembered the map we'd studied briefly in the lobby before we'd left the hotel.

The town was set in a bay off the main body of the lake. The peninsula we were standing on extended into the bay, so we couldn't even see the whole lake from there.

What we were looking at was only an inlet. I mentioned it to Gary.

"Yeah, you're right," he mused.

"Wow," was all I could muster for a comment.

"Wow, indeed," Gary agreed.

We stayed up there for half an hour or so, pointing out significant landmarks to one another and cracking jokes about ice fishing and such, until the breeze off the lake came up and threatened to freeze us where we stood.

As we beat a hasty retreat down the stairs, my eyes fell on a bank of earth that had been cut away at the base of the rock to facilitate the stairway. They'd used heavy equipment to slice across a gravel esker about twelve feet high, exposing the permafrost to the sun, which had been steadily eroding the cut since.

About three feet up, a stone had been uncovered. I could see where the newly thawed dirt around it had sloughed away and fallen in a mini landslide, leaving the rock, which looked to be about a foot across, jutting out from the bank. What caught my eye was the seemingly perfect symmetry of it. I pointed it out to Gary.

"What if it's like that on the other side?" I suggested.

"That'd be cool. Maybe we can come back in ten years, when the whole thing is free and see."

"Why wait?"

"C'mon, you're not going to try to dig that thing outta there?"

"Why not?"

"Well, for starters it might take all day. You'll freeze your butt off. Besides, this is a monument, man-it's like sacred ground, or something."

"Nah, the monument is on top of the hill. This is the bottom of the hill. I'm gonna give it a shot. Maybe it'll come out easy."

"What if you go to all that work and the other side is just a lump?"

"Well, at least I'll know."

"Okay," said Gary, checking his watch, "well, it's six fifteen, so I will be at yonder Wildcat Café, having breakfast. Join me when you give up."

"Alright. See you in a bit," I called to his back as he disappeared around the rock.

I climbed over the handrail and started digging.

It didn't come out easy but I didn't give up, either. It took about ten minutes of hard work, clawing away at the frozen earth with a discarded piece of wood I found under the stairs. I tried to work all around the circular base at first. Then, as I realized just how hard the permafrost was, I began concentrating my efforts at the bottom of the stone. I figured the weight of it would work for me, if I removed the stuff that was holding it up. I was right.

No sooner had I scooped a few inches of stuff away from under the bottom edge, the stone moved. At first it dropped about an inch, leaving a similar sized gap above it. Wedging my stick into the void, I used it as a lever, pushing up on it against the frozen ground above.

The stone came loose in a shower of gravel and I had to do some fancy footwork to avoid having it roll over my foot. To my delight, I saw that it was symmetrical; an almost perfect sphere of grey granite about the size of a soccer ball.

I used my stick to scrape the last bits of gravel off and gave it a quick polish with my gloves. Then I picked the thing up and took it over to the Wildcat Café to show Gary.

"Holy shit!" he exclaimed when he saw it, "it is round!"

"Not round-spherical," I replied, "Pretty cool, eh?"

"Very cool. Now that you've got it, what are you going to do with it?"

"I don't know. I hadn't thought much past just getting it out of the ground."

"I doubt if they'll let you take it up to your room."

"I'll just have to smuggle it, then."

Just then a wide, bearded individual came out of the kitchen with a plate of eggs and bacon, which he place in front of Gary.

"There you go," he said to Gary, "Morning," to me.

"Morning. Any chance I can get one of those?"

"You bet. Say, what do have there? A mountain egg?"

"Mountain egg? Hey I like that. Yeah, man-this is my mountain egg."

"That's what folks call them things around here. People are always finding them in the ground around these glacial eskers. Seems like they start out just normal shaped rocks and then they get caught under the glacier and rolled for a few thousand years until they get ground into spheres. They come all sizes. That's a nice one."

"Wow, that's good to know. I just like it. I think I'm taking it home with me."

"Ooo, I don't know if that's a good idea."

"What do you mean?"

"Well, the native people say that, if you take a mountain egg too far from the ground it's found in, it'll never hatch."

"Hatch? Jesus Christ, I'd like to see that."

"Just saying. I'll get your eggs on."

"Thanks."

"Nice guy," I commented to Gary after he'd disappeared into the back.

"Seems like. So you're really going to carry that thing all the way back to the hotel?"

"Why not?"

"You mean, other than the obvious reasons, like you're going to give yourself a hernia?"

"It isn't that heavy. Besides, I like it. There isn't a hell of lot else of interest around here. You can't even sleep in, 'cause the sun never goes down."

"Oh, it goes down, all right," our host put in as he returned from the kitchen with a plate of food, "just not this time of year. You have to come in the wintertime. Sun goes down then, about two in the afternoon. Don't come up again 'till ten o'clock in the mornin'."

He put the plate down in front of me and I tucked right in. The host lingered, stroking his long red beard. I didn't mind. I had the impression that, like a lot of people that cook for a living, he took pleasure out of watching his customers enjoy his food. I had a good appetite after the long walk in the cold.

"Wow; totally dark for twenty hours. That must be a little hard to take," Gary said.

While our host refilled our coffees from an old fashioned enameled percolator, he went on.

"Hard for some folks, for sure. Some can't take it at all. Them kinds of people don't tend to last up here too long. Spring comes, you see 'em headin' back down south. Them what's made it through the winter at all; some don't."

"How do you mean?"

"Cabin fever sets in, people do some strange things. There's always one or two thinks they can last it out and stay until it's too late to get out and then they just go round the bend."

"Suicide, you mean?"

"Yep; couple or three every winter. You find 'em, rolled up in their bedroll, empty bottle of pills beside 'em, or hangin' from the rafters. One old boy tried to hang his self last January, found out he hadn't built his cabin roof as strong as he thought."

"What happened?"

"Pulled the roof down on his self. Neighbors heard the racket and pulled him out, laughin' his head off. Thought it was the funniest thing in the world. Didn't stop laughin' until spring when they put him on a truck back to the world. Maybe still laughin' for all I know. Warm you up?"

I said yes please and he filled my cup.

"Some people get right creative about it. A few years back there was a guy come up from the states somewheres; nice enough fella. Wanted to set up a commercial smokehouse. Figured he could buy the fish right off the dock, fillet 'em up and smoke 'em, then ship the smoked fish down south. There's a big peat bog just south of town where he harvested the stuff for the smoke fires. Sprinkled some birch chips on top. Birch smells real nice when it burns. Worked real good. Kippered whitefish. Wasn't bad eatin'. We bought some and served it for a season. Folks snapped it up; nice change from bacon every mornin'. He made out well 'till that first winter, then he started to show the signs."

"The signs?"

"Oh, well; folks who don't make it through a winter tend to exhibit certain behaviors right before they slip off into the deep end. Starin' into space, not knowing when they're bein' talked to. Then they start talkin' to themselves, right before the end."

"Yeah? So what happened in the end?"

"Well, he sorta started keepin' to his self more and more, like they do and sooner or later somebody remarked they hadn't seen 'im in a while. Then somebody else said so and at some point, somebody took it on themselves to go down to his place and check. That's what folks do up here, we look out for our neighbors, especially in winter. There's none of us hasn't felt the cold and lonely of a February."

He was wiping the counter with his cloth at that point and he stopped to finish his story.

"They found him hanging from the roof of his smokehouse, with a nice smoky peat fire goin' under him. He was the color of a tarnished penny and tanned like good saddle leather. He'd smoked his self. How's that for creative?"

"It's like something out of a Robert Service poem."

"I wouldn't know; I don't read no poetry."

He said his name was Willie. He had been up North a long time, although he was oddly vague about just how long. Willie had plenty of good stories to tell. Gary and I sat there in the warm café, drinking coffee and listening to him for most of the morning.

When it was time to leave, as I picked up the stone, Willie made one more appeal.

"You should really reconsider taking that thing home with you," he said, "no good can come of it."

"Right, well, I don't think I'm doing any harm by it, either."

"No-you ain't doin' harm, but harm can come of it anyways, maybe."

"Still, I really like it. Thanks for the breakfast and the stories."

"You paid for the breakfast. The stories are free. Thanks for the company, boys."

We said our goodbyes and went out into the dimly lit morning air. On the walk back to the hotel we noticed it was getting colder again. We hurried to get in out of the weather.

As we neared the entrance I took a moment to conceal the mountain egg under my jacket. Gary went straight over to distract the desk clerk with some made-up question, while I made a beeline for the elevator with my treasure. Just as the elevator door was closing, a hand reached in and stopped it. A middle-aged couple got on and we exchanged pleasantries.

The man punched the button for their floor and we did that studious not-looking-at-each-other thing that people do on elevators, though I could tell they were having a hard time not turning to ogle me with my bulging front. I must have looked nine months pregnant.

I got the stone to my room without further incident and put it on the chair by the window, carefully nesting it in with a towel to avoid any falls. I didn't know what it would sound like downstairs if the thing rolled off onto the floor but I didn't want to risk having the security guy come up to investigate.

It was Sunday and the tavern was closed. I hadn't planned on being gone so long on our little sojourn and I'd wanted to get some writing done before lunch but the fresh air and my exertions freeing the mountain egg from it's nest had taken a toll. We'd been up drinking after the gig the night before and things were catching up to me. I needed a nap.

I lay down and covered myself with the woolen Hudson's Bay blanket the hotel put in every room. I was thinking about Willie, the café cook and the stories he'd told as I drifted off into what promised to be a delicious mid-day snooze when a sound close by brought me abruptly back from the abyss.

It was a gruff croak, like a bird sound. It seemed to have come from behind me, so I rolled over on the bed, bringing my face up next to the window. There, not six inches from my nose and separated from it only by the windowpane, was a huge raven. He was perched on the sill, looking in at me intently.

As I recognized the shape for what it was, he let go with another croak. It sounded like someone gargling with marbles.

I recoiled to the other side of the bed, pulling the blanket up over me as if it would provide any protection, should the beast decide to attack. One look at his powerful beak gave me all the assurance I needed that, if he wanted to, he could be through that fragile window glass before I could get to the door.

Not that I was in the habit of being afraid of birds, but this one had taken me by surprise. I wasn't in the habit of being this close to a bird, either-especially one the size of this. With the exception of the turkeys on my uncles' farm, I don't think I'd ever *seen* a bird the size of this raven. He must have been two feet tall and heavy; ruffled looking the way they are.

The raven and I regarded each other silently through the window, me trying to decide whether it would be wise to try to make my way out of the room, while he just stared at me with an unwavering glare that I found quit unnerving. He looked like he might be sizing me up for his next meal.

As much as I wanted to just leave the room and hope he'd lose interest if he had no one to ogle, I feared that any action on my part might elicit an attack. I couldn't decide what to do, so I did nothing until the raven let out another of his ghastly squawks.

That did it. I threw the covers away and leapt to my feet. Pausing only to snatch my shoes up on my way out, I made a dash for the door expecting any second to hear the crash of the window behind me. Slamming the door, I stood panting in the hall. I turned my head to see a maid looking at me from the end of the hall. We regarded each other for a few seconds, then I gave her a friendly wave and started putting my shoes on. She muttered something under her breath and went on her way.

I found Doug and Percy in the coffee shop. I ordered a java and joined them, looking a bit disheveled from the escape from my room, apparently, because Doug asked me if I was all right. I told them about the raven.

"You mean you got that scared over a *bird*?" he asked, incredulous.

"It wasn't just a bird, man-you should have seen the size of it!"

"I've been noticing them around town," offered Percy, "they are pretty big, all right."

"What's that?" asked the waitress, bringing me my coffee.

"The ravens. We've been noticing the big ones around town."

"Oh, yes, they're a caution. You don't want to let your puppies play outside alone. I heard one tried to take a baby-picked it up and only dropped it cause the mother threw something."

"Wow. That's a big bird."

"And the way it just sat there, peering in at me...it just spooked me, I guess."

"I guess. So, what are you doing with the rest of your day off?"

"I don't know. Just taking it easy, I think. I'm pretty bushed."

"Doug and me are going to go check out the Co-op. See if they have anything good."

It was a well-known fact that one of the perks of being on the road and staying in small towns was that the local merchandisers often didn't change their stock for decades. You could find things on a visit to a small town store that hadn't been available in the city for years. It was one of the ways we kept from going too stir crazy on road trips.

It was tempting but I found myself reluctant to go outside when I knew that big black bastard might still be around.

"I think I'll pass. I'll see you guys later."

I spent some time wandering through the hotel, getting to know the lay of the place. It never hurts to know how a building maps out, especially if you're going to be living there for a month. I chatted with a couple of the maids and cadged some extras off their trolleys for my room. After a while I ended up going down to the tavern to do a little work on my drum set.

I had been experiencing some problems with my hi-hat the last few nights. There are lots of moving parts and things that can go wrong on a modern drum set but any drummer will agree that the most common source of trouble was that ingenious device called the hi-hat.

The hi-hat is the machine that allows a drummer to crash two cymbals together without the use of his hands. The first "hats" were low to the ground, ten inches or so high, limited to allowing the drummer to play the two cymbals only against each other. It was called the "low boy" or "low hat." This expanded the drummers' repertoire of sounds by exactly two; he could mash the cymbals down in closed position for a "chick," or clash them open for a ringing crash.

No one knows whom it was that first decided he wanted to play the hat with sticks but by the mid thirties the "hi-hat" was in common use. With the cymbals mounted up at the same level as the rest of the drums, they could be played in either open or closed position, and soon drummers found ways of combining the two, adding a variety of different sounds and combinations and finally giving the modern traps man something useful to do with his left foot.

The design is pretty simple and although the latest models are made considerably more robust than those early prototypes, no one in the drum hardware manufacturing business has yet come up with a hi-hat that will withstand the abuse it receives at the hands (or foot, I suppose) of a rock drummer who is trying to make himself heard over two or three amplified guitars and a big P.A. system.

My hi-hat was a good one; not the best you could get, but the best I could afford and made pretty well. It was one of the first designs to incorporate something new in the field-the neoprene gasket. These wonderful plastic inserts served to make every connection where metal met metal stronger, less prone to slip and more resistant to wear. They did not, however, do anything about the weakest point in any hi-hat; the connection between the foot pedal and the rod.

This was where all the impact of the players' energy was delivered to the device. It needed to be stronger than the manufacturers realized to meet the needs of the modern rock drummer. This vital link was constantly breaking down.

Of course, it wasn't nearly as bad as having your bass drum pedal malfunction. The hi-hat could still be played in the closed position with the sticks, it just felt weird not to be able to play the foot pedal. When your bass pedal went, you were really off balance. Like most professional players, I'd learned to keep a spare bass pedal handy. I suppose one could do the same with the hat but there's only so much room in a trap case. I guess drummers who tour with big concert bands and are paid enough to afford all the equipment they want, would have an extra hi-hat or two set up and ready for emergencies. It must be nice to have somebody else carry all that heavy hardware to and from the trucks, as well.

For a working schlub like me, it was an ongoing game of attrition and a never- ending maintenance schedule.

Right now, the problem was with the connection at the toe of the hi-hat pedal where it attached to the rod. This was done differently on different models and makes. Some used a leather strap. Later, some replaced that with a metal one. Still other varieties had a short length of bicycle chain to serve the purpose. Mine was a hybrid, with five links of chain attached to a metal strap by means of a large rivet. It worked fine when it was working and was relatively noiseless, too; an important consideration that many drum manufacturers seemed unaware of.

The trouble was the rivet itself. While the rest of the stand was made of pretty good steel, the rivet was of some softer stuff. Aluminum, I suspect. Whatever it was, it was too soft for the job and tended to bend and twist under the constant pounding. Eventually a limit was reached and the metal would part at the weakest point, generally in the middle of a set on a busy Saturday night.

After three such occurrences, I had decided to try to deal with the problem once and for all by replacing the rivet with a steel bolt. It had worked fine for a few months and then the bolt had failed, shorn through at the same spot. I told a friends' dad, who was a machinist about it and he told me that the bolt was likely aluminum as well.

"They're making all this stuff in Asia, now," he said, "No quality control at all. A good steel bolt should take that kind of wear for decades. The problem is trying to find one. They've been selling this crap as steel long enough that the old stock is all gone most places. You're lucky to come across any. You'll know it when you do, though; it'll cost ten times as much."

The thought occurred to me that I might have better luck finding old stock steel hardware in one of the small towns we played, so I started making the hardware store my first stop in a new town. It wasn't long before my search was rewarded with the discovery of a little Ma & Pa hardware with a complete inventory of nuts and bolts, all clearly stamped "Shefield Steel." I bought a dozen each of anything they had that would fit anything I had.

It took me half an hour to drill out the busted piece and replace it with a nice new British steel bolt. It worked like a charm and looked like it would last forever.

As I worked up on the stage, I gradually became aware that I was being watched. There shouldn't have been anyone there on a Sunday except for the cleaning staff, so I was surprised to see a man sitting at a table by the dance floor, with a highball glass half empty before him.

He was a big guy, dressed in rawhide. The coat he had on was beaded heavily and fringed on the arms and across the chest. From what I'd seen in the shops around town, it would probably cost a thousand bucks. His pants were doe hide and the muk-luks he wore were decorated with polar bear fur. A Stetson hat was about the only thing he wore that didn't look home-made. He must have come in while I was busy and making noise with my drill.

"Good morning," I offered.

"How you doin'?" came the reply, "looks like you're a pretty handy guy."

He was an older man, weathered and grizzled, resting his arm on an old trapper Nelson-style backpack that rested in the seat next to him. His long legs extended out into the dance floor.

"What, this?" I indicated the newly refurbished hi-hat, "that's just what you have to do when you're on the road. No music repair shops up here, I guess."

"No, you'd be right about that. Gunsmiths, mechanics, boat builders, yes. I don't think you'd be finding any musical instrument repair places around here. Folks mostly rely on their own selves for stuff like that. You gotta know how to improvise up here."

"I guess," I answered.

I went over to the bar and poured myself a glass of water from the spigot. The guy seemed friendly enough and willing to sit and chat, so I went over and took seat at his table.

"Mind if I join you?"

"Not at all, young fella," he said, "tell me, where did someone your age learn to improvise repairs like that? You're not from around here, are you?"

"Nope. I'm from Edmonton. My dad was a farm boy, grew up in Mayerthorpe. In his day they were pretty isolated up there. If something broke down, they generally had to make their own repairs. He used to do the same on things around the house-why run to the hardware store and spend good money on a part, when you could make one just as easily? I guess the habit kind of rubbed off."

"Good habit to have, in these parts. I knew people that would have died if they didn't have the knack. Hunters, trappers; people who make their living off the land, they got to do things for themselves. I tell you who is the best at it; the Inuit. I knew a Inuit guy years back, took me out to hunt for walrus in the pack ice off Hudson Bay. We were in his Umiak; hide boat, wonderful light but strong for all that, and no sooner do we get out in the ice than the outboard motor breaks down."

He paused for a drink. I noticed how tiny the highball glass looked in his big, calloused hand.

"That guy just laid out a blanket on the bottom of the boat and started taking the engine apart, piece by piece, until he found a piece that was broken. Throttle linkage. Then he roots around in his hunters' sack and comes up with a piece of seal bone. Damned if this particular bone wasn't almost the right size and shape to start with but in about five minutes, he's whittled it down to an exact fit. Put that motor back together and off we went."

"Wow. That's amazing."

"Amazing to you or me, sure. To those people, it's just business as usual. Living up in the North weeds out the folks that don't have that kind of skill pretty quick."

"I guess."

"People come up here for all kinds of reasons," he said, "some come for the gold, or the fur. Some come up here for the hunting or the fishing. If they are wise, they leave once they find what they want, otherwise this country will get into your blood and then you're lost. Once it gets into your blood, you can't ever get away, even if you do leave. You come back."

He paused for another drink.

"You see them, every summer, getting off the planes. They think they've come back for some more hunting, or fishing, or to look for gold in a different place but that's not why they're here. You can see it in their eyes, if you know how to look for it; they're here because they can't stay away. They come back to try to understand why it is they can't stop thinking about the place. Why they need to come one more time, and one more time after that."

The big man picked up his glass and drained it.

"Well, I got to get going. Nice chatting with you, son. I hope your repairs hold up."

He stood up and shrugged on his parka, then extended his hand to me. I shook it, standing myself. It was time for me to go, too.

"Thanks for the story."

"Oh, there's lot's where that one came from. I'll see you around."

He made his way to the door and left, the heavy security door banging closed behind him.

I went back to the stage and started cleaning up my tools and stuff. One of the hotel's two security guys came into the bar from the lobby.

"Hi," I said. It always pays to be civil with the security guys.

"Oh, it's you," he replied, "I heard the outside door close. Were you looking for something outside?"

"No, I came through the lobby door, same as you did. That was a customer leaving just now."

"Customer?" he said, "the bar's closed. Nobody should be in here except staff until noon. Who did you say this was?"

"An older guy, a local, I think. Big man, dressed like a hunter. He had a drink; I guess he must have helped himself."

The guard didn't comment on that. He went over to the outside door and tried it.

"You said he went out this door?" he asked.

"Yeah, just a couple of minutes ago. You heard it close, right?"

"I heard something, but it wasn't this door. This door is double locked, as it's supposed to be. The only way to get in or out this door is with a key."

"I didn't see him use a key to get out. He just pushed on it and went out, then it swung back and slammed."

"Not possible. This door's locked. Here-try it yourself."

I did. To my surprise, he was right; the door was locked solidly. I was starting to feel paranoid again.

"That's weird," I told him, "I watched him go out this door. Could it have locked itself?"

"Nope. Doesn't work that way. Your friend must have had a key with him. You just didn't notice him use it."

"I guess. Weird."

"Actually, the weird thing is, he didn't set off the alarm. You have to turn it off before you open the doors or it goes off automatically. Now I have to test it."

He took his walkie-talkie from his belt and addressed it. "Central, this Rob. Testing tavern door alarm."

He went back to the door and, using his key, he opened it. Immediately, a claxon started up somewhere in the hotel. Rob closed the door again and re-locked it.

"Well, that's working."

"So how come it didn't go off when he went out?" I asked.

"Dunno. It should have. Look, if you see any more characters hanging around in here off hours, you let me or the other guard know, all right?"

"Sure. No problem," I agreed, feeling a bit shaken. I decided to go back up to my room for a while and see if I could get a little nap in before we had to play.

As I approached the door to my room, Gary came out of his room across the hall. He was looking uncharacteristically thoughtful as he beckoned to me.

"Hey, man. Got a minute? Yeah? Come on in."

I followed him into his room and sat down. Gary remained standing. Up close, he was looking downright flustered.

"What's up?" I asked him.

"Listen, this might sound odd, or something, but I just need to know; did we go for a walk early this morning over to old town?"

"Yeah, of course we did."

"OK, I thought I might have dreamed it, or something." He paused, staring absently into space and pulling on his bottom lip.

"So, what's the deal?" I prompted, startling him back to awareness.

"Um, well, Listen; did we or did we not have breakfast at that little diner there? The Wild Cat Café; remember the guy there, the owner?"

"Yeah, of course we did. The guy told us some stories about the place, about the town and stuff. We had bacon and eggs, Three bucks. We both paid with fives and told him to keep the change. Why?"

"That's the way I remember it, too."

He went back to staring at the wall.

"So, are you going to tell me what the deal is, or not?"

"I was having lunch in the restaurant downstairs. I told the waitress about this morning and she got really freaked out. Then she got mad 'cause she thought I was trying to bullshit her.

She told me that the Wild Cat Café has been closed for, like ten years. It closed after the owner, who she described as a big guy with a red beard, hung himself in the kitchen."

We looked at each other silently for a minute.

"The Wild Cat Café."

"Yup."

"Why would she say that?" I ventured.

"I went back, man. I walked back to Old Town and I found the place again. It's closed, just like she said. It looks like it's been closed a long time. The roof is half caved in and the floor is collapsing."

"Yeah, but…" I didn't know what to say after that. It was obvious Gary wasn't lying to me, or playing some kind of joke.

"So what the fuck was that, this morning? We imagined the whole thing, both of us?"

"No, I don't think so, man."

"Well, then, what?"

"I'm just not going to think about it anymore, that's what. I don't want to talk about it, either. Just forget about the whole thing, alright?"

"Alright, I guess. Jesus."

"I don't think Jesus had anything to do with it."

I went back to my room, feeling more paranoid that ever. I opened the door and there, on the chair, was the mountain egg.

It was months later, after we'd finished up our gig in Yellowknife and returned to the city. I'd brought the mountain egg home with me as I said I would and found out that it weighed exactly 28.5 lbs. I found that out by having to pay $1.50 per lb. to fly it home by Air Canada Freight.

Joe thought I was nuts spending good money to haul some stupid rock around but I just really liked the thing. Of course, there isn't a lot you can do with a 28.5 lb. piece of granite.

One day, I was going through a stack of albums looking for inspiration, when I came a cross a real rare classic, an LP from the sixties by the "West Coast Pop Art Experimental Band." On the cover were a variety of psychedelic images including a picture of a stone with a little sign that said; "Help, I'm a Rock." I was inspired.

I crafted a small signpost out of one-by-twos and used a piece of shirt board for the message. That night I took the mountain egg to the tavern where were playing and installed it in front of the drums, complete with the sign. It looked great, and had the unexpected effect of keeping my bass drum from sliding forward as I played the pedal, something I had been struggling with for years.

After the gig was done, I took it back home with me.

It hung around the band house until a couple of people tripped over the thing and then it was outside for a while. One day, an extremely bored Percy spent about an hour picking it up and dropping it from chest level, at great risk to his bare toes, until it had made a depression in the lawn. It looked like it was sitting it's own nest, ready to hatch. I left it there.

How was I to know?

About three o'clock the following morning, returning from a late night at the local bar, our roadie, Shane, who was a strapping young guy of notably athletic leanings, saw the mountain egg sitting in the grass and, in the darkness mistook it for a soccer ball.

Shane said later that he had intended on kicking it right over the house. The amazing thing is that he did actually move it about five feet. He also broke every bone in his foot and hobbled around the house for weeks in a lot of pain and a foul mood.

It was shortly after that that the mountain egg went missing from the Klondiker tavern. Whether somebody had decided it was just too much of a hazard to keep around or someone actually stole the thing, I will never know.

I do seem to remember, though, the night it disappeared, seeing a big guy dressed in rawhide sitting at the back of the room as we were warming up for the third set. I was busy tuning a tom-tom, but it did strike me that I had seen the guy before. When I looked again, he was gone.

I miss it. It was my mountain egg. I had always intended to take it back to Yellowknife one day and replant it in its' native gravel, to give it a chance to hatch.

I have this feeling that, wherever it is now, it will somehow find its' way back to the north and fulfill its' destiny. I hope so.

FINE

CONCLUSION

I lie there on my sprung-spring mattress in my dingy hotel room, staring at the peeling plaster on ceiling, trying to remember one good thing about life on the road.

Eventually I fall asleep, worn out from the travel and the labor of moving things and the playing. I awake to a harsh morning light filtered through the dust and grime on the windows as through stained glass. The sounds in the hallway tell me others are up already, checking out or going for breakfast.

It is only with the most heroic of efforts that I'm able to drag myself out of bed and over to the washroom. Only after I wash my hands and face do I remember-no towels.

"Fuck."

Trudging down the hall towards the stairs, I am joined by Gary and Bob. Bob lights a cigarette and leaves it in his lips as he buttons his shirt.

"Can't wait to see what this cook can do to a simple breakfast. I bet the eggs are all hard as silly putty."

"Mmmm, undercooked bacon-my favorite. Do you think they'll let the toast get cold before they butter it?"

"Any luck, they won't have real butter."

"You mean…"

"Yeah, man. Margarine!"

"Mmm, boy!"

Breakfast is everything we'd imagined and less. Chef has somehow managed to burn the bottoms of the eggs while simultaneously leaving the whites uncooked. We eat around the grottier bits, knowing there is no point in complaining.

Nursing coffees that look and taste more like teas, we find that there is little to say about the gig last night. We used to talk about every performance the day after, pointing out any areas that could be improved, mentioning weak spots or complementing one another on a particularly good solo.

We sit, comfortable in one another's presence but still, in silence. Doug and Percy come down and join us. After the usual salutations, the silence descends again, like a pall over the morning.

After a few unsuccessful attempts to break through the fugue, we disperse

to our various rooms. I'm putting my jacket on to go out for a walk when the phone rings.

"Hello?"

"Is this room 212?"

Uh…just a second, I'll check." I go to the door and open it and then remember that I have a tag on my room key. Back to the phone.

"Yes, this is room 212."

"This is the manager. I have some towels for you."

"Oh! Oh, well, thanks, um, I'll come get them, shall I?"

"Sure. I'll keep them at the bar for you. We do try, you know."

"Sorry?"

"I said; we do try. It ain't like the shithole everybody thinks it is."

"Right, well...I certainly appreciate the towels, anyways."

"You're welcome. They'll be here for you when you come for them."

"Right. And, thanks again."

The line goes dead. 'Well, that's something,' I tell myself. I hurry down to the bar and collect an armful of nicely laundered towels in various sizes. It's a bit awkward, having just spoken to the guy on the phone and now having the same conversation in person but I'd rather get it done. I pick up my towels and take them back up to my room.

"Shower today," I promise myself, and head out for a little reconnoiter.

No sooner do I step out onto the street than a couple of guys on Harleys roar past me, riding down the center of the main street. They're wearing colors but I can't make out the insignia, just the standard horseshoe shape. It starts me thinking about a gig we did in the Kingsmen Tavern in Edmonton, years back.

The Kingsmen was well known as the main biker hangout in the city. The Rebels were always well represented there, along with a couple of rival groups like the Coffin Cheaters. It was once the site of an historical rumble between the Rebels and members of the Canadian Armed Forces.

The thing had apparently been brewing for a while, with both groups drinking at the bar and small skirmishes breaking out from time to time.

One hot summer night, a couple of members of the PPCLI got into it with a few bikers inside the bar and were ushered out by the numerous security staff there. Somehow a lone soldier ended up isolated in the parking lot with three or four Rebels, including one who had a particularly nasty reputation.

Well, they beat the poor boy within an inch of his life and tossed him into a dumpster, which precipitated a major confrontation the next night, when thirty or more uniformed members came looking for revenge.

They say the resulting brouhaha took hours to sort out, with numerous injuries on both sides and the entire neighborhood under Marshall law for the night. It was considered a draw in the end but the bikers, after a period of banishment, made no bones about their intention to continue to show their presence in the Kingsmen.

All this was ancient history by the time we came along and got our first chance to play the legendary venue. The Rebels still held court but, unless you were actively looking for trouble, the place was big enough to avoid them.

It was, in fact, the biggest bar in the province. At eight hundred seats, the Kingsmen tavern was not typical of the average 80-200 seat bars in the province at that time. It more closely resembled the huge roadhouses you see in the south. It was the biggest Albertan establishment ever to hold a liquor license, then or now.

The owner was shrewd little guy named Earl who wore gold-plated glasses with rose-colored lenses into which he'd had his initials etched. He was a man of diminutive stature, comically emphasized by the Stetson and the cowboy boots he wore but he knew what was what in his rooms and he insisted on personally auditioning every act he hired.

We were obliged to cart our equipment down to the hotel and set up in an empty conference room and then we waited half an hour until he was free to come and listen to us. We'd planned a half-hour set that would showcase all our best material but after two tunes, Earl got up and said he'd heard enough.

"You're hired," he said, around a pudgy cigar, "you start Monday."

Right from the first night, it was a tough gig. The stage was in one corner of the place and although it was of a good size, as tavern stages went, in that place it just looked tiny.

Our usual friendly banter was lost on the tough crowd and our eclectic mix of material failed to click on any level. There were several regulars who liked to heckle the band, something we weren't used to.

Our usual group of faithful followers made a brief attempt to support us towards the weekend but found they were intimidated by the general hostility of the place. By Friday night we were on our own, facing a room that was at least half bikers.

The atmosphere was close and stifling, like the air before a storm. There was a fight brewing somewhere and everybody knew it.

So, faced with an uncomfortable, unsafe and possibly dangerous situation that we didn't know how to cope with, Captain Nobody did what came natural.

We dropped acid.

Gary scored some stuff that was supposed to be really good and we all took it at the same time-about half an hour before curtain. We were well into the second set before it started to take effect. When we realized just how good the stuff was, there were some mixed feelings about the wisdom of having tripped on it *here* but by then it was far too late.

The only way through was forward, so we resolved to just put our heads down and play our best. Doug remembers that I became so focused on what I was doing that when I went into one of my two drum solos, I got so involved that I failed to notice the looks of confusion on every ones' faces when I came out of the first solo playing the intro and cues for the *second* one.

Then, something magical occurred. We started into a song early in the third set. It wasn't one of our top selections-I can't even recall what song it was but, right from note one, it *clicked*. The whole band was suddenly transported to that most sought-after place wherein everybody is in sync. Every one of us found his keenest focus and began to play his part better than he ever had.

It wasn't the first time this had occurred to the Captain on stage and we were always striving to recreate it but the experience was rare enough that we all seemed to sense it happening at the same time. We exchanged looks, confirming with one another that; yeah, I feel it too. We were in the zone for the whole song.

It had never sounded better but the question now was; could we keep it going? Could we maintain that level into another completely different tune? The next song in the list was suddenly less than ideal to follow with. We looked at each other, trying to think of a better choice.

Gary began the opening guitar intro for "Red House," the blues-based Hendricks 12-bar showcase for his voice/guitar skills. He usually shone on it but that night, peaking on some righteous LSD and completely oblivious to the belligerent audience before us, Gary was brilliant. We all were.

Percy backed Gary's lead work with a chord clinic in the blues, weaving patterns through the infinitely creative stuff Bob was layering on with the piano. Doug and I took turns holding down the simple, traditional 12-bar rhythm and then playing around with rests and spaces, at times only *inferring* the beat while taking the kind of bold liberties in spontaneous phrasing that required the most intimate trust in one another to pull off, at the risk of having the whole thing just fall to the ground.

And Gary soared. His flying V alternately screamed and cried, swooped and dove and soared again to heights we'd never witnessed him achieve but always had known he would.

The last verse was a heart-wrenching monument to the classic blues form, his voice and guitar interweaving and blending until they were impossible to tell apart and when the last line came and the climax led to the inevitable resolution fading into the distance, the silence was full of the knowledge that we had never played *any* song that well, maybe never would play that well again, although we hoped not.

Curiously enough, it was with this complete absorption in our craft, to the utter dismissal of the audience that we finally won them over to us. The people around us might have been happy to give us a hard time when we played some of the more esoteric songs in our repertoire but they were bikers and they knew good Blues when they heard it. The applause was long and heartfelt.

I think they even understood when, even though the night was only about half-way through and we were expected to play another set and a half, we all followed Gary's example and packed up for the night, took our instruments down and left. It was as if there was nothing left to say, after that.

We got hell from the agency and lost a nights' wages and we were never booked to play the Kingsmen again. We didn't care. A pinnacle had been reached, a milestone passed. It was time to move on.

The memory brings a smile to my lips as I continue on down the street. I pass a couple of vacant lots and an abandoned gas station. I'm keeping my eyes peeled for the usual antique store or the local chain store, where I might find an hours' diversion. The only thing I can see that might fit the description is a weathered storefront with a badly hand-painted sign over the door that says; "Ma's Bric 'a Brac."

Entering the gloomy interior, I wait for eyes to adjust. There doesn't seem to be anyone around. There's a counter with an antique cash register. The walls are lined with shelves, displaying the oddest collection of things. There are four or five shelves running the length of the store devoted to nothing but gumboots. Every size available must be represented, posted in big hand-written tags that are taped to the front of the shelf in even spacing.

Across from the boots are the shovels. At least a hundred shovels, hanging in matched groups of six or eight-long handled spades and short handled spades. Snow shovels and wide, square gravel shovels. At the very end of that wall are the picks and a selection of mattocks.

In the center of the room is a display counter heaped high with coveralls. They are arranged by size and stacked neatly, every one in the same white and grey pattern like those worn by trainmen. There must be a gross of them on display.

And that's all. There's nothing else in the entire space save these few items, plentiful though they are.

"How the hell," I ask myself, "can anyone hope to make a living selling nothing but rubber boots, shovels and coveralls?"

"Can I help you?" comes a voice from close-by. I nearly jump out of my skin.

Peering into the darkness, I can just make out the owner of the voice, hidden from me in the corner by the bad lighting.

"Ah, no. I think ...do you have anything else to sell?" I just can't resist.

"Anything else? What do you mean?"

It's a girls' voice. Young, maybe twelve or so. I still can't make out any details of her appearance.

"I mean is this all you sell? Just boots, shovels and coveralls?"

"Yes."

"Well, it just seems... well-bit hopeful, you know? Do you sell a lot of these things?"

"No."

"Well, don't you think you might do better to diversify a little? Try selling a few more things?"

There is a long silence.

"I don't know what you mean."

"Well, I mean..."

"Do you see something you want?" Comes another voice, a loud adult voice from the back of the shop. The speaker is invisible.

"I'm sorry?"

"Do you see something that you want to buy?"

"Uh, no, actually, I was just wondering..."

"Well, then I guess we can't help you, can we?"

I'm getting a bit weirded out but my curiosity keeps me at it.

"Yes, that's sort of what I was trying to point out."

"Shop's closed."

"Sorry?"

"The shop is closed. You'll have to leave."

"Oh. All right. Um, fine. Well, have nice day, then."

I take my leave, out onto the street from whence I'd come, feeling like I'd just taken part in an un-aired scene from "Deliverence" or something. Never a dull fucking moment in small town Alberta, I'm thinking, ruefully. You never knew when you might find yourself taking a trip down somebody's odd little rabbit hole in these places.

The thought starts me thinking of another memory of the past. Playing "One White Rabbit" in Dewey Stocktons' basement, with his sister singing.

The Stocktons lived at the end of 50th street on the south side of Edmonton, in the last house before the river. Dewey and his brother Glen were pretty cool guys and their family was just the right kind of strange to make their place a popular hang-out for us.

They were Mormons, I think-they kept forty days of canned food in the root cellar under the house. Their dad was some kind of executive who worked downtown, commuting to and from his office in his Amphicar; the coolest vehicle in the known universe.

The Amphi-car was one of the many inventions that had come out of World War Two, when the most inventive minds in North America were being funded by the government to design just about anything, if they could convince someone it might help give the Allied Powers a small advantage against the Axis.

The planned invasion of Fortress Europe created a need for amphibious vehicles of all description, to get the fighting men to the beach and across the killing zones the Nazis had put in place. They needed large troop carriers and larger still tank transports but someone in the Allied command reasoned that they would also need a small, car-sized vehicle to get the commanders and picked commando units through the carnage on the beaches and up into the cliffs before they came under fire.

The Allies had no way of knowing, of course, that the Nazis had already been working just such a thing; the "Schwimmwagen" in preparation for the anticipated invasion of Great Britain. One of the engineers who worked on the development of this Volkswagen project was named Hans Trippel.

Mr. Trippel's love of the amphibious car carried over into peacetime and by 1959, he had designed and built a prototype Amphicar. It looked like an oddly shaped sports convertible of the time-squarish and boxy. As the name implies, it was designed to drive in the water as well as on land. This it did, with a few minor drawbacks.

The little four-cylinder motor did pretty well on land, giving the car a top speed of about 70 mph. The handling was acceptable, although no one had a great deal of praise for the suspension. In the water, the Amphicar was somewhat less effective. Its top speed afloat was a snail-like 7 knots, roughly 7mph, so not in any danger of sitting records but hey-it did go on water, and what cool thing that was!

The Amphicar was introduced to North America in 1961 and by '65 there were almost 4,000 of them on the continent. The biggest flaw in the cars' design was that, being an engineer, Mr. Trippel naturally presumed folks would understand that with something like an amphibious car, they might be called upon to perform certain tasks pertaining to maintenance. The car was made waterproof only by the liberal use of lubricating sealant on the door catches and hinges. If the re-application of such were to be neglected for any length of time, the cracks in these areas leaked. If they were neglected for long enough to admit an inflow of water that the tiny bilge pump that Mr. Trippel had so thoughtfully included in the bottom of his car couldn't handle the inflow, the Amphicar would sink.

It was therefore the Amphicars' fate to inevitably become a toy for the collector and for those with the engineering caste of mind, such as Dewey's dad.

The model owned by Mr. Stockton was a convertible, bright red with white trim. The thing that made the car so useful to them was that they lived so close to the river. Dewey's dad could turn right out of the driveway of their house, drive about five hundred yards to the river and, having shifted into aqua mode, keep right on going into and up the North Saskatchewan about two miles, to the canoe launch downtown, which happened to be about five blocks from where he worked.

He took us for a ride one day, down to the river and, with hardly a hesitation, into the water. We went for a brief tour upstream and then turned around and went back to the house. It stands out as one of my fondest memories. It was a great thrill but it didn't hold a candle to playing with Dewey's sister, Ann.

Ann was a knockout. A petite blond with a trim figure that we all went to great lengths to not be caught ogling. This was not made easy by her penchant for flitting about the house in her jammies or, when the parents weren't in, her bra and panties.

We were practicing in The Stockton's basement, having worn out our welcome at all our own parents' houses in succession. It was an open question whether or not we were actually learning anything, distracted as we were by the need to keep an eye out for any possible Anna sightings and the befuddled state that such glimpses left us in.

I imagine Ann was well aware of the effect she had on us and perhaps felt a bit flattered by our attentions but the idea that anything might come of it never occurred to us until the day she came into the practice room in the middle of a rehearsal and asked if she could try singing.

For a room full of band equipment, it was remarkable how quiet things became. We looked at each other and at Ann, standing there in her bathrobe looking like a vision from a wet dream, and none of us could think of a way to answer her request.

She finally walked over to one of our microphones and, speaking into it through the live system asked;

"Do you guys know "White Rabbit?"

Well, we didn't. We'd never played the tune before, nor had any of us listened to it with the intention of learning the parts but we weren't going to let that stand in the way.

What followed was the fastest job of learning a new song ever performed by a band. In two minutes flat, we'd decided on a key, fitted the chord structure together, run over he changes and established the arrangement. Did we know "White Rabbit?"

We did now.

We started the song on an official count-down and, after closing her eyes to focus through the intro, Ann began to sing. Her voice was perfect for the tune; she sounded a lot like Grace Slick, in fact but it wasn't like she was trying to. Her voice had a sulky, more sensual quality on the lower register but, when the louder parts came it darkened and deepened. Better, if I may dare to say so, than Grace.

We played through the tune, which, if you've never heard it, is basically one long, slow Bolero crescendo to a sonic climax at the end. As the last chord died along with Ann's final note, we were all shocked with how good it had sounded.

"Could we do it again?" she asked.

Mere moments before, any one of us would have cheerfully thrown the rest of the band under a bus to hear Ann speak just those words. Everything was different, now.

There were no arguments. With a few minor adjustments and tunings, we started again. It was better this time. More confident. The swell was more controlled, more gradual into the finale. It was really good.

"One more time?"

You bet.

We ended up playing it five times in a row. Each time, it got better and better. By the fifth time, we knew we'd nailed it but everyone wanted to give it one more, just to revel in the sound.

Ann threw herself into the lyrics, letting her passion speak through the song. It was like she was making love to us through the music and we, collectively with her. We didn't want it to end. Finally we had to. The song couldn't be played any better. There was no significant difference between the fifth and the sixth rendition. It was perfect.

We stood there, grinning at each other, at her and she at us. We all knew we'd achieved something wonderful. When we looked at Ann now, she was no less desirable than she had been but now we looked at one another as friends, fellow artists. Where there had only been a sexual attraction now was a respect and admiration that flowed both ways. It had been Ann that had taken the first step through the fog and we all loved her for it.

We packed up wordlessly and went our separate ways. Practice was over for that day.

I've come to the end of the street. Nothing but a feed-lot and a couple of Quonset sheds between here and the edge of town. I cross the street. A truck passes me, driven by a woman with long, curly blonde hair. Once again, my memory is triggered by the sight.

This time I'm remembering a gig we did in the summer, a couple of years back, in the charming little riverside town called "Entwistle." It was a lovely day and we felt like dawdling on the way, so we left early in the afternoon, knowing we'd get to the town with hours to spare. Doug's friend Nora decided to come along and we were all happy to have some female company, as a change from the usual male-only trips we were used to.

Driving along the well-known highway in the bright sunlight, everyone was in a carefree mood. The day grew hot as we travelled and by the time we pulled into town it was sweltering. The task of unloading the equipment and setting up left us all tired and sweaty, with a couple of hours and nothing to fill them before the dance was due to start.

"Let's go for a swim!" Nora suggested.

It sounded like a great idea but the problem was, nobody had thought to bring swimwear.

"Swimming trunks!?" Nora exclaimed, "what the hell for? You guys ain't got anything I haven't seen-let's go skinny dippin'!"

We looked at each other. It was really hot. Without any further discussion we piled into the van and headed to the river. Once there, all our clothes came off and were left on the bank as we jumped into the lovely, cool waters of the Pembina.

The sun was warm, the shade was cool, the water was miraculous and we were so, so happy we'd taken Nora's lead.

That evening, we played as well as we ever had-better perhaps after the relaxing time by the river. Our hair did some interesting things after the soft water worked on it, but we didn't care. We had a good night and drove home tired, tanned and a good deal better for having had the day together.

I chuckle a little at the memory as I cross the street and head back towards the hotel. I'm a bit rattled after the 'Deliverance' tableau in the store. I feel like giving up on my walk. I feel like giving up on the town.

I feel like giving up.

I haul myself up the stairs to the room, stand in the door looking at the bed for whole minutes before entering and lying down. I guess I must have fallen asleep again.

When I open my eyes, there is a late evening feel to the light. I check my watch and see that I've slept the whole day away. It's almost time to play.

The thought makes me groan. The idea of getting up and trying to play music in that horrible little hole downstairs makes me feel like hiding under the bed.

Then I begin to sort through the memories I've been having all day. There is something familiar about them all, something they have in common. The Kingsmen. The "White Rabbit" session with Anna. The summer day in Entwistle.

I get it, by now; my subconscious is trying to send me a message, or something. It's tantalizingly close to making itself known. I can't quite put my finger on it.

I've spent my life wondering why, if one's subconscious mind has something to tell one, it can't just spit it out, already. But NO, we all have to pay attention to all these little random clues and figure it out by ourselves. Self learning, inner growth, whatever; I hate this shit.

I recognize that they are all memories of the times when the music, or the people were more important than the usual stuff. That much is obvious. Only-there's a lot of water under the bridge since any of those times. I'm still here, and the music is better than ever but the usual stuff has become a fucking nightmare.

As I lie there wrestling with my discontent, another memory comes to me, of a single moment. It isn't attached to any other memories. It's just this one isolated moment in time, all by itself. I don't remember where it occurred, or exactly when. It must have been early on in the bands' history but the moment itself comes back to me crystal clear, as if it might have happened yesterday.

We are driving down a road in the very early morning. Everybody's asleep in the back of the van except me and Gary, who is driving. I'm trying to stay awake to help him stay awake but I've run out of stuff to talk about, so we're just driving along in silence together.

We are on our way back from a gig in the country. We must have stayed and played late into the night and then gone to a party at some local fans' place and now we are making our way home in the wee small hours.

The sun is coming up and casting long morning shadows of the pine trees that line the highway across the road. It's early winter. There is a hoar frost on the trees, on the power lines and on the barbed-wire fences. The only sound is the thrum of the engine and the occasional snore from the back.

Just as we crest a small hill, a raven leaves his perch in a roadside tree and glides across in front of us. The suns' rays catch under his wings and tint the feathers with iridescent purples and bronze, just for a second.

Gary and I look at each other, to see if the other one saw. As our eyes meet, broad grins break out on both of our faces. There is no need for words. It's a moment of sharing.

We're twenty years old, young and free and lucky enough to be doing the thing we love most in the world together.

As the memory fades and the mundane reality of my surroundings reasserts itself, I find that it's all been changed. Or, more accurately, I guess-I've been changed. A smile is on my lips. All the heaviness and confusion is gone, replaced by a quiet surety that I am still on the right path, that I'm still doing the thing that I love best, no matter what the circumstances.

It doesn't matter what the crowd thinks of us. It is entirely irrelevant how much we are paid, or how little. So what if the town sucks? Who cares if the room is dirty? What's so important about having a stage to play on?

I get to play. I get to play the music I want to play with as fine a band of musicians as I could ever hope to know and I'm going to get to do it for as long as I want to. We don't have anyone to answer to but ourselves and we know what we want.

And I want to.

I rise from the bed and cross the worn carpet to the door. Only a little while to go, before we start playing again. I can't wait.

The End.

About the Author

Neil D. Martin was born and raised in Edmonton, Alberta. Neil has been a bellhop, a parking attendant, a bus driver, a professional musician, a neon sculptor, a business owner and an ESL conversation facilitator. Neil was a founding member of Captain Nobody and the Forgotten Joy Band. Neil currently resides with his partner, Sandra, in Edmonton where he continues to craft neon signs for fun and profit.

CPSIA information can be obtained
at www.ICGtesting.com
Printed in the USA
LVOW03s2036160318
570149LV00010B/33/P

9 781460 278314